A Brother's

Revenge

Regina Navarra

Copyright © 2008 by Regina Navarra

ISBN 0-7414-5094-1

Cover design by Regina Navarra.

Published by:

PUBLISHING.COM

1094 New DeHaven Street, Suite 100
West Conshohocken, PA 19428-2713
Info@buybooksontheweb.com
www.buybooksontheweb.com
Toll-free (877) BUY BOOK
Local Phone (610) 941-9999
Fax (610) 941-9959

Printed in the United States of America

Printed on Recycled Paper

Published November 2008

To my husband, Gary,

Thank you for all your love and support.
I am very lucky to have you in my life.

To all of my children,
Lewis, Brian, Gina, Steve and Devon

I love you with all my heart
and hope all your dreams come true.

To my daughter, Gina,
To my friend, Darlene,

Thank you for all the encouragement and enthusiasm.

A

Brother's

Revenge

Prologue

William was reading the paper as he did every morning while drinking coffee and eating breakfast. His blood began to boil when he came across a picture of Richard Marks III with his wife and two children. He read the article which fueled his hatred as it detailed the Marks family history and the corporation Richard now controlled. The article described his children in detail stating how smart his son was and how they expected he would follow in his father's foot steps, taking over the company when he was old enough. His anger was overwhelming as he continued to read the article and looked again at the picture of Richard's arrogant and pompous expression. "How dare he look proud of himself while denying Toby even existed?"

Rage coursed through his veins at the memory of what Richard had done to his young, innocent sister. He had seduced her, leaving her pregnant to fend for herself and her new born son. He had gone to great measure to avoid responsibility for either one of them using his power and money to avoid the authority of the courts that would have otherwise ordered his financial assistance.

His sister, Sarah, had been forced to drop out of college and work full time right up until she went into labor. His nephew, Toby, was born healthy however Sarah had suffered hemorrhaging directly after his birth. William had stood by and watched as his sister turned grayish white, moaning with pain. The nurses had taken the baby and ushered him out of the hospital room so they could attend to the unexpected emergency.

Sarah spent several extra days in the hospital trying to regain her strength after losing a dangerous

1

amount of blood. The doctor had suspected the complications were caused by her being forced to work long hours on her feet late into her pregnancy. William had vowed that day he would pay back Richard Marks III for what he had done to his sister. William helped Sarah as much as possible as he finished college while working as much as he could.

After graduation he decided to change his name from Blake to Moore to avoid any possible interference from Richard Marks when he began his work in the business world. After tangling with Richard in the courts, he knew if they crossed paths in business Richard would make things very difficult for him. He was determined to make a good life for Sarah, his nephew and himself after having to struggle for so long.

Shortly after beginning his new career, he had some risky investment opportunities come his way that had fortunately paid off big. Having a knack for business investing, it was not long before he was living comfortably, constantly adding to his new found wealth. As soon as he was able he had bought his first home insisting that Sarah and Toby move in with him. They lived together ever since becoming closer than ever as they shared the daily responsibilities required in caring for Toby.

William read the article that ended with an announcement that Richard's younger sister, Elizabeth, was about to graduate from a prominent boarding school. He looked at the picture thinking she was very attractive and didn't look at all like her brother, having auburn hair with fair skin while Richard had darker skin with brown hair. William had been unaware that Richard had a sister and after reading the announcement of her impending graduation, realized the opportunity for revenge that he'd been waiting for all these years had just knocked on his door.

Chapter One

Elizabeth Marks sat in her cap and gown with her fellow classmates feeling proud as she waited for her name to be called. It was a beautifully sunny day with an occasional breeze that felt lovely on her young face. She watched her classmates one by one as they went up the steps of the polished wood stage to receive their diplomas. Finally they were graduating high school and were looking forward to the summer off before attending college.

After the death of her parents she was sent to the all female boarding school, only going home in the summer and on some holidays to visit her only remaining family, her brother, his wife and their two children. Elizabeth was looking forward to attending the co-ed college where she had been accepted.

Her brother, Richard Marks III, was eight years older than Elizabeth and they were quite different. Elizabeth was petite and gentle with auburn colored hair and green eyes while her brother not only inherited their father's dark hair and brown eyes, but also his harsh and crusty demeanor. Elizabeth took after her mother, in personality, looks and gentle heart. Her memories of her father weren't comforting ones. He was always working and never seemed to have much to say to her being satisfied that her mother gave her enough attention. Her father had been Chairman of the Board of the company her grandfather had started years before. His son Richard Marks III, was expected to graduate from Yale University and begin his career at Richard Marks Corporation, as his father and grandfather before him.

Her mother, however she missed dearly. She was completely devastated when she was told that both of her parents had died in an airplane crash while returning from one of their monthly ski weekends. She was told that the small private jet had experienced some type of engine problem and due to low visibility the pilot was unable to safely land the craft. The exact cause of the crash was never determined since most of the plane and the passengers were incinerated in the explosion caused by the crash.

She soon turned angry and resentful towards everyone around her. After getting in trouble at school a few times in the months that followed the death of her parents, her brother decided she was better off at an all female boarding school he had visited in Simsbury, Connecticut while on a business trip. Her brother could not and had no desire to relate to his thirteen year old little sister who was struggling with the emotions caused by the death of her parents combined with the changes that occur in a girl of that age. To him, she was just a nuisance he inherited along with his parents' money.

Richard Marks III still considered his sister a nuisance and obligation as he sat in the stands discussing business on his cell phone barely taking notice of his sister as she proudly took her turn receiving her diploma. His wife, Susan, sat quietly beside him with their two children, Richard Marks IV, who was five and his older sister, Sophia, who was almost eight. Richard insisted on having a second child even after his wife had major complications with her first pregnancy and almost died. Richard Marks had to have a son to carry on the family name and run the family business. His wife Susan was relieved that her second child was a son so she wouldn't have to repeat yet another difficult pregnancy and labor.

At age thirty four, married with two children and a devoted wife, Richard was much like his father. Ruthless in business, uninterested much of the time regarding his wife and daughter, only showing interest in his son who he was already being groomed to take over his work when he is old enough. No desire or care to be bothered with the day to day emotional needs of his young daughter satisfied that his wife supplied all the attention she needed.

His wife, Susan, the daughter of a prominent business associate was properly brought up and groomed as the perfect type of wife for Richard, subdued and obedient, yet sophisticated and glamorous. Susan married Richard at age twenty-two the summer after she graduated from college. They dated for six months when he proposed and then married one year later. In earlier generations Susan may have been considered a "Stepford" wife. She knew just how and when to behave for the appearance and reputation of her husband and his position. Always the gracious hostess with a beautifully kept home and well behaved children, Susan was happy and took pride in her duties as wife and mother. Of course, none of them were ever in need of anything in the material sense. Richard made sure they were provided with the best of everything. His family always had the best clothing, the best cars, and the best vacation homes to entertain and impress his business associates which were always chosen for either their business or social standing.

A handsome gentleman, forgotten long ago by Richard Marks III, sat at the top of the metal bleachers observing the ceremony and Elizabeth with interest. He watched her receive her diploma and noticed her older brother's indifference to his own family which further infuriated him, reminding him again why he was there. William Moore was a successful stock broker, handsome and quite wealthy. Confident and handsome, with dark wavy hair combined with a tall and muscular physique created a very powerful and intimidating presence. After years of practice entertaining business clients and the ladies he had perfected his techniques used not only to be charming when he chose but to be brutal in his business practices to obtain what he wanted. William was extremely intelligent, had graduated from Berkley University with honors which he had attended on full academic scholarship. He made his money through hard work, intelligent decisions mixed with some wise and sometimes very risky investments. The risks he had taken, fortunately worked out quickly to his advantage and he soon became quite wealthy. William Moore was a man who always seemed to get what he wanted, one way or another.

He sat watching the young women as they received their diplomas but was only interested in observing one of the graduates. Extremely beautiful and graceful with long wavy auburn hair and a petite figure, Elizabeth descended the stairs with her diploma, glancing in the direction of her brother with a wide smile full of pride. The look that came across her face for an instant when she realized her brother was on the phone, not paying attention to the ceremony and didn't see her receive her diploma almost made William feel sorry for her – almost.

Elizabeth's heart sank as she realized her brother didn't care enough to even pretend to watch her be presented with the diploma she received with honors, graduating third in her class. Elizabeth was very innocent and young in many ways. First sheltered most of her life by her mother, then by her brother when he sent her to the boarding school for the protection and solitude an all girls school would provide. Elizabeth was also very intelligent and had realized years before her brother considered her to be nothing more than an obligation he would rather not have. Elizabeth had worked hard at her studies to do well so she would one day be able to leave the cold and uncaring shelter her brother provided, make her own way in the world and start a family of her own. Elizabeth was a very kind hearted person and wanted to do something to help people. She was considering becoming a nurse or doctor and had even toyed with the idea of joining the Red Cross or some other non-profit organization. Her brother wouldn't stand for it of course having all control over her financially until she turned twenty-one years old when she would receive her inheritance from her parents. At that age she would inherit an adequate amount of money to keep her from ever needing help from anyone as long as she spent her money wisely and found a career that provided at least a modest income. She dreamed of the day she would be able to spread her wings and fly away to find the happiness she believed was waiting for her somewhere. Happiness she hadn't felt since before her mother had passed away.

After the ceremony was complete she said good-bye to her friends and classmates then greeted her family. Congratulations and false affection came from her brother providing the expected fuss for those people surrounding them, some of important social standing and some current or prospective business contacts. Her brother and his wife always made sure to put on the proper and expected show when in the public eye.

Since her belongings were already packed and sent off to be delivered for them, they climbed into the limousine where Elizabeth endured the very long and quiet ride from Simsbury to Stamford, Connecticut. As a graduation celebration they all went to dinner at her brother's favorite restaurant which wasn't too far from their home. It was a very fancy, elegant restaurant near the water. They were seated outside on the patio which provided a beautiful view of the water, and access to the warm summer breeze and bright blue sunny sky.

They sat and ate their gourmet meal with little conversation. Elizabeth was satisfied to stare out at the water and watch the small waves hit the sandy shore and splash up on the rocky landscape. Elizabeth loved the ocean and boats. She looked forward to the times they spent on the family yacht despite the lack of affection from her brother. She could spend hours at the front of the boat letting the wind blow through her long hair without a care about the tangles the breeze would cause and how she would look after. Although Elizabeth was always well dressed and groomed she had no idea of how beautiful she was and didn't share in the obsession of vanity so many of her classmates and their families seem to possess.

Mid-way through the meal Elizabeth excused herself to go to the powder room located inside the restaurant. On her way back to join her family, Elizabeth walked through the bar area admiring the shiny polished stained wood and tall matching wood stools. Elizabeth collided with a man as he turned unexpectedly from the bar, spilling his drink in the process. Elizabeth stumbled slightly as the man tried to steady her, only causing her to stumble forward into his embrace. "Oh," was all Elizabeth could mutter as she looked up into the man's face, caught off guard as her heart did several strange leaps in her chest. She felt robbed of her breath as the man smiled down at her and apologized. Elizabeth felt her cheeks turn red with the heat of embarrassment.

"Excuse me miss. I wasn't looking where I was going."

"It's fine," was all she could manage through her suddenly dry lips. Elizabeth still stood within his steadying grasp as he held her arm. She stepped away as she realized this then awkwardly continued back to her table trying to control her pulse and shaky hands. Elizabeth didn't understand her reaction to the very handsome stranger and was mortified by it. She was still blushing when she returned to her family and attempted to gracefully hide her confused and flustered emotions. For the first time in her life, she was grateful that her family paid her no mind. She spent most of the remainder of her day trying to understand her emotions and trying to forget the handsome man with the brilliant smile and gorgeous hazel eyes. This didn't come easily to Elizabeth which further frustrated her. That evening after unpacking her belongings she tossed and turned trying to sleep. Sleep didn't come easily but when she was finally able to sleep she had haunting strange dreams that only further awakened feelings that she had never before experienced.

William Moore was very satisfied with the first contact he had with Elizabeth. "This is going to be much easier than I thought," he said to himself in the dark as he puffed on a cigar. Elizabeth was definitely not experienced with men and with William's expertise in the world of women he felt certain that she was attracted to him instantly. He would soon make his next move, starting a friendship that would put his plan into action. William fell asleep that night feeling very confident.

Chapter Two

Elizabeth woke feeling very restless and agitated. She took a shower and styled her hair while trying desperately to shake the visions of her dreams that repeatedly popped into her mind. She chose to wear a white sundress with white sandals, allowing her hair to flow naturally with its long silky waves. Elizabeth went downstairs and was served her breakfast in the large overstated dining room with its crystal chandelier and thick window draperies. Elizabeth hated to eat in the dining room but her brother insisted. Whenever her brother was away on business or on vacation with his wife she would eat in the kitchen with the servants and have lengthy conversations with them. Her brother didn't believe in getting emotionally involved with the servants, scolding her whenever she spoke to them about anything that wasn't regarding their various duties they performed each day.

After forcing her breakfast, she decided to take a walk down the beach in an attempt to clear her head. "Maybe I'll walk down to the marina, order an iced tea and watch the boats." At this thought, Elizabeth quietly slipped out the French doors and onto the back patio. She walked past the luxurious oversized heated pool and crossed the perfectly attended lush green lawn to the stone stairway that led down to the beach. Elizabeth walked in the direction of the marina which was a mile or so down the beach. She took her time enjoying the sun and watching the children run in and out of the surf. She enjoyed the luxury of having a semi-private beach available anytime she felt the desire to be near the water, which was quite often. The beach was probably the only thing she missed while she was away at school.

Elizabeth strolled slowly along, stopping occasionally to pick up a sea shell that caught her eye or just to sit and watch the waves rolling up the shore. Eventually she made her way to the local marina and ordered an iced tea. She sat at a table near the railing that provided a clear view of the boats coming and going. She sat sipping her iced tea, feeling much more relaxed than when she awoke that morning.

While watching a couple as they maneuvered their sailboat into their slip a shadow fell over the table. Elizabeth instinctively looked up to see what was blocking the sunshine she had been enjoying and felt her heart skip a beat as she came face to face with the handsome stranger that had haunted her dreams. He smiled down at her, "Well, hello again."

"Hello," Elizabeth replied nervously.

"I wanted to come over and apologize for my clumsiness last evening. I'm sorry if I embarrassed you." He said gently.

"Not at all," she said as her pulse raced and she tried to avoid his eyes. At that moment a waiter brought two iced teas and a plate with a mix of fresh fruit and cheeses. "Excuse me, I didn't order this."

"Compliments of Mr. Moore, Miss," the waiter explained as he made a quick exit.

"I hope you don't mind, I took the liberty of ordering drinks and a snack in the hopes you would allow me to join you to make up for last evening." William flashed a brilliant smile that few women could resist. As Elizabeth's heart again skipped a beat, all she could do was gesture towards the opposite chair for him to join her.

Graciously he sat down and took a long sip of his drink. "Thank you for gracing me with your company, if only for a few moments. My name is William Moore." He extended his hand.

Elizabeth automatically took his hand intending to shake it in the traditional fashion, "My name is Elizabeth Marks. It's nice to meet you, Mr. Moore."

He gently turned her hand in his and brushed his lips lightly against the top of her hand in a most charming greeting. "Please call me William," he replied with a devilish grin that seemed to radiate through his eyes.

Elizabeth nodded, "William," she replied as she gently removed her hand from his grasp afraid he would feel her pulse racing. She awkwardly began sipping her iced tea unsure of what to say or how to react. He seemed completely at ease however and immediately began to question her. She answered his questions about where she grew up, told him she just graduated and slowly began to relax with him. Elizabeth was actually enjoying talking to William on various topics and suddenly realized that an hour had flown by.

Between her walk and the time spent conversing with her handsome companion she was away from the house for more than two hours. "I believe it's time for me to return home. Thank you for the company, William," she said, smiling as she stood to leave.

"Must you go now? I was so enjoying our conversation. I was hoping you would allow me to show you my boat. It's docked here in the marina. You did say you love boats, did you not?"

Elizabeth hesitated but couldn't help but consider going with him. She looked at her watch. "I would love to however I really should get home," she replied.

He pulled out his most practiced pout and looked like a child who had just had his feelings hurt. "Oh how disappointing. Are you sure you won't reconsider? It won't take long. I'm very proud of her, only recently purchased her and haven't had much opportunity to show her off..."

Elizabeth was shaken by the affect he had on her and couldn't resist once he stood looking down at her with those eyes. "I guess I could, but not for long. I must get back soon before someone starts to worry."

"I won't keep you longer than you're willing to stay," he replied smiling, making her heart skip a beat once more. He led her down the docks while they chatted about the different boats that were docked along the way. William was surprised just how much knowledge she seemed to have regarding boats for being so young and commented on it.

"I grew up here and have always loved boats. I have read books on the subject and always pay close attention when people discuss boats."

When they arrived at his boat she was surprised to see it was larger than she expected. She was also surprised that it was an older type of boat with a lot of wood on the inside which she always thought made the boats seem so much more comforting. It was a beautiful boat with a small galley, a nice sized bedroom with a queen size bed and a comfortable size salon with a table for eating and a couch that turned into a bed. There was nothing overdone or flashy about this boat. It was a perfect, comfortable, cozy home on the water. She smiled warmly at him as she expressed her appreciation for his taste in boats.

He broke into a proud smile as he told her the details of how he obtained her and all the work he had done on the wood work and upholstery. "You wouldn't be interested in taking her for a ride, would you?" he asked her innocently.

Elizabeth was very tempted but had to force herself to decline. "I'm sorry. I really can't. Thank you for the invitation, maybe another time."

Disappointment was apparent on his face as he replied, "I understand. I have kept you long enough." Then with a sudden look of hope, "Would you possibly be interested in meeting me here tomorrow? I could make you lunch then we could take her for a ride?"

She was slowly warming up to him after seeing the obvious disappointment on his face when she was leaving and the excitement at the prospect of her joining him tomorrow. Elizabeth hesitated again, unsure of whether she should continue to see the charming and handsome William Moore. As she considered his proposition she found she couldn't bring herself to say no. "I'm not sure I can make it tomorrow."

"I'll tell you what, if you can make it, meet me here at say… eleven. If you're not here by Noon I'll assume you were otherwise engaged."

"Agreed. Thank you for the company today. I really enjoyed myself." Elizabeth walked towards the doorway that took her back to the dock. She took a step up onto the side of the boat ready to hop over to the dock when a small wave from a passing boat made her stumble. William grabbed her waist to steady her. His touch sent shivers up her spine and sent her heart racing. Overwhelmed by the unexpected emotion she froze in his grasp. Sensing her reaction, William instinctively turned her slowly towards him, looking deep into her eyes. She seemed to be glued to that spot, unable to move as he hypnotized her with his hazel eyes. He leaned down and gently kissed her. She didn't resist, couldn't resist. Her whole body seemed to come alive all at once. She leaned into the kiss and reveled in the sensations his kiss created. After a few moments, William slowly pulled back and looked down at her with a soft smile. He gently turned her around, assisting her over the side of the boat and onto the dock. "I hope to see you tomorrow," he said with a smile, smoothly hopping over the side of the boat and going back inside.

Elizabeth walked back to the beach and returned home in a haze, still reeling from the kiss that had evoked a reaction of such surprising magnitude. Although Elizabeth was innocent in the area of men, she had been kissed several times by boys that attended the occasional dances that were held at the boarding school she attended. She had no real reaction to the boys' attempts to win her affections.

Elizabeth knew she shouldn't go to the marina the next day for lunch with William but wasn't sure how she would keep herself from going, already feeling an excited knot in her stomach at the thought of being alone with him again. She thought about him all the way home, wondering if another kiss would feel just as wonderful. Suddenly, she couldn't wait for tomorrow.

William went back into his boat feeling quite satisfied that he had a very productive day. He was surprised several times when he caught himself sincerely enjoying Elizabeth's company and intelligent conversation. He also admitted that he wasn't as immune to her kiss as he would have liked. "A man is always a man and she is quite a beauty after all," he mused. Tomorrow he'd be more guarded. Tomorrow he would start the next phase of his plan. All he needed was for Elizabeth to show up for their date. William thought about whether he believed she would show up, remembered her reaction to his kiss, and then confidently told himself, "She will, without a doubt." William made some business calls then went shopping for supplies for the boat trip he had planned for the next day with Elizabeth.

Elizabeth entered the house through the same French doors in which she had left. "Where have you been? We have been waiting for you for quite a while now," her brother scolded.

"No where special. Just wandering the beach and marina, enjoying the day," she replied, trying to hide that he had startled her.

"Why didn't you let someone know where you were going?" he asked with more irritation than before.

"I'm sorry. I didn't expect to be gone so long but the day just got away from me," she explained trying to deflate his irritation with her so she could escape to her room.

"Well, be sure not to disappear again without letting someone know where you're going to be. Now go get ready, we are having dinner guests," he informed her coldly. "Please dress elegantly and be on your best behavior." Disappointed that she had to endure a night of entertaining his boring friends and business associates, she simply nodded, escaping to her room to shower and dress. Once in the privacy of her room, she let the irritation she felt towards her brother fester. "I am not a child or one of his servants," she fumed. "I can't wait until I graduate college so I can get away from him!"

Elizabeth looked through her enormous walk in closet. It was a warm evening so she picked out an emerald green dress with spaghetti straps that flattered her figure and brought out the color in her eyes. She chose matching green high-heal sandals and simple emerald earrings to finish the look. She clipped her long hair up, permitting several strands to hang delicately along the sides of her face. She looked absolutely stunning and was completely unaware when everyone stopped to stare as she joined the guests on the back patio for cocktails.

Elizabeth was introduced to the guests she didn't know after greeting several she had met previously. In total they had nine guests, four couples and one gentleman. She did her best to be attentive to their guests but her mind and heart wanted nothing more than to escape the company forced upon her. She sipped on her iced tea as she tried to pay attention to the conversation around her. Her brother introduced her to more of the guests which included a prominent banker her brother had dealt with on several occasions, along with his wife and son who had just graduated college. He would soon begin his new career at the same bank where his father happened to be the Vice-President. A few moments later she found herself seated at the dining room table next to the banker's son, Jonathan Parker.

Jonathan had short light brown hair and wore a dark brown tailored suit with matching tie and white shirt. He looked exactly how he should for an up and coming bank executive. He spent the rest of the evening drumming up conversation with Elizabeth, asking her question after question to keep her attention. She politely responded to his inquiries and listened as she ate the elegant meal that she couldn't appreciate. Her mind kept wandering back to William and that kiss.... and tomorrow.

Eventually everyone moved into the living room for coffee and dessert, Jonathan continuing to stay by her side. Elizabeth excused herself to use the powder room only to find Jonathan immediately at her side upon her return. She assumed he wanted to talk to someone closer to his own age since most of the other guests were much closer in age and older than her brother.

As the evening came to a close and the guests slowly began to leave, Elizabeth gracefully thanked each guest for coming. The last to leave were the Parker's. "Thank you for the wonderful conversation. I had a wonderful time. I'm looking forward to seeing you tomorrow," Jonathan said as he turned to leave with his parents.

Elizabeth said good night but was confused. "Why would he look forward to seeing me tomorrow?" she thought.

After the Parkers started down the driveway she immediately approached her brother who was smoking his late night cigar as he sipped his late night brandy. "Richard, do we have plans this weekend I'm unaware of?" she asked.

"Yes, as a matter of fact. We've all been invited to the Parker's vacation home in Maine for the weekend and I've accepted their invitation," Richard replied.

Desperately looking for a way to avoid the outing so she could keep her date with William she calmly asked, "Do you mind terribly if I don't attend this weekend outing? After all I just got home from school and would like some time to simply relax."

Richard immediately grew angry at her request. "You will accompany us this weekend and enjoy yourself. You'll have Jonathan's company for the weekend. You both seemed to get along very well this evening," Richard replied sternly.

"Jonathan was very nice but I...."

Richard cut her off mid sentence. "You will go with us. No more discussion! Now take yourself to bed and pack your things. We will leave at seven." Elizabeth knew not to bother arguing with her brother when he had that tone in his voice. It would only make things worse. She went to her room feeling angry and frustrated, desperately trying to think of a way out of the weekend outing. Maybe she could pretend to be sick but doubted her brother would fall for that after she made it known she didn't want to go. Elizabeth reluctantly began packing her things as she accepted that there was nothing she could do. She would miss her date with William tomorrow and didn't have any way to let him know why. She may never see him again she thought sadly. He may simply assume she didn't want to see him again. Elizabeth didn't sleep well that evening, again haunted by disturbing and erotic dreams.

Chapter Three

The next morning, Elizabeth awoke to the sound of banging. She had overslept and her brother was pounding on her door and yelling for her to get ready. "All right, I'm up! I'll be right down!" she yelled at the closed door irritably. Elizabeth quickly showered and dressed in the outfit she had picked out the night before. She reluctantly took her suitcase and descended the long staircase to join her family downstairs.

The entire ride she felt irritated and resented being ordered to attend the weekend solely to impress his business associates. She felt like a mannequin on display in a department store window with the one and only purpose was to look pretty. It was almost ten o'clock and the closer it came to eleven the more restless she became. They arrived at the Parker's summer home just before eleven and were greeted happily by their hostess. They were all given a brief tour of the immaculately decorated Cape Cod overlooking the bay then were provided a nutritious brunch on the back patio which she found no joy but managed to appear interested in her surroundings. If it wasn't for the beautiful weather and her love of the water Elizabeth wouldn't have been able to produce even a smidgen of interest and would have embarrassed her brother terribly.

William Moore was preparing his own sumptuous meal to present to Elizabeth assuming, with all confidence that she would be there on time or shortly after. The meal would consist of a mix of fresh fruits, warm croissants, and cheeses accompanied by champagne cocktails mixed with citrus juices. Hoping the champagne would loosen her up a little and make her more receptive to his invitation of a ride on his boat. William had the table set elegantly with a white tablecloth and candles, providing the romantic mood he needed to seduce Elizabeth. Satisfied with the meal and mood he had created, William turned on some background music to complete the romantic atmosphere he wanted.

Checking his watch he noticed it was eleven o'clock so he went to the sun deck at the back of the boat to await the arrival of his guest. He relaxed in a lounge chair with a glass of champagne cocktail only to find the minutes passing without an appearance from Elizabeth. As the moments passed he became increasingly irritated that she hadn't appeared. Finally at Noon he realized she wasn't coming which didn't set well with his ego or his plans. Frustrated and angry he paced back and forth wondering what went wrong. He was so sure he had her right where he wanted her and yet she didn't show up. He decided he would wait around another hour on the chance she was simply detained. After another frustrating hour of waiting William finally wrapped up the food he had elegantly placed about his dining table, blew out the candles that had burnt almost half way down, then angrily slammed the dishes back into the his cabinets breaking a glass in the process.

William was a man who was used to getting what he wanted and remained in a terrible mood the rest of the day while he replayed all his moves over and over in his mind trying to figure out what went wrong. "Maybe I came on too strong and scared her away," he thought, but he didn't think so. "I'll just have to come up with another way to see her again." He immediately began planning his next course of action.

Elizabeth finally accepted the fact she had missed her date with William and there was nothing she could do. She decided to make the most of her day. Jonathan Parker escorted her down to the beach after they all finished settling into their assigned guest quarters. They walked along the beach discussing books, politics, and business. Jonathan was excited that he would soon begin working at his father's bank. He seemed to have a passion for it, talking with great enthusiasm and detail regarding his prospective career in the banking industry.

The more time she spent with Jonathan the more she liked him. He was polite but not as stuffy as she first thought. They went swimming in the ocean for a while then relaxed on the sandy beach. As they stretched out on the beach blanket absorbing the summer sun, Jonathan turned on his side looking her over while her eyes were closed to block out the bright sun. He had a good view of her as she stretched lazily in the sun, fully appreciating her beauty and tempting figure. Elizabeth was blessed with a modest figure just right for her petite body. All her curves perfectly proportioned to her height and bone structure.

Elizabeth slowly opened her eyes when a shadow crawled over her face, finding Jonathan leaning over her in close proximity. He was looking at her with desire in his eyes and a soft smile on his lips. Elizabeth smiled back at him taken by surprise when he leaned down and kissed her softly. She wasn't sure how to react to this unexpected affection. She allowed herself to return his kiss more out of curiosity than anything. She enjoyed his kiss but didn't have the same reaction as when William had kissed her. He pulled himself up to search her face. Elizabeth awkwardly looked away not sure what to say to him.

"I like you very much, Elizabeth," Jonathan admitted to her. "I only hope you feel the same way as I do."

Elizabeth blushed with embarrassment and was unsure how to respond. She shyly kept her head lowered and nervously ran sand over and over through her hand. Jonathan put his hand gently on her shoulder. "You have nothing to fear with me. I don't mean to scare you or pressure you in any way. Can we just enjoy each others company this weekend and try to get to know each other? Maybe with time you will begin to share my feelings?" he asked hopefully.

She raised her head to look at his kind and hopeful face. Her heart softened at the kindness she saw in his eyes. "Okay, Jonathan. We'll see how things go. But for now I'd like to remain friends."

"I would be privileged to acquire your friendship," he replied gallantly. "Would you like to walk for awhile?"

"That sounds nice," she said as she gathered her things. They spent another hour walking along the shore talking about various subjects they both found they had interest in. When they returned to the house to shower and dress for dinner Elizabeth was surprised to realize that she really enjoyed her afternoon with Jonathan. He was kind, intelligent and she had felt quite relaxed in his company, with the exception of the awkward moment when he kissed her.

She took her time and enjoyed the shower she needed to wash the salt water and sand off her skin and out of her hair. The Parker's had informed them upon their return that they would be going out to the country club for dinner and dancing. After the day she had spent with Jonathan she was actually looking forward to the evening. She styled her hair and applied a modest amount of make-up then dressed in a white strapless evening gown she had packed. The soft white gown enhanced her tan skin. She chose delicate pearl jewelry and white sandals to complete her outfit.

Promptly at six o'clock Elizabeth joined everyone in the library where they were having cocktails. As she entered the library everyone suddenly got very quiet which made Elizabeth slightly uncomfortable. At that moment, Jonathan appeared and immediately complimented Elizabeth on how stunning she looked. "I can't wait to dance with the prettiest lady in the entire state of Maine!" he exclaimed.

Elizabeth smiled, blushing in response to the fuss he made over her. "Thank you. You look quite handsome yourself," she replied sincerely.

They all piled into the long stretch limousine that would take them to the country club for dinner. Seated in close proximity to Jonathan along the way and at dinner Elizabeth was slowly warming to his affectionate attention. Throughout the evening she was given constant attention from Jonathan filled with stimulating conversation, compliments and dancing. Jonathan proved to be a very good dancer spinning her around the room quite smoothly over and over throughout the evening. Elizabeth was beginning to feel very flattered that he seemed to adore her and wanted nothing more than to enjoy her company.

Quite warm and breathless from the dancing they decided to go outside onto the patio and enjoy the summer breeze. Elizabeth took a deep breath, allowing the air to cool her damp skin. She looked up at the beautiful night sky illuminated by the stars and light of the moon. Elizabeth was feeling quite happy and relaxed as she allowed herself to take an admiring glance at her escort. "He is quite handsome," she thought to herself. He turned and looked down into her smiling face. She was no longer nervous when she saw the look of desire cloud his eyes. She slowly leaned upward and allowed him to kiss her. Jonathan pulled her close and kissed her deeply. Elizabeth responded to his embrace but was disappointed when he pulled away to try to catch his breath.

"Why did you stop?" she asked confused. He looked into her eyes with the same flame of desire, "I care about you deeply and don't want to do anything to hurt you, Elizabeth. I don't want to rush you into anything and besides, this isn't exactly the proper place to further explore our feelings in such a manner. Do you not agree?"

She blushed brightly when she realized the full meaning of what he had said. Elizabeth nodded in agreement. "You're quite right, Jonathan. Maybe we should go back inside and join the others?"

"Go on ahead. I need a moment to collect myself," he replied with a mischievous smile. She laughed and retreated inside after giving him a quick kiss on the cheek. Elizabeth was growing quite fond of Jonathan, forgetting all about the date she missed that morning.

She went to the table where the others were seated and joined them with a smile on her face. Everyone grew quiet and seemed to be looking at her questioningly. "Is something wrong?" she asked her brother quietly.

"Not at all," he responded. "We're all so pleased that you and Jonathan seem to be getting along so well."

"Jonathan is very nice and easy to talk with," she replied looking curiously at her older brother. Everyone smiled approvingly at her comment.

"Good, good." Her brother replied looking very proud.

"Am I missing something?" she asked her brother quietly as she surveyed the others at the large round table.

"What do you mean?" Richard replied innocently. Elizabeth was about to push the issue when Jonathan appeared. He placed his hand gently on Elizabeth's shoulder as he took his seat beside her with a smile meant solely for her.

The group again looked proud of themselves as they gave each other secret knowing looks. Elizabeth didn't notice this time as she smiled at Jonathan. They all finished their coffee and desert then went back to the limousine waiting to take them back to the house. Everyone was in good spirits on the ride home, gathering in the library for the traditional cigar and late night brandy. Elizabeth said good night to the Parkers and her brother then climbed the stairs to retire for the evening. Elizabeth was about to shut the bedroom door when she heard footsteps behind her. Elizabeth turned to find Jonathan standing just outside her doorway with a grin on his face. "I wanted to say good night. I'll have to leave early tomorrow morning to prepare for some business appointments I have early Monday morning," he told her with regret. "I really had a wonderful time with you today. I was hoping you would allow me to call you this week?"

Elizabeth smiled brightly, "That would be lovely Jonathan. I enjoyed myself as well."

"Maybe I could come and see you next weekend?" he added hopefully.

"I think that would be nice," Elizabeth responded. A broad smile crossed Jonathan's face as he stepped closer to Elizabeth.

"Good night Elizabeth. I'll call you this week," he whispered softly as he leaned down and kissed her. She said good night and shut her door. She was happy with how the day had turned out. She was amazed at how fond she was of Jonathan after only one day. She slept fitfully that evening and woke refreshed and relaxed. The Marks enjoyed a late breakfast then thanked the Parkers for their hospitality. They would all be back home in by mid-afternoon. Elizabeth spent the ride home thinking of Jonathan and how she had enjoyed his company. She was looking forward to seeing him again.

They all sat quietly looking out the windows of the limousine at the passing landscapes while her brother was as usual working. He made some phone calls, went through some paperwork, and checked his emails on his laptop as they drove along. Susan being bored after a while complained to her husband that he never stopped working. 'Look at this beautiful scenery for crying out loud. It's so lovely out."

Irritated by the interruption he snapped at his wife. "Well, if I didn't have to play match maker to find a suitable husband for my sister I could've gotten my work done on time."

Elizabeth was stunned by the abrupt statement. She stared at her brother with horror on her face. "Is that what this weekend was about? Finding me a husband?" she asked. "Well?"

Richard looked at his younger sister not even embarrassed by his slip. "That's right. Do you think I want to take care of you for the rest of your life? Jonathan is a very suitable match and he comes from a proper background. What difference does it make anyway? You seem to like him just fine."

"I liked him fine enough, but I have no intention of marrying him or anyone else anytime in the near future. I intend to go to college and start a career," she told her brother stubbornly.

"A career?" her brother sneered over his paperwork he shuffled in irritation. "The only career you will have is taking care of your husband and giving him a proper heir."

Elizabeth looked at her brother in disbelief, horrified to realize he actually meant was he was saying. "I will not be anyone's puppet Richard. I will go to college before ever considering marriage to anyone and when that day comes it will not be to a chauvinistic control freak looking for a Barbie doll for a wife!" she said angrily.

Her brother simply laughed at her and went back to his phone calls. This further infuriated Elizabeth. "How dare he treat me like this?" she thought to herself. She was incredibly irritable the rest of the drive home. She couldn't wait to escape the close confines of the limousine which despite its luxurious size suddenly seemed to shrink to the size of a small sardine can.

Elizabeth ran to her room the moment the limousine pulled up in front of the house. Behind closed doors she allowed her emotions to take over. She fumed and sobbed for almost an hour before dragging herself into the bathroom to shower and dress. Shortly afterwards she heard a knock at her door. "Who is it?" she called.

"It's Susan. May I come in?" her sister in-law asked from the other side of the closed door.

"Yes." Elizabeth reluctantly replied.

The door slowly opened and Susan took a look around and then studied Elizabeth face. "Dinner will be ready soon but I came to tell you that you have a phone call."

"Who is it?" she asked.

"It's Jonathan," Susan replied.

"Could you please tell him that I'm not feeling well and I'll call him back later? I have a terrible headache. I don't think I'll be down for dinner either. I thought I would take some aspirin and rest for a while." Elizabeth replied coldly.

"Now Elizabeth, I understand how you feel but do you really want to further irritate your brother? If you don't take the call he will assume you're simply being stubborn."

"Thank you for your concern Susan. Would you excuse me now so I can get some rest?" Elizabeth replied firmly.

"Alright then, I'll give him the message. Shall I have someone bring your dinner to your room?" Susan offered trying to be understanding.

"No, thank you," was all Elizabeth could manage through her frustration.

Susan scurried off leaving Elizabeth angry all over again. After a few moments she couldn't take anymore, feeling trapped in her room and decided to take a walk along the beach to clear her head. The sound and smell of the ocean and feel of the sand under her feet always made her feel better. She always escaped to the beach whenever she needed time to herself.

Elizabeth quietly made her way downstairs leaving through the servants' entrance to avoid being seen by her brother or his wife. She walked quickly at first in case anyone spotted her then slowed her pace. Elizabeth was so deep in thought thinking about everything that had happened over the last two days that she didn't realize she had walked all the way down to the marina. She looked around and decided to sit at the bar and order an iced tea.

She sat on the dock recalling the last time she was sipping an iced tea at the marina. "Was that only two days ago?" she thought. So much had happened over two short days. She met William, met Jonathan and then found out her brother was trying to marry her off to the man most likely to improve his social standing. Elizabeth was feeling hurt and frustrated over her brother's coldness towards her.   All she was to him was an obligation he couldn't wait to be rid of.

As she finished her tea she decided to take a walk down the dock. She strolled along until she came upon the boat she had admired only two days before. She wondered if William was there. She called out his name but no one answered. She tried to peek through the windows but couldn't see much past the drapes hanging to provide privacy. She wondered if she should simply climb aboard and knock on the closed door. She was trying to make up her mind whether to leave or wait to see if he would come back when she heard footsteps and then a voice behind her. "May I help you?"

She turned recognizing his voice instantly. "William, how are you?" she asked nervously.

"Fine, how are you?" he asked her coldly.

Elizabeth knew by the tone in his voice that he was upset with her for not making their date the day before. "William…." He wouldn't look at her so she touched his arm. "I'm very sorry I didn't make it yesterday. I was…..unavoidable detained. Please forgive me. I wanted to be here, truly I did."

He looked at her as if he were considering whether he should forgive her or not but said nothing. Elizabeth only felt worse and decided it was a mistake to have come. "I'm sorry. I guess I should go," she said softly as she turned to leave.

"Don't go." Elizabeth looked at him for a moment then took his hand as he silently helped her onto the boat. The moment they were out of public view William pulled her close and tight to him looking into her eyes. She saw something in his eyes that both excited and scared her. She couldn't find any strength after the rotten day she had to fight the feelings she had for him. She looked up at him, knowing she wanted more. All her nerves came alive as he slowly bent down to kiss her. This time she allowed herself to enjoy it, responding with all the passion she felt for him. With a groan he lifted her, put her on the couch and lowered himself on top of her. He enjoyed her response as he kissed and caressed her. Elizabeth responded in turn and ran her fingers through his hair then up and down his back, exploring the taunt muscles all over his body.

William abruptly pulled himself up and off of Elizabeth without warning. She looked at him confused. "What's wrong?" she asked.

Running his fingers through his own hair in frustration he groaned and turned away from her. Elizabeth sat up on the coach and re-adjusted her clothing. She was confused and embarrassed. "William what is it?" she asked again.

He poured himself a whiskey, took a large swallow then turned to face her. "I want you too much Elizabeth. I don't want this to be a fling or simple flirtation. I did nothing but think about you since the night I bumped into you at the restaurant and when you didn't show up yesterday I was beside myself. I need to know that this is more to you than just a game."

Elizabeth was stunned and didn't know what to say. After a few moments thought she replied, "I have very strong feelings for you William. This is not a game I'm playing." She walked towards him with a smile on her face. Feeling brave, she took the glass half full of whiskey from him, taking a large swallow for herself. She smiled up at him, took his hand and led him into the bedroom below.

They explored each other, allowing their passion to lead the way. William slowly and expertly seduced Elizabeth teasing her with his caresses. They slowly removed each other's clothes piece by piece, allowing time to explore each newly exposed area of flesh. Elizabeth's defenses were destroyed and she could no longer resist the passionate emotions William invoked within her. She was being carried away on a sea of exquisite sensations unable to stop herself. As their passion grew with each moment Elizabeth was coming closer and closer to complete surrender. William softly caressed her soft skin and slowly let his hands travel over her flat young stomach to the moist area at the top of her thighs, gently teasing her with his fingers as she moaned with pleasure.

Once satisfied that she was at the point of no return he gently rolled on top of her preparing to take his satisfaction. He looked down at her and smiled gently, "Are you sure, Elizabeth?" he asked looking into her eyes.

"Yes, please William, yes," she responded huskily as she pulled him down towards her. He began to move gently, trying not to hurt her as he slowly applied pressure. Elizabeth stiffened as the pain took her by surprise. Feeling her stiffen William entered her with one swift movement as she cried out in pain.

"Are you okay?" he whispered. All she could do was nod as he gently began to move within her. The pain was soon forgotten, replaced by the pleasure he gave her.

William made love to Elizabeth, making her cry out over and over. Finally, she was overwhelmed by the sensation of her climax. When he knew she was about to reach her peek, he began to move more swiftly, thrusting hard into her as she moaned repeatedly. He looked at her innocent face and found himself angrily thrusting into her more roughly than he had intended until he also reached his climax. Panting, he slowly rolled over surprised and angry at the mixture of feelings he was himself experiencing. Elizabeth let the tears roll down her face caused by the massive amounts of emotions she just experienced.

Elizabeth rolled over and cuddled up against him with a smile. She was confused when he immediately pulled away from her, went into the bathroom and slammed the door. Elizabeth sat up in amazement. She didn't understand his sudden coldness after the tenderness of the moment and emotions they just shared. First she was hurt and confused then angry. "I can't believe this. How could I be so stupid?" She leapt out of the bed with tears rolling down her face and quickly found her clothes then got dressed. She stared at the closed bathroom door for a moment then angrily grabbed her handbag, running off the boat and down the dock. Not only embarrassed but extremely hurt and angry, she quickly made her way out of the marina and down to the beach, careful not to let anyone see the tears still streaming down her face.

William stared at himself in the mirror full of guilt and hating himself for feeling this way. "Get it together man!" he told himself sternly. "Stick to your plan. You have her right where you want her." He forced himself to think about why he was doing this in the first place. He thought of his sister then. The embarrassment and heartache she had suffered for years, struggling to take care of her son alone. He thought of the man responsible for his sister's heartache and allowed the anger to re-fuel his ambition to continue with his plan of revenge.

He regained his composure, splashed some cold water on his face and opened the bathroom door to find the bedroom empty. He quickly looked around and found Elizabeth's clothes were gone. "Shit," he said out loud, grabbing his clothes to get dressed. He slipped on his shoes and bolted off the side of the boat and up the dock. "She only has a few minutes head start," he thought. If he hurried he may be able to catch her and repair the damage before it was too late. "How could I let myself get emotionally involved?" he again scolded himself for being so stupid.

He ran down the docks and made his way to the beach scanning the people along the way but the thick sand forced him to slow down. After a while he spotted Elizabeth up ahead so he picked up his pace. When he almost reached her he yelled her name, "Elizabeth, wait!"

Elizabeth turned slightly and saw William jogging up behind her. She stubbornly kept walking and quickened her pace as she tried to wipe the tears from her face. "Elizabeth, please," he begged as he finally caught up to her and grabbed her arm. She tore away from his grip and continued on down the beach. "Elizabeth, please wait. I'm sorry. I didn't mean to hurt you!" He again took her by the arm in an attempt to stop her. She angrily swung around and slapped him hard across the cheek. William was momentarily stunned by the sting and froze. She glowered at him without saying a word and turned away once again.

This time when he caught up to her he roughly pulled her into his arms allowing her to flail away as she repeatedly smacked her fists into his chest and struggled to get out of his grip. He let her pound on his chest until her strength was gone and she crumbled into his arms sobbing. "I'm sorry baby. I didn't mean to hurt you. I guess I got a little overwhelmed and scared of my feelings for you," admitting inwardly that most of what he just said was true. "Please forgive me?" he asked as he lifted her tear stained face up so he could look into her eyes.

"I don't understand William. After everything you were suddenly so cold. I thought you had used me and played with my feelings just to get me into bed."

William gave her a small apologetic smile, "Elizabeth, I'm sorry for making you feel that way but believe me it wasn't you. I adore you," he told her in an attempt to regain her trust. "Please come back to the boat with me. I can cook you something to eat... Please," he begged with one of his practiced smiles he used to get his way. Elizabeth's resistance began to melt away. She reluctantly agreed still feeling slightly muffled by the incident.

William took her hand then they quietly walked back to his boat together. He pulled her into his arms and kissed her gently when they reached the privacy of the boat. Looking down at her, he again felt a pang of guilt as he noticed how puffy and red her face and eyes were from crying. Elizabeth excused herself and went to freshen up in the bathroom while William began searching for something he could make them to eat. He settled on a Swiss cheese and mushroom omelet that he served with melon slices and toasted English muffins.

They ate the meal he cooked in silence both realizing how hungry they were from their earlier exertion. Elizabeth rose and began clearing the dirty dishes into the sink. William grabbed his plate, placed it in the sink, putting his arms around Elizabeth as she washed the dishes. "I can take care of these later," he whispered in her ear as he began nibbling on her lobe.

"Keep it up and you most certainly will have to take care of these later," she replied as a shiver went down her spine. He turned her around and began kissing her lips while stroking her back side. Her body responded immediately to his touch as he pulled her even closer to him. He lifted her up in his arms and carried her back to the bedroom. Elizabeth was once again swept away by a sea of sensations and emotion. They made love again until they were both spent and satisfied. This time he pulled her close making sure not to repeat his earlier mistake. They were trying to catch their breath when Elizabeth suddenly sat upright, "What time is it?"

"It's almost eight-thirty," William told her.

"Oh my god! I have to get home. I completely lost track of the time." Elizabeth was scurrying about the room trying to gather her clothes. "William where did my..." she began when he dangled one of her undergarments in the air. She went over to get it from him but he grabbed her, pinning her down on the bed.

"Did I say it was time for you to leave," he said teasing her still bare breasts with his tongue. "William, please I have to go.... Oh...." Elizabeth moaned than groaned as he let her go. She stayed there for a moment, not wanting to leave.

"You better get before we get started all over again," he told her huskily.

She rose from the bed and began dressing. "Elizabeth, can I drive you home? I have a rented car parked right outside the marina."

She nervously shook her head as she finished dressing. "No. I'll be fine. Thanks."

She ran into the bathroom to brush her hair and freshen up. She needed to be sure she looked normal when she returned home. She came out of the bathroom to find William half dressed. "Well Elizabeth, are you even going to give me your telephone number or are you just going to pop in and out as if I'm a cabaña boy?" he asked with a smirk on his face.

She looked up at him realizing he was teasing her when she saw he was smiling. She retrieved her handbag and quickly scribbled her number on the scrap of paper she found. "Here you are. Call me whenever you'd like. I have to go," she quickly kissed him trying to escape but he grabbed her arm.

"Hey, wait just a minute. What's the rush here? Oh my god…. You're involved with another man?!" William accused trying to turn the tables on her to strengthen his hold on her.

Elizabeth laughed and again tried to pull away. When he didn't release her she looked at him and realized he was serious. He looked very angry or was that jealousy on his face? She sat down next to him on the bed and looked him right in the eye. "I am not seriously involved with any other man except my over bearing and very controlling older brother." She saw the muscles in his jaw and shoulders relax so she kissed him again and left. "Call me."

As William listened to her footsteps moving quickly up the dock, he smiled widely glad that he hadn't ruined everything. Elizabeth is very beautiful and he was enjoying seducing her much more than he had anticipated but would not allow himself to truly care about her. He was determined to finish what he started.

Elizabeth walked home as quickly as she could, doing her best to be as quiet as possible as she entered the house hoping she wasn't missed. As she tip toed up the stairs toward her room her hopes were dashed by the booming sound of her brother's angry voice behind her. "Elizabeth! Where have you been?" he asked.

She turned to face her brother while she tried to think of an explanation for her absence. "I took a walk on the beach."

"You've been gone a long time for a simple walk. I went to your room right after dinner to speak to you and you weren't there. That was hours ago," he said not satisfied with her explanation.

"I got a little carried away and ended up down at the marina. I ran into a friend from school and just lost track of time. I'm sorry if you were worried."

"This is the second time you disappeared without letting anyone know where you were going Elizabeth. Please don't let it happen again," he said angrily. Elizabeth nodded and tried to flee to her room but was stopped again by her brother. "Jonathan called twice this evening for you Elizabeth. He called before dinner when you refused to take his call then again later. You will not embarrass me with your rudeness. Next time I expect you to take his call," he ordered as he walked away.

Elizabeth went to her room wanting nothing but some time to think about everything that has happened to her in the last couple of days. She began to worry that what she allowed herself to do with William was a mistake. She felt like she was on a roller coaster the last few days. She wasn't only frustrated with her brother for trying to pawn her off on the Parkers but was also confused by her feelings for both William and Jonathan. The two men were so completely different. William made her feel alive and daring while Jonathan made her feel comfortable and safe. She also knew her brother wouldn't approve of William since he had his mind made up that Jonathan was the appropriate husband for her.

She sat on the balcony of her room looking up at the stars trying to make sense of her feelings. She had been so reckless today with William. They both had been reckless. Since they hadn't used any type of birth control that day, fear gripped her at the thought that she could be pregnant. Elizabeth's fear subsided as the memory of their love making left her hungry for more. William certainly had gotten under her skin. They would definitely have to be more careful in the future….if they had a future. Completely exhausted from her emotions, Elizabeth finally crawled into bed and curled up under the covers.

Chapter Four

William woke early the next morning after sleeping soundly in the bed he had shared with Elizabeth the day before. He decided to visit Elizabeth at her home instead of calling her. She may be upset at the unexpected visit but decided he would deal with that when the time came. He was sure he had Elizabeth wrapped around his finger after yesterday anyway and felt confident he could charm her into just about anything.

He was in a great mood and was ready to move into the next phase of his plan. He sat outside sipping his coffee and ate his breakfast of toast and jam while he planned his day.

Elizabeth woke up feeling quite confused and full of doubt about her actions of the previous day. She showered and dressed then joined her family in the dining room for breakfast. She ate her grapefruit and toast with little enjoyment as she sipped a cup of hot coffee. They were all quiet this morning which suited Elizabeth just fine. She was not in the mood to argue with her brother this morning. She still hadn't come to terms with all that had happened and couldn't understand how she could be attracted to two completely different men for completely different reasons at the same time.

When Elizabeth was just finishing her breakfast, she heard the telephone ring. "Excuse me, Elizabeth. You have a telephone call," Sally, the young maid informed her.

"Thank you." Elizabeth left the table without bothering to ask who it was. "Hello, Elizabeth speaking," she said into the receiver.

"Elizabeth! You're not easy to get on the phone. I understand you weren't feeling well yesterday. Feeling better today I hope," replied Jonathan Parker.

"Yes, I'm feeling much better today Jonathan. Thank you for asking," she replied.

"Is everything alright? You don't sound very happy to hear from me," he asked sulking at her lack of enthusiasm.

"Oh, Jonathan, I'm sorry. I just have a lot on my mind and I didn't sleep very well last night."

"I am sorry to hear that. Anything I can do to help?" he offered.

"No. I just have some things I need to work through," she said warmed by his concern.

"Nothing too serious I hope?"

"No. Nothing too serious," she lied.

"Well please let me know if I can help. Even if you just need an ear or a shoulder, mine are always available," he replied hoping she would open up to him.

"Thank you. I'll keep that in mind," she told him.

"Elizabeth…..I was hoping you would allow me to visit this weekend. I have some late meetings on Friday but I could drive down early Saturday?" he asked nervously still unsure if his attention was completely welcome.

She hesitated for a moment unsure if she should encourage him any further, but found she wanted to see him. "Maybe if I see him again I'll be able to figure things out," she thought to herself. "That would be nice, Jonathan," she replied with mild enthusiasm.

"Great! I'll see you on Saturday around lunchtime," he responded with obvious delight. They said good-bye then Elizabeth returned the phone to its cradle, startled when she turned to find her brother standing behind her.

"What things could you have on your mind that need to be worked out?...Besides how to style your hair that is," he asked sarcastically.

"You were listening to my conversation Richard?"

"Yes and it's a good thing you allowed Jonathan to visit this weekend. I will not have you embarrassing me," he replied dryly.

"Richard, I am not a child! I did not allow him to come see me for your benefit!" she said angrily.

He glared at her for a moment then waved his hand to dismiss her as he went to retrieve his brief case so he could leave for the office. His casual dismissal of her further frustrated Elizabeth. She was about to return to her room when she heard voices in the foyer. As she listened chills ran down her spine. She thought she recognized the male voice talking to her brother. She slowly walked in the direction of the foyer trying to listen to the voices more closely. She was sure that it was William's voice she heard.

"....do not think that would be a good idea, Mr. Moore," she heard her brother say sternly. She took a deep breath and walked into the foyer.

"Elizabeth, apparently you've been making some new acquaintances since you've been home. Mr. Moore just requested my permission to visit with you this morning. Of course, I told him that would not be possible since you are engaged." Elizabeth's mouth hung open in disbelief at what her brother just said. She looked at William who was obviously hiding his fury and quietly glared at her. Elizabeth was so furious with her brother for lying to William and so stunned by the situation she didn't have any idea how to handle it or what to say.

"I apologize for the intrusion. I wasn't aware of Elizabeth's engagement but it was nice to meet you Mr. Marks. Good luck to you Elizabeth. He's a lucky man," he replied with hidden sarcasm only she realized was there. She couldn't manage to say anything when William turned to leave.

"Good day Mr. Moore," her brother said dryly as he shut the front door firmly behind the unwanted guest.

Elizabeth just stood there and stared at her brother, not believing he had stooped to lies to get rid of someone simply because he wanted her to marry Jonathan. "Why did you lie to him and say I was engaged?" she demanded.

"I did not lie. You are engaged," he replied coldly.

"I am no such thing Richard and you know it!" she cried.

"Oh but you are, my dear. I have had this arranged for years now. Of course, we were hoping the situation would present itself in a much more natural fashion." Elizabeth couldn't believe her ears.

"I will marry no man unless I make that decision! Do you understand me Richard! No one!" She ran up the stairs crying hysterically. Richard dismissed her out burst with a simple shrug of his shoulders and wave of his hand then went off to work without a second thought for his distraught sister.

Elizabeth threw herself on her bed sobbing uncontrollably. She couldn't believe her brother actually thought he could pre-arrange a marriage for her! She would not stand for it! She cried and fumed for an hour before she was able to finally calm down. She went into the bathroom and splashed cold water on her face. She looked in the mirror to find she was literally a mess. "You will no longer do this to me, Richard," she said to her reflection in the mirror. Elizabeth freshened herself up, changed her clothes, went down the stairs, out the back door and down to the beach. She knew exactly where she was going and why. She would not allow her brother to ruin things with William before she even had a chance to figure out what she wanted. She walked as quickly as the sand would allow her feet to go, holding her shoes in her hand. When she reached the marina she brushed off her feet and replaced her shoes then made her way to William's boat.

Without hesitation she stepped onto the boat yelling his name as she entered the salon that opened up to the modest kitchen area. "William? Are you here?" she yelled as she surveyed the room and found no one. She stepped down to check the bathroom and bedroom but again found no one. Frustrated that he wasn't there she was unsure what to do. After she considered her options for a few moments she decided to get comfortable and wait for him to return whether he liked it or not. "After all I did nothing wrong. I am not engaged." She said to herself in the empty room knowing she must convince William that her brother had lied to him. She found herself feeling quite tired so she removed her shoes and stretched out on William's bed, taking a deep breath and smelling the pillow that held the lingering scent of his cologne. After a while Elizabeth fell asleep feeling exhausted from the emotional morning and spirited walk from the house to the marina.

William pulled into his assigned parking spot at the marina after taking a long drive in his convertible to clear his head and recover from his failed meeting with Elizabeth. He had been pleased but not surprised that Richard didn't recognize him after all the years that had passed. He was surprised and angry that Elizabeth lied to him and was not honest about her engagement. Although he was sure she was attracted to him, he was no longer confident that he had her wrapped around his finger as he assumed before. He was certain that he was her first lover but outside of that maybe she wasn't as innocent as he first expected. He climbed aboard his boat carrying the take-out food he had picked up on his ride. He heard a soft sound coming from his bedroom while he was unpacking the food. He walked towards the bedroom quietly with fists clenched ready to pounce on any intruder. His arms fell to his side as he recognized the sleeping body lying on his bed.

He watched her sleep for a few moments wonder-ing how long she had been there before walking over to the bed softly shaking her. She slowly opened her eyes as she looked around remembering where she was and why she was there. William stood over her with his hands on his hips glaring at her. "What do you think you're doing here?"

"William, I had to come. I had to see you and explain things," she said as she sat up and followed him out to the salon.

"You don't have to explain anything. Your brother did it for you," he said coldly.

"My brother lied to you William. I am not engaged. He just wants me to marry the son of one of his business associates so he was simply trying to get rid of you. I have told him more than once I will not marry anyone for those reasons," she explained.

"Do you honestly expect me to believe that? I asked you just yesterday if you were involved with someone else when you were trying to rush out of here and you said no. Now I show up to surprise you and invite you to breakfast then your brother tells me you're engaged? What do you expect me to think?" He responded playing with her emotions in an attempt to strengthen his hold on her.

"I understand you're having doubts but you have to believe me." She walked over to him and looked up into his eyes, "Please believe me. I am not lying to you! I'm crazy about you and want nothing more than to be with you."

"Then come away with me Elizabeth. We can take the boat and travel for a while. We can take some time to really get to know each other without your brother's interference. What do you say?" He stood looking down at her with a look that said "now or never".

Elizabeth was startled by his request and didn't know what to say. "Well?" William persisted. "If things are as you say then you're free to do what you want. You say you want to be with me, then be with me," he said firmly, intentionally challenging her with his statement.

She looked at him thinking about her brother and how angry he would be if she left with William. The thought of defying her brother made her want to go just to spite him however she realized she was tempted simply because she wanted to be with William.

"Okay. I'll go with you William," she smiled then laughed as he hugged her, twirling her around. He bent down and kissed her hard on the lips.

"What will I do for clothes? I have no money with me either." She asked him after realizing that she could not return and retrieve any money or clothes without drawing attention to her plans.

"No worries, darling. We'll buy you some clothes and I have more money than we'll need. But for now, you don't need either money or those clothes you have on," he responded as he tossed her over his shoulder and carried her into the bedroom. She couldn't help but laugh as he tossed her onto the bed with a wicked grin spread across his face.

He climbed on the bed and crawled towards her like a panther about to pounce on his prey when Elizabeth remembered something that had concerned her the evening before and earlier that day. "William, I have something else to ask you. As you know you're my first lover," she said blushing shyly, "and we didn't use anything to protect us yesterday. I don't have any protection with me today either. Do you have anything?"

He smiled at her, "You need not worry about getting pregnant my dear. I had a vasectomy years ago."

William began to kiss and nuzzle her neck and earlobe but Elizabeth questioned him further. "Does this mean you can never have children?" she asked disappointed since she always wanted children one day.

William gave up nibbling her neck for a moment, "A woman I had been intimate with tried to claim her child was mine years ago. A simple DNA test proved the child wasn't mine and she was simply after my money. I think she thought I would simply pay her off to be rid of her. After that I had the vasectomy but not before I had plenty of sperm frozen so I could one day have children of my own. I can't however get anyone pregnant by the traditional method."

She was happy to hear he was able to have children even if it wasn't in the traditional fashion since she desperately wanted children one day. She was also relieved to know that she had no chance of being pregnant from her escapade the day before.

Realizing she could enjoy herself without worry she turned towards him with a mischievous smile on her face and began to kiss and nibble his ear lobes. They made love until they were both dripping with sweat and satisfied. They showered together and made love again under the cool stream of water then reluctantly got dressed. William took her to dinner and then shopping for some clothes as he promised. On their way back to the boat, they also stopped at a late night grocery store to buy some supplies.

They unpacked all their supplies then she made some space in his drawers and closets for her new clothes. They were both exhausted and decided to turn in so they could get an early start in the morning. Elizabeth was anxious to get as far away from her brother as soon as possible. Once in bed and the lights were off, William rolled over to cuddle up against his new roommate. It didn't take long before he found himself making love to her once more. Afterwards they fell asleep holding each other, exhausted from their day.

Richard Marks III was pacing furiously back and forth in the library with a glass of whiskey in his hand. He couldn't believe Elizabeth had disappeared again and hadn't yet returned. It was very late and already dark outside. She had left no word with anyone in the house. He wasn't happy about the visit from the gentleman earlier that morning requesting a date with his young sister and suspected he had something to do with his sister's disappearance. Richard had already called a private detective earlier in the day to run a back ground check on the man but hadn't yet received the requested information. "He will be sorry if he had anything to do with my sister's disappearance," Richard vowed to himself. At nearly midnight he was completely beside himself with rage. "If she is not in her room by the time I wake up in the morning, I'll call the police and report that man as a suspect in her disappearance!" Raging irrationally he took the last swig of his bourbon throwing the glass angrily into the fireplace before stomping upstairs to bed.

Chapter Five

William woke early the next morning knowing he would need to set sail as early as possible. He was sure Elizabeth's brother was aware of his sister's absence by now and it wouldn't take long for him to suspect Elizabeth was with him after their meeting the previous morning. William quietly left the bedroom trying not to disturb Elizabeth before he had the boat out of the marina and well on its way in case she lost her nerve. He moved around the boat quietly, making coffee while he removed the lines that kept the boat secured to the dock. He took his coffee, started the engine and smoothly maneuvered the boat out of the slip, making his way to the open sea.

He had been carefully tracking the weather in the hopes his plan to take Elizabeth away would work although he hadn't expected her brother to assist in his efforts. An hour into the trip Elizabeth woke up startled to realize the boat was already moving. Panicking for a moment, she collected herself then went to the bathroom to freshen up. She was feeling a little nervous when she joined William on the upper deck. "Good morning," she greeted him awkwardly. She instantly relaxed when he flashed a big smile and kissed her softly on the lips.

"Did you sleep well?" he inquired.

"Yes actually. I think you wore me out," she said playfully.

He looked at her grinning, "I plan to wear you out today, tomorrow and the next day...and the next day..." She couldn't help but laugh at his promise.

"Did you eat anything yet?" she asked. He shook his head in response, "I wanted to get going and I thought I would wait for you."

"Okay. You drive and I'll make us something to eat," she told him returning back downstairs. She surveyed their supplies and decided to make a cheese omelet with toast. She placed the food on a wooden serving tray with two small glasses of orange juice then brought the tray to William on the upper deck. They ate their breakfast while quietly enjoying the ocean breeze and the slow rocking of the boat against the ocean waves. When they were finished Elizabeth took the dirty dishes below and began to clean up. As she washed and dried the dishes she thought happily how relaxed she was and tried to push all thoughts of her brother to the back of her mind. She was sure that he was aware of her absence by now and probably beside himself. She sadly admitted to herself that his main concern would be the embarrassment her absence would cause in regards to his arrangement with the Parkers. She felt slightly guilty that she wouldn't be there when Jonathan came to visit her on Saturday but she knew now which man she wanted to be with.

Richard Marks, III woke early and immediately went to Elizabeth's quarters to be sure she had returned. He didn't bother to knock on the door and swore loudly when he found her quarters empty and that her bed hadn't been slept in. He left her quarters extremely angry and went to make some calls. "When I get a hold of that girl she will regret ever defying me!" he said out loud in frustration.

Richard called his contact at the local police department and explained the situation, stressing the importance of keeping the issue quiet. He gave the policeman her description and the description of the uninvited visitor, Mr. Moore. The policeman asked him some questions about her various friends and social habits which Richard answered to the best of his ability.

The officer informed him that technically because of her age she could not be considered missing until forty-eight hours after she was last seen however due to their friendship he would begin to make inquiries immediately. Richard thanked him and continued to make some calls regarding his sister's disappearance.

He called the private detective next, telling him to complete the back ground check immediately. He ordered him to begin searching for his sister and Mr. Moore. Afterwards, Richard went back to his normal work day while he waited for news on his sister's where-a-bouts.

Elizabeth settled into a routine of cooking and sun bathing while William planned their trip with strategic stops for fuel and entertainment along the way. They docked in Atlantic City where he treated her to day of pampering at one of the casino's spas then an evening of dinner, dancing and some light gambling. Elizabeth was happier than she had ever been in her life, enjoying William's constant affection and attention. Having not received any real affection from anyone since her mother had died she was devouring every bit of the attention he offered.

Each day flowed into the next as they made their way down the coast towards Florida. Elizabeth trusted William completely doubting nothing he said and questioned nothing he did. She gave him her heart and body completely, sharing stories of her childhood including how she had felt when her parents died and Richard sent her to the boarding school. Everyday seemed to bring them closer together. They made love almost every morning and almost every evening during the first week of their adventure.

They reached Florida where William decided they would stay for a while. They spent their days walking the beach and swimming in the ocean. One of the days William rented a convertible and they drove around enjoying the sites. He spoiled her with a shopping spree, buying her some new clothes. They went to dinner at one of the restaurants they came upon where he presented her with a delicate gold and diamond bracelet that was accented with small gold hearts. Elizabeth was ecstatic with his generous gift, hugging and kissing him with a big smile on her face. It was the first real gift of jewelry she ever received from a man that she cared about. "I love it William. I'll treasure it always," she told him as he put it on her wrist.

William was feeling very proud of himself. His plan was working better than he ever thought possible. Elizabeth was completely under his spell and if all went well he would only have to keep up the charade for another week or so. He pictured Richard and his reaction to not only his sister's disappearance but when he found out who he really was. This brought a smile to his face that quickly faded as he remembered his own sister's struggles and heartache that resulted from carrying the child of a man who deserted her and her unborn child not only emotionally but financially as well. Richard Marks III had gone to great lengths to avoid any responsibility for the child what so ever. After a DNA test Richard insisted upon turned out negative, William's sister sobbed hysterically swearing to William that Richard was the only man she had ever been with. William visited the lab technician in charge of the test and managed to find out that Richard had bribed him with a combination of money and black-mail since the technician was actively cheating on his wife with one of the female staff. William had tried to have another DNA test ordered by the courts but after being denied his request he suspected that Richard Marks also had the judge in his pocket.

His sister endured the heartache of being coldly tossed aside like an old blanket when she told Richard she was pregnant then endured the pain and struggle of being an unwed young mother with only a high-school diploma, forced to drop out after her second semester in college to work and care for her child alone. William provided them as much assistance as possible but since he was also working his way through college it left his sister and her child living a very poor lifestyle. His sister suffered during childbirth due to complications they suspected were due to emotional stress and having to waitress up until the moment she went into labor. He vowed that one day he would make Richard Marks, III pay for what he had done to his innocent young sister.

William was torn from his thoughts when he heard his name called from below. "William, lunch is ready," Elizabeth yelled. William now being wealthy himself was used to a higher standard of cooking than Elizabeth could provide. Since she had always had someone else do the cooking for her, he politely ate everything she served him with enthusiasm making sure to thank her after each meal she prepared.

He made every attempt to make her trust him fully which was turning out to be very easy. Is this what Richard had done to his unsuspecting sister years ago when she was also innocent, naive and fresh out of school? He looked across the table at Elizabeth feeling slightly guilty. He quickly pushed aside his guilt, determined that he would have his revenge even if innocent Elizabeth had to suffer, getting caught in the middle.

Richard received a call from the detective he hired who had found out nothing except William Moore was a wealthy and successful broker without so much as a traffic ticket. He advised Richard that if Elizabeth was with him she probably went willingly. Richard had completely lost his temper at the thought his sister would have gone with him and defied him so blatantly. He ordered the detective to find this man whether her sister was with him or not. "The police can handle things if something has really happened to her. You concentrate on finding William Moore and do it fast!"

The police had made little progress although they had determined she was most likely not hurt since they checked all the local hospitals and morgues. Sergeant Barnett who had been contacted directly by Richard suspected that where ever his sister had gone she probably went willingly, knowing how Richard Marks could be. When the Sergeant questioned Richard if there had been any arguments that would have caused her to want to leave, he was told to mind his business and do his job. After Richard's response to his questions he was sure that there had been some type of argument that resulted in his sister's disappearance.

Sergeant Barnett had obtained a picture of Elizabeth then started up and down the beach questioning different people along the way to see if anyone recognized her or had spotted her recently. Eventually they made their way to the local marinas and finally got lucky after questioning one of the bartenders at the marina where William had docked his boat. The bartender recognized her immediately and told them she would come and sip an iced tea from time to time. "Did you ever see her here with anyone?" the Sergeant asked.

"Usually she was by herself but was joined by a gentleman once."

"When was this and do you remember what he looked like?" questioning him further.

"It was a couple of days ago I think. The man was fairly tall with dark hair. I had seen him around the marina before but don't know his name. You can check with the front office, maybe they could provide more information on the guy," he suggested to the officer.

Sergeant Barnett made his way to the front office where he questioned them about Mr. Moore. He requested to speak to the manager, showing his badge to the receptionist. The receptionist called the manager's extension and informed him there was a policeman that needed to ask him some questions. The manager appeared after a moment and extended his hand, "My name is Tim Wilmar, Manager. What can I do for you officer?"

"Sergeant Barnett," he corrected the manager, "I need to know if you have any information or records regarding a man named Mr. Moore. We are trying to locate him in regards to a missing person case we're investigating," he explained.

"Oh my, who's missing?" asked the manager. "The name is confidential at this point. Could you please check your records?"

"Of course, Sergeant. Please have a seat for a moment while I look into it." The Sergeant impatiently took a seat in the office lobby.

Only a few moments later the manager returned with some papers in hand. "It appears we had a Mr. Moore in our records. According to our records, he leased a slip here on a week to week basis. About two days ago he paid his bill and departed," he told the officer.

"Is there anyone who would know if he left with a woman on board?" asked the Sergeant.

"We don't keep records of their guests however you could question some of the people in the slips that were next to him. They may have seen someone," he suggested then provided the Sergeant with a copy of the records which included the slip location and boat registration information.

"Thank you for your assistance Mr. Wilmar." He left the office making his way to the docks to question the neighboring boaters.

The Sergeant made his way down the docks to the slip where William Moore had his boat only a couple days before. He questioned the boaters on each side, having no luck with the first however the second was much more informative. The neighbor informed the officer that they had seen him with a woman.

The sergeant showed them a picture of Elizabeth, "Is this the woman that you had seen him with?" he asked.

"Yes. That's her," the woman confirmed.

"Do you know if she was with him when he departed last week?" he questioned further.

"I'm sorry. We weren't here when he departed so I couldn't say either way."

"I see," the Sergeant said disappointed he couldn't confirm for sure if Elizabeth had indeed left with him. He asked a few more questions about William and Elizabeth but didn't gain any other information that was useful. "Thank you for your help."

Since he had confirmation that Elizabeth had been on the boat before and the date of his departure was the day after her disappearance, the Sergeant was fairly certain she had left with William Moore. He would have to contact the coast guard and some marinas up and down the coast to try to track him down. "At least I have something to report to Richard," he thought to himself, although he wasn't looking forward to giving Richard the news, knowing he would be furious.

The Sergeant called the Coast Guard first so they could keep a look out for the craft. Then he called Richard to inform him of what progress had been made. As expected, Richard was furious after receiving the news but agreed that the date of William's departure and the date of his sister's disappearance wasn't a simple coincidence. He informed Richard of his call to the Coast Guard and let him know he would be researching marinas up and down the coast trying to track them down or at least get a clue of which direction they were headed.

Richard hung up the phone then dialed his private detective, sharing the new information. "I want them found! Do you hear me? I don't care if you have to rent a boat and visit every marina between here and the moon. You find them!" he exclaimed angrily into the telephone.

"Okay Richard. I'm on it." The detective, Harry Finch, hung up the phone and decided it was time to call in a favor. He dialed the number of an FBI friend he had and asked him to run a check on the guy, recent credit card use, and any other information he can get. The standard back up check he was able to run is no where near as detailed as an FBI check. His friend agreed and told him he would get back to him as soon as possible. "Great, this is a high-priority case – a real nasty high roller involved. The kind that you don't want to get angry," he stressed.

"Understood. I will get this to you ASAP."

After hanging up with his friend he went to his computer and searched marinas along the coast. He found a couple in each direction and began to make some calls in the hope he would find out what direction they were headed. By now they could be half way to Florida, he thought to himself. After a couple of calls he found a marina that remembered the name in Atlantic City. The front desk clerk told him that the information was confidential and they weren't permitted to discuss anything in detail but she believed she remembered the name and the gentleman. "Do you remember what the man looked like?" the Sergeant asked the clerk. "Tall, dark hair, and quite handsome in fact, which is why I remember him so well. Unfortunately he was with some cute little red head so I was out of luck," the clerk informed him. Finch stood up at the statement not expecting to hit pay dirt so soon.

"You wouldn't happen to have the name of the woman he was with?"

"No, not required. Sorry."

"Would you be able to tell me if they're still there?" he again questioned the clerk.

"I'm sorry. As I said we aren't permitted to discuss that information. In fact, I probably wasn't supposed to tell you what I have already. I'm sorry I can't be of more help. Have a nice day," then the clerk hung up on the detective. He jotted the name and address of the marina down on a piece of scrap paper then called the airline for the first flight out to Atlantic City. He would rent a car there and start tracking them. He knew from personal experience that he could get more information in person when he was able to slip some money into the clerk's hand.

Chapter Six

William figured Richard would be on his trail soon so he didn't spend much time in one place until they got to Florida. Elizabeth was still happily going with the flow, not questioning anything he did. He took her to dinner at the marina restaurant and then took her dancing. They were having a wonderful evening until an old love song was played by the DJ at someone's request. Elizabeth was suddenly taken back to when her parents were alive and remembered her parents dancing to the tune at one of their summer evening garden parties. She remembered how she thought her mother looked like a princess as her father twirled her smoothly around the patio they used for a dance floor. Tears welled up in Elizabeth's eyes and she ran off to the ladies room without an explanation. William was confused by her sudden onslaught of tears and waited patiently for her to return to him. After about ten minutes she came out of the ladies room still looking upset. "I'm sorry William. Could we go back to the boat now?" she begged quietly.

"Sure," he replied putting his arm around her waist, escorting her from the restaurant. Once they were outside in the dark he attempted to find out why she ran off. "Elizabeth, what's wrong sweetheart? I'm confused. One minute we were having fun, the next you're in tears in the bathroom."

"It's nothing. Just forget it," she told him softly.

"Just forget it? I see," he removed his arm from her waist and walked stiffly next to her. Elizabeth felt him pull away and stiffen next to her which made her feel even worse. She looked up at him, saw that his jaw was set and knew she had upset him. They reached the boat and Elizabeth quickly climbed aboard, retreating to the bathroom as fresh tears rolled uncontrollably down her cheeks.

William was again surprised with Elizabeth's emotional outburst. He went aboard the boat and went in search of Elizabeth. He could hear her sobbing from the hallway and softly knocked on the door. "Elizabeth, what's wrong and don't tell me to forget it this time," he questioned through the closed door.

"Please leave me alone for a while. I'll be fine!" she hollered back at him.

"Fine!" he replied frustrated and stomped off to pour himself a glass of bourbon. William grabbed a cigar and went up on deck. William felt helpless and didn't know what to do. He was a little insulted that she wouldn't confide in him. He couldn't figure out why he was so upset. Was it because he actually cared what was wrong with her or was he just insulted because she didn't trust him as much as he thought?

A good half-hour went by before Elizabeth finally emerged from the bathroom and joined him on the deck. "I'm sorry William. I'm feeling a little embarrassed," she told him softly.

"What's wrong Elizabeth? Please tell me," he begged.

Elizabeth sat on the chair next to him and took a deep breath of the fresh ocean air. "I just had a bad moment. It happens once in a while when something catches me off guard and reminds me of my parents. They died when I was almost thirteen and then my brother sent me to the boarding school," she said in an attempt to explain her outburst.

"What was it that reminded you of your parents?" he asked her curiously.

"It was the last song we danced to. At one of their summer garden parties my parents had danced to that song. It was one of the few moments I remember seeing my parents looking happy just being together. To me it seemed that my father was always working even when he was at home."

"I'm sorry about your parents. How did they die?" he asked softly.

"They died in a plane crash. They were returning from a ski trip and something went wrong with the engine. Since it was snowing the pilot wasn't able to safely land," she explained sadly.

"What was it like at the boarding school?" he asked with even more curiosity, wanting to hear what her childhood was like without her parents.

"Well, I didn't want to go. Richard sent me there after I got into a little trouble at school. I guess you can say I was angry and acting out in reaction to my parents' death." Suddenly angry she continued to tell him about her brother. "I think it was just the excuse Richard needed to send me away. I don't think he wanted me around then and he doesn't now. In fact, I would doubt he would even be looking for me now if it wasn't for the fact he has some type of arrangement worked out with one of his business associates. He actually has an "arrangement" for me to marry their son! I can't believe he is so cold and uncaring! I have no family that cares for me anymore!" She began to cry once again.

William hugged her, suddenly wanting to protect her from the evil Richard Marks. He knew full well how cruel and heartless he was but to treat his own flesh and blood with such disregard made him even worse. Holding Elizabeth as she cried filled him with guilt that was completely overwhelming. She was truly an innocent victim that didn't deserve what he was doing to her just to get back at her brother. How could he have been so stupid to believe he could be as cruel as Richard Marks? He wanted to confess everything to Elizabeth but couldn't bring himself to tell her, knowing it would probably destroy her to know how he had deceived her.

William tucked Elizabeth into bed and held her until she fell asleep. William wanted to fix everything he had done but wasn't sure how to do it. William tossed and turned most of the night trying to figure out where to go from here. Her explanation of her parents' death troubled him. He wasn't sure why but couldn't shake the odd feeling. Maybe he had read about it when he was younger or maybe it was just his sudden need to protect her that made him feel this way. William admitted to himself that he cared deeply for Elizabeth and no longer had the desire to continue with his original plans. He would still love to see Richard Marks get a taste of his own medicine but could no longer follow through with his plans knowing Elizabeth would be hurt in the process. He realized Richard had already hurt his sister enough.

It had been only a few short weeks since she had given her heart and body to William so willingly and it took only those few short weeks for Elizabeth to capture his unwillingly heart. When William finally fell to sleep right before sunrise he was haunted by dreams of Elizabeth crying, asking him how he could do such a thing.

Harry Finch arrived at the Atlantic City Airport exhausted from his flight, not having slept since he had gotten the information on Elizabeth. He immediately rented a car, bought a map, driving directly to the marina to interview the staff face-to-face. It didn't take long to obtain the information he was looking for once he bribed the desk clerk with a one-hundred dollar bill. He found out that William Moore was there for only one night a couple of days before. Harry concluded they were probably heading towards Florida but had no idea how many stops along the way they would make or if they would turn around and head back to Connecticut.

Harry decided to check into a hotel so he could do some homework and make some calls before deciding how to proceed. He began searching for marinas on his laptop from Atlantic City to Florida and wrote each address and telephone number down in his notebook.

While he was doing his research his cell phone rang. "Hello. Harry Finch speaking," he answered.

"Harry, this is Tom. How are you?" the caller replied.

"Not bad, Tom. Have you managed to find out anything?" he asked his friend from the FBI.

"As a matter of fact I found out some very interesting information about your mystery man. William Moore was born William Blake. He changed his name right after graduating college. He has one sister, Sarah, about three years younger. His father died unexpectedly in a car accident when he was in his early teens and his mother passed away from cancer right before he graduated high school. He has no record however, no tickets, nothing. He is quite wealthy by the looks of his financials. He made a lot of money in the stock market."

Harry absorbed the information then asked, "Why would anyone with a clean record change his name right after college?"

Tom had asked himself the same question. "Don't know. There have been no recent credit card transactions that would help you locate him either. There was only one rather large cash withdrawal the day before he left the marina in Connecticut. This guy is probably smart and doesn't wish to be tracked down. I have a couple more things I can check out. If I come up with anything else I'll let you know." Harry thanked Tom and hung up.

Harry decided to call Richard and update him on how the search was going but wanted to call a few marinas first in case he got lucky. Harry looked at his list, randomly calling different marinas, some in Florida and some in between. None of the marinas that he called had ever heard of William Moore. Harry realized he was starving and extremely tired. He decided to call Richard in the morning after he made a few more inquiries. In the meantime, Harry took a break to take a shower and get something to eat. He was exhausted and decided to call it a night.

The next morning Harry continued making calls to the various marinas on his list. He started checking for information under both names, Blake and Moore, assuming he may use another name if he suspected they could be looking for them. Finally he got lucky with a marina in Virginia who told him that Mr. Moore had stopped for only one night and was long gone. He crossed out all marinas on his list that were above Virginia and concentrated his attention on the marinas in the direction of Florida. After another long day of making calls to dozens of marinas that provided no further information Harry called it a night since the marinas would be closing soon anyway.

Elizabeth woke feeling much better and well rested. She rolled over and watched William sleep for a while but decided not to disturb him. She slipped out of bed and freshened up in the bathroom being careful not to wake him. She made a pot of coffee and a piece of toast. Elizabeth poured herself a hot mug of coffee and took her toast up on deck to enjoy the morning air. There were already some boaters moving about, some making their way to the marina restaurant for breakfast. Elizabeth felt happy again as she watched birds fly high into the sky then swoop down at the water in an attempt to find their morning meal.

She sat drinking in the sweet smell of the salty ocean air, thinking how lucky she was to have William. He had been so sweet to her the evening before trying to comfort her during her emotional outburst. After a while, William emerged holding his own hot cup of coffee. He leaned over and kissed the top of her head. "Why didn't you wake me?" he asked her with sleep deprived eyes.

"I didn't have the heart. You looked like you were sleeping deeply. You didn't even stir when I got out of bed," she said smiling up at him from her chair. "Did you sleep well?" she asked.

"So-so. It seemed to take forever to fall asleep but I'll be fine. What would you like to do today?"

Elizabeth thought for a moment. "How about we just have a lazy day? Maybe pack a lunch and relax on the beach?" she suggested.

"That sounds like a great idea," he said thinking he could get a nap later on the beach.

"Great. I'll pack us a cooler with lunch after I fix us some breakfast," she responded with enthusiasm. Elizabeth went about making breakfast while William tried not to doze off on the deck. She made them both some scrabbled eggs with toast, serving it on the deck. After they consumed their eggs and toast Elizabeth cleaned up then surveyed their supplies for something scrumptious for their picnic lunch. She found some fruits in the refrigerator and decided to make a fruit salad to pack in the cooler which included grapes, cantaloupe and apple slices. Then she made some chicken salad from a can of chicken breast meat she found in back of one of the cabinets. She put the chicken salad in a plastic container and packed some bread for the sandwiches. She made sure to pack up some napkins, plates and silverware along with cups for drinks. Elizabeth made a batch of homemade iced tea and poured it into a travel cooler made for liquids she had found under the sink. She was quite proud of what she managed to put together for their picnic and went in search of William to tell him she was ready. She went up on deck and laughed softly when she found William curled up on the lounge chair sleeping. Elizabeth decided not to disturb him and went for a walk.

She quietly climbed over the side and onto the dock, making her way to the marina. She decided to order a glass of lemonade and sit at one of the tables outside in the sun. She had just sat down when she heard a woman's voice calling her name. She looked around to see who could possibly be calling her since she knew no one except William in Florida. As she turned she spotted a small group walking toward her and instantly recognized the girl waving as one of her classmates from boarding school. The girl had long straight dark hair that went half-way down her back. "Elizabeth! How are you?" Tina Mason exclaimed as she hugged Elizabeth tightly.

"Fine, Tina. How are you?" she replied as she was released from Tina's friendly embrace.

"I'm great. You remember my parents don't you?" Elizabeth turned and greeted Mr. and Mrs. Mason. "We're here on vacation for the next week. What are you doing here?"

Elizabeth searched her mind frantically for a response to her friend's innocent question. "I'm also on vacation." Elizabeth replied hoping to avoid any further questions.

"Are you here with your brother? It would be wonderful to all get together for dinner!" her friend said excitedly.

Elizabeth again had to search frantically for a reason she couldn't have dinner with her schoolmate and her parents. "Oh, that would be wonderful except we are leaving in a little while. In fact I should probably get back now and help everyone get ready," she lied and felt awful for doing it.

"Oh, how disappointing!" her friend replied. "Please be sure to call me in a couple of weeks and maybe we can visit." Elizabeth was relieved that her friend didn't push the issue further agreeing to call her in two weeks to make plans to get together.

"Take good care of yourself, Tina. It was nice seeing you again Mr. Mason, Mrs. Mason," she hugged Tina goodbye and watched them shuffle off, thankfully in the opposite direction that she needed to go. Once the Mason's were out of sight Elizabeth quickly made her way back to the boat where she found William still sleeping.

She didn't hesitate to disturb him this time. "William, William, wake up!" she said, shaking him anxiously.

William woke with a start, "What is it?" he looked around with confusion on his sleepy face. He looked at Elizabeth and the worried expression on her face then sat upright suddenly awake and alert. "What's wrong?"

"We have to leave immediately," she said firmly.

"Why? What happened?" William asked seriously. "Is it your brother?"

Elizabeth sighed deeply, "No. But I just ran into a friend of mine from school and her parents. They're acquaintances of my brother."

William absorbed what she told him and thought for a moment. "What did you tell them?"

Elizabeth explained the whole conversation and how she managed to avoid an invitation to dinner with her family. "They're here for another week and I told them we were just leaving. If I run into them again it will definitely be a problem." Elizabeth finished explaining while pacing the deck nervously.

"You're right. We'll have to leave," he agreed after only a moments thought. "I'll go pay the bill and we'll set out right away. I guess we won't be having that lazy day you planned for us after all," he said with disappointment, "Can I have a rain check?" he said playfully trying to lighten her mood. Elizabeth couldn't help but smile at the childish pout he attempted to make with his lips.

She kissed him softly, "You can count on it, mister!"

William went inside to clean up still feeling very guilty and not knowing what to do. He couldn't shake his instinct about her parents' death either. William went to the front office to pay the bill and while he was away from Elizabeth decided to make a call. He dialed the number of a friend that worked at a newspaper in New York and asked him to find out anything he could about the death of Richard Marks II and his wife. "No problem. It might take me some time though. I'm pretty swamped here," he told William.

"Thanks. I'll be waiting to hear from you."

When he returned to the boat Elizabeth had everything else in order. They set sail, making sure to stop on the way out for fuel and again made their way to the next marina they would visit. Several hours later, they stopped at another marina a little farther down the coast of Florida and docked the boat. "This should give us enough distance away from your friends," he told Elizabeth confidently. Once again they settled into their new location but were both too tired to go out to eat. Elizabeth decided to serve the picnic lunch she had packed earlier that day as an early supper which they devoured in no time.

They rested lazily on the deck, sipping the home-made iced tea Elizabeth made that morning while watching the sky slowly turn dark as rain clouds approached blocking the rays of sunlight they had been enjoying. The rain began slowly but was shortly followed by thunder and lightning. The wind picked up splattering the deck with rain which forced them inside. "Well, what do we do now?" William asked her with a suggestive grin on his face.

Elizabeth smiled in answer and walked towards the bedroom. "I have a feeling we'll be able to find something to do with the rest of the day," she replied playfully. They spent the rest of the evening in bed making love until they were both exhausted. They fell into a fitful slumber and didn't wake until late the next morning.

William woke first watching Elizabeth sleep as a fresh wave of guilt washed over him. He was still trying to figure out how to repair the damage he may have caused. If he tells her the truth he was sure to lose her. "Maybe I should marry her before Richard finds us and interferes," he thought. If she was pregnant as he had intended he couldn't live with the damage and heartache it would cause her. He imagined what it would be like to be married to Elizabeth and was surprised at how happy the thought made him. He decided it was the only way. "I'll ask Elizabeth to marry me."

At that moment Elizabeth woke with a soft smile on her lips. "What are you looking so happy about?" she asked him playfully.

"Just being with you makes me happy," he told her sincerely. "How about we go up to the restaurant for some breakfast? After that I have a few business errands to take care of, so you'll have to do without my company for a few hours. Do you think you can survive my absence for a little bit today?" he asked grinning at her.

"I think I can manage for a while." She answered dryly, rolling her eyes dramatically. "Breakfast, however sounds wonderful. I'm starving," she informed him as she stretched her stiff muscles.

"Well let's get a move on then!" William said ripping the covers off them both and jumping out of bed. Elizabeth laughed at his sudden burst of energy, joining him in the bathroom to freshen up before going to breakfast.

They went to the restaurant and drank hot coffee as they waited for the food they ordered. William kept looking at her with a grin on his face. He reminded her of a child with a secret he couldn't wait to share. "What's going on?" she asked him curiously.

"What do you mean?" he replied trying to pretend he didn't know what she was talking about.

"Out with it, William! You keep looking at me with a shit-eating grin on your face and I demand to know what's going on!"

He gave her one of his charming smiles, "I'm quite sure I don't know what you mean."

She looked at him suspiciously as he cracked a grin he couldn't suppress. "You're full of it, mister."

He laughed and kissed her hard on the mouth. "If you say so, miss," he returned smoothly refusing to tell her before he was ready. They finished their meal and paid the bill. William escorted her back to the boat leaving shortly afterwards to complete his errands. He gave her a quick kiss, "Don't wander too far my love. I'll be back soon," he told her as he jumped onto the dock grinning ear to ear.

She looked at him and laughed. "He sure is in a great mood today," she said to herself as she went to pack a beach bag. She grabbed some sun block, a blanket and her sunglasses along with a book she had bought on one of their stops but never bothered to read. She packed a small cooler with some fruit, cheese and something to drink. She changed into her bathing suit and made her way down to the beach to enjoy a couple of hours of leisure. She found a quiet spot where she arranged the blanket then smoothed sun tan lotion on her skin to avoid being burnt by the Florida sun. She settled into a comfortable position on the blanket, feeling relaxed as she absorbed herself in the book she had brought along.

William had rented a car for a couple of days then set off on his mission. He asked the clerk at the car rental office if he knew of any good jewelry stores in the area. The clerk suggested a store only fifteen minutes away and gave him general directions. William reached the store in no time and went in search of the perfect engagement ring. He carefully looked at all of the rings on display before selecting a beautifully designed gold ring with a one karat marquise cut diamond in the center with smaller accent diamonds on either side. He was very proud of his choice, trying to pick something that expressed his love but also reflected Elizabeth's personality. Of course he could have afforded an over sized, over priced, gaudy ring bought for show but he knew that wouldn't be something Elizabeth would want. The ring he chose was classy, delicate and just the right size for her small hands. He only hoped the size was correct although the jeweler assured him they could bring it back to get it sized free of charge.

Before he left the jewelry store with his tiny package in hand he inquired if they knew of a reputable salon where he could treat his soon to be fiancé to a day of leisure. They suggested one that was conveniently located between the jewelry store and the marina. He also inquired about the local restaurants, wanting an elegant place to propose. The jeweler suggested a French restaurant that was quite close to the salon. He drove to the salon and inquired about their services and if they had availability for the following day. Luckily they just had a cancellation and had an opening for one of their mid-level spa packages that included a massage, facial, manicure, pedicure and a hair styling at the end of the day. He made the reservation for eleven the next morning. They told him she would be done somewhere around four o'clock. The timing worked out perfectly. William could take her to an early breakfast, drop her off for her spa day then pick her up and take her to an early dinner then dancing afterwards.

Before returning to the marina he went into the restaurant the jeweler had recommended and looked the place over. It looked very romantic and their menu had wonderful selections. He spoke briefly to the hostess and made reservations for the following evening at five. He also stopped at the local grocery store to pick up a few things so they could enjoy a leisurely evening on the boat. Tomorrow would be a full day and he wanted Elizabeth well rested and relaxed.

He returned to the marina in the late afternoon hiding the small ring box in his pocket before climbing out of the rented car and grabbing his shopping bags. He returned to the boat to find it empty so he immediately hid the small precious package in his chest of drawers and then unpacked the groceries he had purchased. William wondered where Elizabeth was and felt a moment of panic at the thought that she may not come back. He told himself he was being silly and went for a walk in search of Elizabeth. He strolled down the docks to the bar at the front of the marina to see if she was there. When he searched the crowd and didn't see her, he headed towards the beach. He strolled along the beach, scanning the area and spotted her lying on a beach blanket reading a book.

He watched her for a moment before he approached with tenderness in his heart. "Have you been out here all day?" he asked her. Startled she looked over her book into William's smiling face.

"What time is it?" she asked not remembering to bring a watch. She had been so wrapped up in the book she was reading that she had lost track of the time completely.

"It's around four. Must be a good book," he teased.

"I've always enjoyed reading and I guess I lost track of the time. When did you get back?" Elizabeth inquired.

"Not too long ago actually. I picked up some things at the grocery store for dinner. I thought I would cook you dinner for a change," he told her.

"You do enough for me William," she replied smiling at his thoughtfulness.

"Are you ready to go back now or did you want to stay longer?" he asked.

"I think I have been out here long enough. It's a good thing I remembered sun block or I would be mistaken for a lobster about now," she replied. William helped her gather her things then they strolled back to the boat together. Elizabeth went to shower off the sand and salt water while William cooked them a satisfying pasta dinner.

Chapter Seven

Harry Finch woke early the next morning and ordered room service so he could continue making calls to the marinas that were still left on his list. He ate his ham and eggs as he dialed number after number until he finally got some information at a marina in Florida. He was told that Mr. Moore had left the day before. "Damn," Finch said out loud as he hung up. He scratched off all of the marinas on his list located above Florida. He only hoped they were still heading in the same direction and hadn't turned back. The list consisted of only three marinas in Florida. Upon speaking to the clerk at the second to last marina on the list, he was informed that Mr. Moore arrived the day before and was still docked in the marina. "Would you like to leave a message for Mr. Moore?" the clerk asked.

"No thank you. I think I'll surprise him. Thank you for your assistance." Finch responded then hung up.

The next call Harry made was to the airport and booked a flight to Florida at three o'clock. Now the only thing to do was to call Richard and give him the news. He dialed Richard's telephone number and was placed on hold by Richard's secretary. A moment later Richard was on the line, "Harry, what have you come up with?" Harry was not surprised at the lack of a proper greeting.

"I have tracked Mr. Moore to a marina in Florida. I have already booked a flight that takes off at three," he informed Richard not bothering to go into details at the moment.

"Good. God knows, you couldn't be any slower. I don't know why I keep you on my payroll. When you get there I want you to make sure Elizabeth is with him. Once that's confirmed you contact me immediately. Don't approach them unless instructed. Is that clear?" Richard replied sternly.

"Certainly." He replied irritated at Richard's comments. "There is something else you should know. Through some of my contacts I found out some interesting information about your Mr. Moore."

"Well, what is it?" Richard asked impatiently.

"Although all the initial information I received is accurate, no tickets, no record of any kind, it appears your Mr. Moore changed his name. He was born William Blake. His only living relatives are his sister Sarah and her son." Harry informed him. There was a long silence and Harry thought he had lost Richard. "Richard are you there?"

"Yes, I'm here. Continue as instructed Finch. Goodbye." Harry was stunned when he heard the phone go dead.

"That was strange," he thought. He quickly dismissed Richard's reaction as he packed his bags and prepared for his flight to Florida.

Richard Marks hung up the phone and sat in his office as the blood drained from his face. His secretary knocked on the door and popped her head in to inform him his next appointment just arrived. She looked at him with concern realizing he looked extremely pale. "Mr. Marks are you feeling alright?" she asked with concern.

"Yes I'm fine. Give me a few minutes then I'll see Ms. Wright," he barked. His secretary quickly exited the office knowing he was in a mood over something. Richard quickly composed himself. He took several deep breaths then buzzed his secretary to send in Ms. Wright. "Please send in Ms. Wright and cancel the rest of my appointments this afternoon," he instructed his secretary.

"Yes, sir," came the reply through the speaker.

After dinner, William surprised Elizabeth when he told her he had booked her a spa appointment for the next morning. "You spoil me William!" Elizabeth exclaimed. "You don't have to do things like that to keep me happy you know. I'm happy just being with you," she said as she kissed him gratefully.

This sincere response sent another wave of guilt through William. "I know but I wanted to do something nice for you. I rented us a car and we'll be going to dinner afterwards so be sure to bring a nice dress to change into when you're done."

"It sounds wonderful. I'll go pick something out now then I'll have to thank you properly," she told him playfully.

"Now that sounds wonderful!" he replied with enthusiasm. She laughed and went to pick out an outfit for the next day making sure to pack the gold bracelet he bought her earlier on their trip to wear with her outfit.

Richard finished up his last appointment and went home early so he could figure out how to handle the situation. He hadn't heard the name Sarah Blake in years and thought he had been successful in ridding himself of her. Apparently her brother who had been a thorn in his side years ago would not let things go even after this long. He considered that it could be coincidence that he was now involved with his sister but quickly dismissed the possibility. After all William Blake had threatened him years ago that one day he would find a way to get back at him. He dismissed Blake's threat then however realizes that may have been a mistake. "How is he planning to use Elizabeth to get back at me?" he wondered. He went over the possibilities in his mind, none of which pleased him. He would just have to fly to Florida and expose him to Elizabeth as a liar and gold digger. "Hopefully it won't be too late," he thought to himself. He called the airport himself and booked a flight for early the next morning then called his secretary and informed her he would be going out of town on personal business.

Harry Finch checked into a hotel near the marina where Elizabeth and William were docked. He quickly unpacked and made his way to the marina in his rented car where he had dinner in the hopes he would spot Elizabeth. He constantly scanned the people coming and going from the restaurant but didn't see either Elizabeth or William Moore. After he ate his meal and paid the bill he took a stroll around the docks to see if he could spot them. Trying to appear as if he was just strolling around checking out the sites he walked each dock scanning each boat for Elizabeth. Unfortunately this method didn't work out and he didn't have any luck spotting them. It was getting dark and it would become more difficult to spot them so he decided to try again early the next morning.

William and Elizabeth sat inside enjoying the meal William had prepared then sat quietly in the salon on the sofa chatting. "I seem to remember something about a proper thank you mentioned earlier," William teased Elizabeth.

"Did you get that in writing Mr. Moore?" Elizabeth teased as she climbed on top of him, straddling his lap seductively.

"Yes, but I'm not sure where I put it," he replied as he pulled her closer to him.

"That's a shame," she teased as she began to get up from her position with a pout on her lips. "Looks like you're out of luck then," she said trying not to laugh as he pulled her back onto his lap and kissed her.

She returned his kiss with pleasure and began teasing him by rotating her hips slightly and pressing her breasts seductively into his chest. William groaned, grabbed her backside and carried her into his bedroom with her legs wrapped around his waist, kissing her all the way there. They never left the boat that evening thoroughly wrapped up in each other. They fell asleep in each others arms again that evening and slept soundly.

Harry Finch arranged for a wake-up call for six o'clock in the morning to insure he got an early start. He woke the next morning to the phone ringing and was out the door within an hour. He again went to the marina and sat outside on the patio with his coffee then went into the restaurant for breakfast at nine, again scanning all the customers hoping to spot Elizabeth.

Since they had fallen asleep relatively early the evening before, William and Elizabeth woke early. They stayed in bed together, taking time to discuss the day ahead. Elizabeth was excited to have a day of pampering followed by dinner and dancing with William. They finally dragged themselves out of bed and Elizabeth went to take a shower before her spa appointment. A few moments later while she was washing her hair, William joined her in the shower and immediately assisted Elizabeth with washing, taking time to make sure every little spot on her wet body got an equal amount of soapy attention. Elizabeth enjoyed this immensely and began to do the same for him. This excited William and soon they were making love in the small shower under the spray of hot water. They finally rinsed off all the soap then got out of the shower smiling as they dried each other off.

When they were finally dressed and ready to go, William took her to breakfast at the marina restaurant as promised, putting Elizabeth's outfit she packed in the car beforehand so they could leave right after their meal. It was half past nine and they had plenty of time for a leisurely breakfast before William had to drop Elizabeth off for her spa appointment. After they were seated in the restaurant they ordered coffee and omelets with toast. They sat enjoying their meal, engrossed in conversation, not noticing the gentleman in the far corner of the restaurant watching them intently.

Harry Finch was just about finished his breakfast and had decided to inquire at the front office for information on William Moore when he spotted Elizabeth across the room being seated by the hostess. She was with a man he could only assume was William Moore by the description he had been given by Richard. "Finally," he thought to himself. He sat and watched them, taking extra time finishing his meal and coffee. He asked for the check but was sure to request another cup of coffee allowing him more time to keep an eye on Elizabeth. He tried to call Richard but got his voice mail so he left him a vague message that he had found her and for him to call him back as soon as possible. Harry hadn't been informed that Richard had already booked himself a flight to Florida therefore didn't realize that Richard was on a plane at that moment.

Eventually Harry moved to the patio to avoid being noticed and sat in a spot where he could watch them casually through the window. When they finally received their bill and got up to leave an hour later Harry was ready to discretely follow them back to the boat. He was surprised however when they went to the parking lot instead and he had to hurry to his vehicle so he could follow them. He was a professional and knew how to follow someone without being noticed, making sure to stay several cars behind. He followed them all the way to the spa where he watched Elizabeth get out and go into the salon while William drove away. He had to decide quickly which one to watch and decided to follow William since he would probably be picking up Elizabeth again later.

Elizabeth kissed William, got out of the car and went into the salon to begin her spa treatment. She was excited and always enjoyed the pampering provided by a good salon. William drove away, deciding to pamper himself a little, stopping at a barber shop he had noticed on the way. He got a haircut and a hot towel shave that always relaxed him. After that he stopped at a man's clothing store and purchased a new shirt and tie to wear that evening. He had a couple of nice suits on the boat he kept for special occasions. On the way back to the marina he stopped at a Florist to purchase a dozen long stem roses for Elizabeth.

He finally made his way back to the marina where he put the roses in some water to keep them fresh and laid out his new shirt. He took out his little ironing board and pressed his new shirt then pulled out the suit he was going to wear, allowing it to air it out since he hadn't worn it in several weeks. He then pulled out the little box with the engagement ring and opened it one more time. As he looked at it he felt happy again at the thought of Elizabeth being his wife and was sure she would like his choice. He made sure to place the ring box in his jacket pocket of the suit he had chosen to wear.

William was feeling happy but nervous and was unsure what to do with himself for the next couple of hours before he had to get dressed and pick up Elizabeth for dinner. He decided to fix himself a cocktail and relax on the deck. He rehearsed his proposal over and over in his mind until he felt comfortable with how he wanted to ask her. He would wait until after their meal and then ask her hoping, of course, that she would accept. He couldn't face the idea that she would say no so avoided the thought altogether.

Harry Finch had followed William back to the marina and down the dock to the boat. Watching from a distance as he climbed over the side holding roses and the bag he had when he came out of the store. Once William was on the boat he quietly walked up to the boat, writing down the slip number, the name of the boat and what kind it was in case they should slip away from him again. By the looks of things they had no plans of leaving any time soon Finch surmised. He walked back up the dock and sat at the restaurant outside so he would see if Moore left again. He tried calling Richard but again got his voice mail. He left him another message with the location of the marina and asked him again to call as soon as possible with instructions.

As William sat on the patio sipping his bourbon his telephone rang. "Hello," he answered.

"William?" answered the voice on the other end.

"Yes, this is William," he replied too distracted to recognize his friend's voice immediately.

"William, its Mike Zimmerman." William sat up forgetting that he had asked his friend to find out information about Elizabeth's parents.

"Hey, Mike, how are you?" he asked.

"Good. I'm sorry it took so long for me to get back to you but I have been really swamped here."

"No problem, I understand. Did you find out anything?" William asked.

"Yeah, actually it's kind of strange. Didn't you tell me they died in a plane crash?" he asked William.

"That's what I was told." William replied.

"Well they didn't die in a plane crash. They were murdered at a ski resort. The suspicion was that it was a professional hit, according to the papers, but the case was never solved. I even contacted the policeman that was in charge of the case," his friend informed him.

"What did he tell you?" William asked puzzled by the information.

"He was reluctant to talk but he did say that he was reassigned suddenly when he was finally getting somewhere. He insinuated that there were politics working against him and he was forced to give up the case. When I asked him if he thought it was a professional hit as the papers said, he got real quiet and wouldn't reply which to me, means yes. He was definitely afraid of something or someone if he said too much," Mike told him.

"This doesn't make any sense," William commented to his friend.

"Well, if you don't mind me asking, who told you they died in a plane crash?" he asked.

"Off the record, Mike?" William asked cautiously.

"Of course," he responded. "Keep this between us but I'm dating their daughter who was around thirteen when they died. That's what she told me. Now either she said that to avoid admitting her parents were murdered or someone, most likely her brother, told her a big fat lie."

"Maybe the brother told her that to spare her feelings?" Mike suggested.

"Not this brother. He is as selfish and mean as they come. If he told her a lie it was for his own reasons and nothing to do with his sister's feelings, believe me," William replied. "Do you have anything in print you could fax me about what happened?" he asked his friend.

"Sure, what's the number?" William provided his friend with the number and thanked him.

"Could I ask you one more favor Mike?" William asked.

"Sure. What do you need?" his friend responded.

"When you have some spare time could you dig a little deeper? See what you can come up with in regards to her brother, Richard Marks III, in relation to his parents' death."

"Sure, William. This one has certainly caught my interest," Mike replied.

"Nothing is to be printed Mike. This one is personal and will be kept quiet. Got it?" William said firmly.

"No worries, William. I understand. I'll get back to you if I find out anything else." William thanked his friend and hung up pondering the information he was just given. "Why would Richard tell her his parents died in a plane crash?" he thought to himself. After going over the possibilities in his mind he wasn't happy. He could not picture Richard telling her that to save her feelings. He was not the type that cared. A chill ran up his spine and a creepy thought came into his mind. "Could Richard have had something to do with his parents' death? Could he be that cold and cruel? He did stand to inherit the entire fortune and sending his sister to a private school could have just gotten her out of the way to avoid any questions and finding out how her parents really died." He accepted that this was a possibility but hoped for Elizabeth's sake he was way off track.

He looked at his watch and realized he needed to get ready, forcing himself to concentrate on much happier things. While he was getting dressed he heard the fax machine ringing and went to retrieve the papers Mike was sending him. He scanned them over with a frown on his face then put them away in his bedside table for safe keeping.

Harry Finch was patiently sitting at the marina watching for any movement from William when his phone rang. "Hello," Harry answered.

"It's Richard. I just got your message. Where are they now?" he asked. Again Harry wasn't surprised at the hard and unfriendly greeting from Richard.

"Right now your sister is at the spa and William is on his boat at the marina. I'm waiting for William to leave again to go pick her up," he informed him.

"I am checking into my hotel now and then I will drive there and meet you. Make sure you keep your phone on and if they move you let me know where they are." Richard replied firmly.

"You're here in Florida?" Harry asked surprised.

"Yes. I flew out this morning. Keep me informed of their movement and I'll call you soon when I get on the road," Richard replied and hung up before Harry could say anything else. At that moment Harry looked up to find William walking towards him wearing a suit and carrying the roses he saw him with earlier. Harry watched him out of the corner of his eye as William walked towards the parking lot. Once William passed and was out of his view Harry got up and slowly headed in the same direction. Once he saw William getting into his car he picked up the pace, jumping into his car to follow him again.

William, being preoccupied with his own thoughts about his upcoming proposal, again didn't notice the man following him. He drove to the salon and asked the receptionist if Elizabeth was ready. She informed him a moment later that she should be out shortly. They were just finishing her hair and then she was going to get dressed. "Thank you" he said as he took a seat in the lobby. He waited patiently for about twenty minutes before Elizabeth finally appeared. He was stunned by how beautiful she looked in the elegant emerald green evening dress she wore. They had styled her hair half up with the other portion hanging down in spiral like waves around her neck. Elizabeth smiled widely when she saw him and did a proud little twirl to provide him a view of every angle. "You're stunning!" he told her, providing the approval she was hoping for. He pulled her close and kissed her softly.

"You don't look too bad yourself," she replied with enthusiasm.

"Shall we go?" he asked extending an elbow. She smiled at him and slipped her arm through his, allowing him to escort her to the car. He opened the car door for her, allowing her to slip into the vehicle. Shutting the door behind her, he made his way to the driver's side of the car. He climbed in and reached into the back seat presenting the roses to Elizabeth.

"They are lovely! William, thank you," she replied feeling much too spoiled. She kissed him softly then settled into her seat as he put the car in drive and headed to the restaurant.

Finch dialed Richard's number again, informing him that they were together and in the car. He told him he would call when they arrived wherever he was taking her. Shortly after, he followed William into the parking lot of a French restaurant and watched as William and Elizabeth entered the restaurant together. "Well, they should be here for a while," he thought. He parked his car in a spot where he could see both their car and the entrance then called Richard to let him know where they were.

"Good. Give me the address of the restaurant. I'll be there as soon as I can," Richard told him, hanging up immediately after receiving the location of the restaurant.

Elizabeth and William were seated in the elegant dining room in a quiet corner as he requested the day before. They took their seats at the table that was set with a beautiful white table cloth. A small floral arrangement held a small candle in the center providing a relaxing and romantic atmosphere to set the proper mood for his proposal. The restaurant was illuminated by dimmed lighting and candles with soft, slow music playing in the background.

They looked over the menu while the waiter went to get the champagne William ordered for them. The restaurant was so elegant and quiet it came natural to whisper, everyone afraid to disturb the peaceful atmosphere. A moment later the waiter returned and poured them each a glass of champagne then took their order. After the waiter departed Elizabeth smiled softly at William. "This place is so lovely William. How did you find it?" she asked curiously.

"I just asked around while I was doing errands yesterday. I was hoping you would like it," he responded proudly.

"I do like it. You spoil me! First with the spa then flowers and now this fabulous restaurant," she replied feeling very appreciative at his efforts to make her happy.

At that moment the waiter returned with their salads which they ate while chatting about their day. William told her he went to the barber and bought the shirt and tie he was wearing. "I did notice your hair looked shorter when you picked me up but I was stunned into silence by how handsome you look," she whispered playfully.

William smiled at her as the waiter removed their salad plates. William took her hand across the table and gently caressed her fingers with his own. "I'm afraid that I adore you, Elizabeth. I hope you know that. I never want to lose you," he told her softly with a gentle love in his eyes.

Elizabeth blushed softly at his tender expression of his feelings for her and smiled back at him. "I adore you as well. I will stay with you as long as you will have me," she responded, meaning every word.

Before William could respond the waiter returned with their meals and placed them on the table. The food smelled delicious and they were both very hungry since they hadn't eaten since breakfast.

William ate his meal while admiring Elizabeth, trying to silently rehearse his proposal again. Now that their meals were there and the time was coming he began to get nervous, anxious and excited all at once. Elizabeth noticed a strange look on his face and asked if he was alright. "Yes sweetheart. I'm great," he told her with one of his brilliant smiles that always made her heart jump in her chest.

Elizabeth still felt something was going on since William seemed to be acting a little strange all of a sudden. She studied him closely as she finished her meal noticing that he actually looked a little anxious. She wondered if there was a business matter that was bothering him. She was about to ask him again, when the waiter arrived to refill their champagne glasses and remove their dinner plates. "Would you care for some dessert?" the waiter asked before retreating. Elizabeth and William both declined and watched the waiter leave with their plates.

William felt as if he was going to burst with emotion, shifted in his seat and took a deep breath. Elizabeth noticed his anxious movement and again asked if he was alright. "Yes. I hope so. That is…. Elizabeth, I am in love with you. I know we haven't known each other that long but I love you."

Elizabeth was deeply touched by his expression of his feelings for her and was about to respond when he reached into his jacket pocket and pulled out a small box. William reached for her hand and looked into her eyes. "I

love you Elizabeth. I want you with me always...."
William rose from his chair, kneeling beside her and
opened the ring box, "Will you marry me?" he asked,
stunning Elizabeth with his proposal.

She stared at him, glancing at the ring then back at
William. "William, I don't know what to say," she
stuttered shocked by his unexpected question.

"I was hoping you would say yes?" he replied
nervously still on one knee. Elizabeth looked into his
eyes and was overwhelmed by what she saw there.

Before she could think of all the reasons she
should say no, she found herself responding, "Yes! Yes,
William. I will marry you," she told him softly as a tear
ran down her cheek.

He smiled proudly then put the ring gently on her
finger. "Do you like it?" he asked relieved that the ring
was the right size.

"I love it William!" he rose from his knee and
pulled her close into his arms as he kissed her tenderly.

William released her and happily shouted, "She
said yes! We are getting married!" he said to everyone in
the room. There was a small round of applause from the
fellow diners congratulating them both when a loud
angry voice rang out behind them.

"The hell you are!" Elizabeth froze as she recognized the voice and looked up at William. William had
already turned to face Richard Marks III.

Chapter Eight

Outside the restaurant Harry crouched in the bushes with his camera and telephoto lens. Following his instincts after Richard had simply told him over the phone to get lost and send him the bill that something wasn't quite right. He decided to stick around for the show and protect his interests. In his experience the richer the person was the less you could trust them. So he sat taking pictures as Richard pulled up in his limousine outside the restaurant. Richard climbed out of the vehicle followed by a much larger man. They were joined by a second very large man that had arrived in another vehicle parked on the side of the restaurant. Finch watched as Richard said something to the two men who then positioned themselves on either side of the entrance to the restaurant while Richard went inside. He started to snap picture after picture of the whole scene planning to keep them as collateral should Richard try to stiff him on his bill.

William looked at Richard with disgust and anger on his face, taking Elizabeth's hand, pulling her close to him. William stood his ground and showed no sign of fear, while Elizabeth was already starting to tremble. Richard walked up to them, looked William in the eye then simply acted as if he didn't exist. "Elizabeth lets go. Now!" he ordered.

Elizabeth didn't know what to say, overwhelmed by her brother's sudden appearance. When Elizabeth didn't respond William decided to step in. "She's not going anywhere, Mr. Marks. We are engaged and she will be staying with me," William replied firmly.

"Mr. Moore is it? Or is it Blake? I am confused how to address you," Richard sneered at William and then turned to his sister again. "Elizabeth, this man is using you! He and his sister tried to get my money years ago and now he has changed his name and is trying again by going after you since his sister failed with me," Elizabeth was stunned by Richard's accusation and looked at William expecting a denial. William said nothing and Elizabeth took her hand from his grasp.

"William? What's he talking about?" All the guilt William had been feeling overwhelmed him as he looked at Elizabeth. "William is it true?" she demanded.

"I am not after your money Elizabeth," was the only explanation he could provide.

Richard pulled out some papers and handed them to Elizabeth. "See for yourself," he stated coldly.

Elizabeth scanned the papers and was shocked by what she read. She looked up at William, "Is your name Blake?" she demanded.

William looked at her with regret and guilt in his eyes. "I was born William Blake. Elizabeth, please let me explain. Things are not as Richard is making them out to be. I love you. Come with me and I'll explain, just trust me."

Elizabeth looked into his eyes and could not see past the fact that he had lied to her all this time. Suddenly angry with herself for being so naïve and stupid she couldn't bare to look at him again. Elizabeth grabbed her bag and walked out of the restaurant with her brother not bothering to look back even once as William called her name. Elizabeth felt numb as she climbed into the limousine and sat quietly looking out the window while they drove away. She couldn't see anything through the tears she was trying to hold back, not wanting Richard to see her cry. She didn't see William as he ran out into the parking lot after her a moment too late as the limousine was already moving.

"William?" a deep male voice said from behind. William turned to see who was addressing him stunned by a swift blow to his stomach knocking the wind out of him. He endured repeated blows from two men as they followed their orders and beat him black and blue. When they were satisfied that William had enough, spitting blood from his mouth and gasping for air while lying crumbled on the ground, they made one simple statement before leaving. "Mr. Marks wants you to stay away from his sister." With one more kick to his ribs they left him there to lick his wounds.

The pain William felt at that point was nothing compared to the pain he felt for hurting Elizabeth. He attempted to get up but only stumbled to the ground. He looked up at the sky but everything was whirling around him, "Elizabeth, I'm so sorry," was his last thought before everything went black.

Harry Finch was appalled at the events he witnessed but was glad he decided to hang around and take photographs. He witnessed Richard exit the building with Elizabeth in tow then watched while his two thugs intercepted William in the parking lot and beat him bloody. Finch was about to intercede thinking the thugs just might kill him when he noticed the parking attendant rush into the restaurant. He continued taking photographs making sure to get a photograph of the license plate of the vehicle driven by the thugs. Harry slinked away just as the police showed up and was glad he would have something to use against Richard if he needed it.

William woke for a moment to the sound of sirens but couldn't tell where they were coming from, blacking out again. The parking attendant had seen the men beating on William and had called the police. By the time they had gotten there the assailants had already left making sure the beating was received swiftly. The officers called an ambulance immediately and took statements from several of the staff including the parking attendant.

Elizabeth had no idea what had just happened to William and barely noticed when her brother received a call from his hired hands informing him his message had been delivered. Elizabeth was grateful that her brother didn't say anything to her. Richard had already reserved a room for her next to his at the hotel. He had already booked a flight for both of them to return to Connecticut early the next morning. When they reached the hotel Elizabeth was ushered to her room. "Get some rest. We'll be leaving at six tomorrow morning for the airport," her brother said as he went in his own room.

She entered her room where she found a set of night cloths and one outfit left on the bed. She numbly took the night clothes into the bathroom and turned on the shower. As she undressed she slowly removed the bracelet and ring William had given her and placed them in her handbag. Once under the spray of the hot water she allowed all her heartache to flow, sobbing until no tears were left. She dried herself off and dressed as if she were a robot, feeling numb. She went to bed and fell asleep immediately from pure emotional exhaustion. At that moment she did not care if she ever woke up again.

William was in and out of consciousness all night in the hospital disturbed by haunting dreams of Elizabeth. He was tossing and turning violently in his sleep and screaming Elizabeth's name until the doctor was finally forced to sedate him. The doctors found he had a concussion and several broken ribs. He finally regained consciousness around noon the following day and immediately tried to get up but was forced back into bed when the room spun around him. The doctor came in to see him shortly after having been told by the nurse he was awake.

The doctor informed him of his condition and told him he would need to stay at least one more day for observation due to the severity of his concussion. William argued but was too weak to do anything but deal with his guilt and shame. He decided he deserved the beating he received for hurting Elizabeth so when the police showed up to question him that afternoon he didn't bother to tell them the men were hired by Richard Marks. William felt completely helpless and only blamed himself for the situation he found himself in. He returned to the restaurant by cab the next day to pick up the rental car and returned to the marina feeling weak and beaten. He slept for the majority of the following two days still tired, weak and sore from his injuries.

Elizabeth woke to the telephone ringing at five the next morning when her brother called to wake her so they wouldn't miss their plane. She climbed out of bed still feeling exhausted and dressed in the only outfit available to her other than the evening dress she had worn the night before. She placed the remaining items she had in the small overnight bag that had also been left for her. She took her belongings and met her brother in the hall. They checked out of the hotel, climbed into the limousine then drove to the airport. Elizabeth slept through the entire flight back to Connecticut and was silent all the way home. She went directly to her room wanting nothing more than to sleep forever and forget about William and his deception.

She woke in the afternoon to find a plate with a sandwich and fruit but touched nothing feeling nauseous at the thought of food. She sat on the balcony outside her bedroom for a while finding no comfort from her beloved ocean view. Eventually she returned to bed and slept again haunted by dreams of William. To her relief she had been left alone and not bothered by anyone all day but wasn't as lucky the following morning.

This time she woke to a knock on her door and without waiting for a reply her brother appeared through the doorway. While she was still in bed she was informed they were having guests that evening and she was expected to attend. Elizabeth tried to object finding she had a horrible headache and was feeling quite nauseous. "I'm not feeling well Richard..." but before she was able to say more her brother cut her off coldly.

"I am unconcerned with how you feel after what you put me through. You will attend dinner and be a gracious hostess. Please dress nicely. Jonathan will be there. By the way, to save us both some embarrassment, I told Jonathan you had taken a vacation with one of your friends from school. No one knows that you were actually tramping yourself down the coast to Florida with that scoundrel!"

Elizabeth was stunned at his cold and cruel statement. She boiled at his cruelty but before she could say anything he left. "Be downstairs by six," he ordered as he slammed the door behind him.

Elizabeth climbed out of bed, angry again at her brother for the way he treated her. "Tramp?" she thought to herself. "How dare he?" Suddenly overwhelmed with a nauseous feeling, she ran into the bathroom where her body violently rejected what little was left in her stomach. Afterwards, feeling quite dizzy, she made her way back to her bed, crawled back under the covers, falling back to sleep almost immediately.

The next time she woke was when one of the servants knocked lightly on the door and entered with a small tray with some cheese, crackers, and fruit along with some hot tea. "Miss Elizabeth," Annabelle said softly in an attempt to try to wake her up. "Miss Elizabeth," she repeated as Elizabeth stirred and slowly opened her eyes. "Are you not feeling well Miss? I noticed you've been in bed for almost two days and you didn't touch the food I left for you."

Elizabeth rolled over and sat up feeling better than she had earlier that morning and finally felt a little hungry. "I'm feeling better I think, Annabelle. Thank you."

Annabelle was still concerned as she noticed Elizabeth looked a little pale. "Why don't you try to eat something before you get out of bed? You will feel much better then you can get dressed for the dinner party. Your brother has sent me to make sure you're ready on time."

"Oh right, the dinner party. What time is it?" Elizabeth asked as her earlier conversation with her brother came back to her and set her blood boiling again.

"It's four o'clock," she answered as she placed the tray in front of Elizabeth and poured her a cup of tea. "Now try to eat and I'll be back in a bit to collect the tray and check on you," she said as she left the room.

"Check on me? Don't you mean watch me as Richard ordered?" Elizabeth mumbled. She grumbled under her breath as she ate some of the cheese and crackers. Elizabeth wasn't looking forward to having to play the happy hostess for her brother. She was still feeling very tired and couldn't shake the sadness that had taken hold of her heart when she found out William had deceived her and used her. She felt stupid and foolish but she had truly loved William. He had made her feel so alive and free. He made her feel safe which was only an illusion, concluding that the quick proposal of marriage was just to get her family's money. She doubted she would ever trust another man again.

She fought back the threat of tears and went to take a shower. Under the water however the tears came once again as the vivid memory of the intimate shower she shared with William sprang to her mind, making her heart break feel sharp and new. After a few moments she forced herself to put all thoughts of William to the back of her mind. She finished her shower and went to prepare for the dinner party. She allowed her sadness to change to anger as she brushed her long hair and looked in the mirror. She wasn't only angry at William but Richard as well. If he hadn't tried to marry her off maybe she wouldn't have run off with William so impetuously. Although she still had every right to be angry and hurt by her brother's actions she knew the only one she could truly blame was herself.

She finished getting ready at six o'clock, took a deep breath, smiled at her reflection in the mirror and went to greet their guests. Elizabeth played the part of the perfect hostess greeting everyone with a smile, asking them how they were and pretended to be interested when they told her stories of their recent business deals or vacations. The most difficult guest to greet was Jonathan Parker. He approached her slowly after waiting for her to do the appropriate rounds so he wouldn't be interrupted when speaking to her. "How are you Elizabeth?" he asked with an undertone in his voice meant only for her. Elizabeth felt a pang of guilt when she remembered their last meeting and that she had taken off after making plans for him to visit.

"I'm well, Jonathan. How have you been?" she asked having a hard time looking him straight in the eye.

"Not as well I'm afraid," he stated with a look that told her he was upset with her. She took a look around at the guests, some of which were now looking in their direction and decided to invite Jonathan for a walk so they could talk more freely.

"Would you like to join me for a walk, Jonathan?" she asked walking towards the garden not really expecting an answer.

Jonathan walked quietly beside her down the garden path. Once they were a safe distance from the guests he put his hand on her arm and gently turned her to face him. "Why did you leave without a word? We agreed to be friends and we made plans to visit. I don't know about you but I don't treat my friends that way," he said with anger in his voice. "Did I do something wrong? Is there someone else you're seeing?"

She looked up at him and felt guilty again when she saw the hurt in his eyes. She looked away not quite sure how to answer his question. She wondered if he was aware of their families' arrangement and decided to find out. She took a deep breath and looked him in the eye before replying. "Jonathan, are you aware of my brother's understanding with your parents in regards to us?" she asked almost accusingly.

"What do you mean, 'understanding'?" he asked.

She studied his face trying to tell if he was being honest with her but couldn't be sure. She wondered if she would ever be sure if a man was lying to her after William. "Are you telling me you have no idea that my brother and your parents have arranged all this? That their plan is for us to get married?" she asked again this time with anger in her voice.

"What? I don't doubt that my parents were trying to play match-maker, but an arranged marriage? That's ridiculous!" he stated raising his voice slightly.

"According to my brother they have had this planned for a while now," she informed him.

He looked at her wondering if it were possible. "Even if that were true, what does that have to do with you leaving without a word or explanation?" he demanded in return.

"Everything," she replied. "I am not a piece of meat to be bought by the highest bidder, Jonathan. Whether or not you were aware of the agreement, it's a big part of why I left and didn't call you. If you truly had no idea then I apologize for my rudeness."

Jonathan sat on a nearby bench unable to believe his parents would have an 'arrangement' with Richard Marks. "Is the thought of marrying me so repulsive that you ran away at the thought?" he asked feeling suddenly offended.

She looked at Jonathan and remembered how sweet he had been the last time they were together. "No, Jonathan. It's not that, believe me. It really had nothing to do with you at all," she told him honestly.

Jonathan sat quietly for a moment and looked at Elizabeth as she sat next to him. He turned towards her and took her hands in his. "Elizabeth, the last time I saw you we had a great time and I thought we were starting a very special friendship. Who cares what everyone else wants? Why can't we continue where we left off and see where it takes us? Not because of your brother or my parents, just because we care about each other. I already know I care about you."

She was surprised at his suggestion but could see that he meant it. She felt warmed by his affection for her but wasn't sure she could pick up where they left off after everything that happened with William. "I'm not sure that's possible, Jonathan," she responded gently not wanting to hurt him.

Jonathan stood up in frustration and looked down at her, "Why not? We were becoming friends before you knew about their stupid agreement. Why does that have to interfere? Unless…" he stopped speaking as he looked at her questioningly.

"Unless what Jonathan?"

"…..unless this is just your way of getting rid of me? Be honest with me Elizabeth."

She looked at him not knowing what to say. "No Jonathan. It's not just my way of getting rid of you."

"Then why can't we pick up where we left off? Try to get to know each other? Be friends?" he demanded.

Elizabeth couldn't bring herself to tell him the truth about William, but couldn't think of any other excuse. "Maybe you're right, Jonathan. Maybe it shouldn't matter but somehow it does."

"I am right. It doesn't matter. They can't force either one of us to marry if we don't want. Why throw away a great thing just to spite them?" he argued trying desperately to make her see reason.

Elizabeth was out of excuses and felt simply exhausted by his determination to remain friends. "Alright, Jonathan. You win. We'll continue to get to know each other and see how it goes. I think I need things to go slowly under the circumstances. Is that agreeable to you?" she asked.

Jonathan smiled and kissed her quickly on the lips. "Whatever you say!"

Elizabeth couldn't help but laugh at the sudden joy on his face that he didn't bother to hide. "We should probably go back and join the party."

"If you wish," he said taking her hand in his as he led her back towards the house. They returned to the party and he spent the rest of the evening at her side. Elizabeth was exhausted and relieved when the final guests, the Parkers, left for the evening. "May I call you tomorrow?" Jonathan asked quietly on his way out. She nodded and said goodnight.

Elizabeth turned to go to her room but was stopped by Richard on her way to the stairs. "Nice performance, Elizabeth. You really should get an academy award. No one had a clue that only a few days ago you were prancing around like a harlot," he sneered. She noticed her brother had a little bit more to drink than usual so she didn't bother to respond except with a polite 'good night'.

William woke up feeling better but still felt horrible for what he had done to Elizabeth. William felt helpless, as if he lost everything that mattered in one moment. He felt no more anger or need for revenge, only regret and heartache. William didn't feel up to driving his boat all the way back up the coast to Connecticut. His ribs were still extremely sore so he decided to inquire at the marina office about delivery services. He made the arrangements for someone to drive his boat to Connecticut in the next day or two then booked himself a flight home for the following morning. He returned to his boat to get ready for his departure. "Home would be a good place right now," he thought to himself.

In the late afternoon the following day, William handed the cab driver the money for his fare wincing from the pain in his side when he picked up his suitcase. He entered his house, feeling better just being there. A moment later he was greeted enthusiastically by his nephew. "Uncle Willy! Uncle Willy!" The young boy ran up to his uncle and hugged him hard. "Where have you been? You were gone a long time!"

"I missed you too Toby," he told his nephew wincing slightly as he bent to return the hug. "Where is your mom?" he asked the eight-year old boy.

"She's out in the garden picking tomatoes. Let's go surprise her!" he exclaimed and took his uncle's hand, pulling him towards the back door. "Come on, Uncle Willy!" he yelled pulling harder when William tried to playfully resist.

"Okay Toby," he couldn't help but laugh at his excited nephew.

"Mommy! Mommy! Look who's here!" Toby exclaimed when he spotted his mother across the yard. Sarah Blake turned from her garden with her basket of tomatoes and smiled as she spotted her brother. Her smile slowly faded as she approached her brother and noticed the fading cuts and bruises on his face.

"What on earth happened to you?" his sister asked concerned.

"It's a long story. I'll tell you about it later. How's everything here?"

"Fine. I was just about to start making dinner. Hungry?" she asked noticing something was different about her brother. Sarah Blake adored her brother. He always looked out for her and they were very close. He was always wonderful and patient with Toby which only strengthened her love and admiration for him.

Sarah was of average height with brown curly hair and hazel eyes and looked a lot like her mother. William took after their father inheriting his height, bone structure and good looks but inherited the wavy dark hair and hazel eyes from their mother. They both had fond memories of their parents but had shared a lot of hard times after his father died. His mother worked two jobs for the next five years until she was diagnosed with cancer, dying six months later. His mother had been insistent on him finishing school and going to college on the scholarship he earned with all his hard work. He didn't want to ever have to struggle again so was determined to do well in school and make his mother proud. He helped take care of Sarah until he went away to college at which time she finished high school while living at their grandparents' house after their mother passed away. William urged her to do well in school so she could also go to college on scholarships. She did just that until her unexpected and unplanned pregnancy forced her to drop out of college at the end of her first year.

Once Toby started school William insisted on paying for her to go back to school part-time to get her degree. He took care of Sarah even now insisting that she move in with him when he bought his first home over six years ago. Toby was just a toddler and he didn't want them living in the horrible neighborhood his sister was able to afford. From then on William's wealth only grew and he provided them all the comfort his money could buy. Sarah was so grateful to him she made sure to keep her grades as high as possible and did everything she could to earn her keep around the house. He asked nothing of her financially or otherwise but Sarah insisted on doing the house work and cooking as her contribution.

Toby was a very happy and bright boy despite the lack of a father in his life. William did his best to be there for him as much as possible since his mother never married. Sarah put all her energy into her son and her studies. She occasionally dated but never found any real interest in any of the men that asked her out. Toby had Sarah's brown curly hair but inherited his father's eyes. At only eight years old he was quite tall compared to kids of his own age and at times reminded his mother of William when they were growing up. She remembered how happy William was as a child, not having a care in the world until things changed when their father died. William took the responsibility on himself to be the man of the house. Making sure things got fixed and the lawn got mowed, sacrificing a lot of things a teenage boy should be doing to help take care of his family, always spending time with Sarah and making sure she did her schoolwork. When their mother began to work a second job to make ends meet William took on even more responsibility making sure Elizabeth had dinner every night, clean clothes and made sure she remembered to take a bath and brush her teeth.

William felt more relaxed being home and enjoyed talking to Toby and Sarah while she prepared dinner for them. Sarah filled him in on school, the little funny stories about Toby and things he did or said since he had been away. Although he was quite happy to be there with them he couldn't shake the awful feeling he had in his gut. He felt as if the weight of the world was on his shoulders and he could not bear to take another step forward without falling to his knees.

Sarah noticed her brother wasn't himself and made a mental note to pursue the subject after she put Toby to bed that night. They ate together at the table, teasing each other and making jokes more to entertain Toby than anything. After they ate William offered to do the dishes but Sarah refused. "Why don't you take Toby outback and play for a while. When I'm done cleaning up I'll take him up for his bath." Toby jumped up and grabbed his uncle's arm before he had a chance to reply. William went outside with his nephew unable to withhold a smile at the child's enthusiasm. His nephew let go of his arm and ran to get his baseball and the two gloves his uncle had bought them the year before. "Can we play catch Uncle Willy?" he asked as he held up a glove to his uncle.

"Sure Toby," he answered as they left the screened porch to throw the ball around the back yard. The large fenced yard provided plenty of space for them to throw the ball. There was a modest size in-ground pool off to one side and a swing set on the other that William installed immediately for Toby after he purchased the house. The roomy screened in porch housed a wooden picnic table and a matching wooden bench swing where they could sit and relax while watching Toby play. William stood in the back yard playing catch with his nephew, suffering the constant reminder of his heartache each time he threw the ball and felt the pain it caused his ribs. He suffered through the pain for no other reason than to please Toby but was relieved when Sarah yelled for him to take his bath.

William went into the kitchen to get a cold glass of iced tea, wiping the sweat from his face with a cold wet paper towel. He took his glass into the living room and gently put his feet up on the coffee table trying to avoid causing himself anymore discomfort. William's house was decorated with simple but modern furnishings meant more for comfort than looks. He liked his home to feel warm and comforting so he had chosen fluffy overstuffed couches and matching chairs with stained wood tables and warm colored carpet and drapes. Most of the house was decorated in the same manor, although he had a large dining room decorated with a very fancy dining set and crystal chandelier, which was only used occasionally when entertaining large groups mostly around the holidays. They almost always ate their meals in the roomy kitchen that got its warmth and character from its stained wood cabinets and ceramic tile floor. The modest table and oversized hutch was also made of wood stained in a tone that matched the cabinets and woodwork beautifully. The big sliding glass door that led to the back porch allowed the sunlight to brighten the room in a very welcoming way making the room appear larger than it actually was.

Although William was a very wealthy man he still preferred things simple and well made instead of fancy and overpriced like his boat, preferring the simpler warm style of boat compared to the newer fancy models made of fiberglass. He sat on his couch unable to avoid thinking about Elizabeth. How could I have been so stupid? How could I have been so rotten? He desperately wanted to take it all back and spare Elizabeth the pain he caused her. Now all was lost and he probably would never see her again. He felt like his chest would burst open at the thought and threw his head back against the wall in utter frustration. He looked up to find his sister standing there, hands on hips, staring at him. "Toby would like you to go up and say goodnight. I just put him to bed."

"No problem," he replied as he rose from the couch trying to avoid his sister's questioning gaze.

"William, when you're done, why don't you join me on the back porch? I'll fix us both a cocktail," she suggested.

"Sounds good," he replied quickly escaping to the safety of his nephew's bedroom. Sarah went into the kitchen and made a small pitcher of their favorite summer cocktail. She placed the pitcher on a tray with two glasses full of ice and went to sit on the swing and wait for her brother to join her. "You will tell me what's going on William," she said out loud as she sat on the empty porch.

After a good fifteen minutes William finally joined her on the porch. Sarah handed him a cocktail as he sat in the swing beside her. "Toby all tucked in?" she asked.

"Yep," William replied as he took a long sip of his cocktail, trying to avoid looking directly at his sister.

Sarah turned towards her brother and looked him square in the eye, "Alright William. Tell me what's going on. You disappear for weeks and you show up with cuts and bruises. Something is wrong. I know it."

Chapter Nine

William didn't want to tell his sister what he had done but could not lie to her either. When his attempts to dodge the issue failed, he decided to tell her everything although he knew she wouldn't be happy. She told him years ago to let things go but he didn't listen. William looked at his sister, taking a deep breath before beginning his explanation. "I did something horrible. You're not going to be happy with me. I'm not happy with me," he began then stood up suddenly pacing back and forth.

"William just tell me what happened," Sarah replied firmly.

He was surprised when she reminded him of their mother, comforting yet firm. He continued pacing as he explained to her the mess he had made. "It all started a couple of months ago when I read an article in the paper. Richard Marks was interviewed for something and there was a photograph of him with his wife and two children," he paused to look at his sister who now had his full attention.

"Go on," she said worried about what he might have done once he mentioned Richard.

"I got so angry all over again about Toby and all that, seeing him in the paper looking pompous with his children and wife, as if Toby didn't exist. It just enraged me. I read the article and it mentioned that his younger sister Elizabeth was about to graduate from some boarding school not too far away." William paused and ran his hand through his hair in frustration. He couldn't bring himself to look at his sister as he told her about his plan of revenge and how it was working until he fell in love with Elizabeth and then broke her heart in the end. He told her he asked her to marry him and she had accepted. He told her about Richard coming along and how she left before he could explain things. He ended with the story of how he received the cuts and bruises. When he finally looked at his sister, she sat with her mouth hanging wide open looking absolutely stunned by what he just told her.

"I told you it was horrible and you wouldn't be happy. I feel terrible and don't know what to do about it," he said to his sister hoping she didn't hate him.

Sarah sat silently for a few moments trying to absorb everything her brother just told her. "How could you do such a thing?" she asked in disbelief.

"I don't know. I was just so angry and the worst thing is she doesn't know what really happened. Richard made it out like I was just after their money like he did years ago when you were pregnant with Toby. She wouldn't even look at me or let me explain once he showed her the papers from the lawsuit!" he explained feeling worse than ever.

"That poor girl! How could you deliberately set out to do to someone else what he did to me? How?" Sarah asked now the one pacing in frustration. "How could you believe for even one second that you had it in you to be as cruel as Richard?" she asked him now furious with him for what he had done.

"It was really stupid. You don't have to tell me, that much I know. What I don't know is how to make things right," he told his sister with regret.

"I'm not sure you can ever make things right. I just don't know…" she trailed off and shook her head with sheer disappointment in her older brother. For the first time in her entire life she was ashamed and angry with her brother. Sarah didn't know what else to say to him at that moment. "I'm going to bed William. Good night," she said as she entered the house and left him feeling even more miserable.

William felt much worse after telling his sister and seeing her reaction. If Sarah could hate him for what he did there was no doubt in his mind that Elizabeth would hate him forever. He climbed the stairs feeling completely defeated and crumbled into his bed not bothering to even change his clothes. He fell asleep from pure emotional exhaustion not being able to withstand the guilt he was carrying. He was haunted with dreams of the two women he loved, his sister and Elizabeth, both asking him "Why?" then walking away, without ever looking back.

Elizabeth woke early the next morning when a wave of nausea forced her from bed and into the bathroom. She emerged a few moments later wondering if she had caught some type of flu. She went back to bed and slept for several hours before waking up feeling better. She showered and dressed deciding she would take a walk along the beach since it was such a beautiful day. She went downstairs and had some toast in the kitchen since her brother had already left for the office. Elizabeth was glad not to have to see her brother this morning after his cruel comments he had made the evening before.

She left the house, descending the stone stairway to the beach when she realized someone was behind her. She turned to face one of her brother's body guards walking a short distance behind her. "What do you think you're doing?" she asked him firmly.

"I have been instructed to watch after you Miss Marks," he replied.

"I don't need watching so be on your way," she ordered.

"Sorry Miss Marks. I have strict instructions from your brother not to let you out of my sight." Fuming at her brother's intrusion on her privacy she went down the beach and tried to ignore her newly acquired shadow that was forced upon her. She found it terribly irritating being followed about and found no peace walking along the shore. She gave up her attempt to clear her head, now more miserable than before. She returned to the house and escaped to the privacy of her room. Elizabeth decided to sit on the balcony where she found herself feeling like a caged animal. She was becoming more and more resentful of her brother each day and wished only to be free of him. Before William, her brother paid her no mind, now every time he spoke to her he was either ordering her around or insulting her.

She thought about Jonathan and their meeting the day before wishing she didn't agree to continue their friendship. How could she encourage him further knowing her heart was broken? She thought about the time she spent with William and how happy she had been. He had been so gentle and caring. Tears ran down her cheeks as she remembered the first time they made love. She still couldn't believe it had all been an act to gain her trust to get her family's money. She remembered that special moment when he proposed and appeared so sincerely happy when she said yes. Her heart felt as though it broke into a million pieces all over again as she thought about William's deceit, yet found she still ached for the feel of his arms around her. She felt like such a fool having fallen for him so fast and easily. Elizabeth admitted that she may have approached the relationship in a much slower fashion if her brother hadn't made her so angry after informing her of the arrangement he had made for her to marry Jonathan Parker.

The days passed slowly for Elizabeth, now feeling more like torture, enduring her brother's repeated digs at her regarding her affair with William while making sure that Elizabeth kept seeing Jonathan. Although her visits with Jonathan were probably the only thing she now enjoyed, she still felt that she was being forced into their friendship. She realized Jonathan probably hadn't known about the arrangement so she did her best to treat him kindly while trying not to encourage him too much, stressing she wished for only friendship.

The only time her brother's bodyguards weren't following her around was when she was with Jonathan. She was looking forward to attending school at the end of the summer simply to escape the coldness of her brother and his watch dogs. In an attempt to avoid her own mind and the constant memories of William, Elizabeth began reading book after book while lying on the beach or sitting on her balcony. Most days this distraction worked but on her bad days nothing seemed to keep her from thinking of William. Elizabeth was barely eating, still feeling sick each morning when she woke. She felt tired and depressed most of the time, feeling like a robot going through the motions of its expected duties, finding no joy or satisfaction in her days.

William woke the next morning to the sound of his nephew calling his name as he bounced on his uncle's bed in an attempt to wake him. William opened his eyes and couldn't help but smile at the enthusiasm the boy had so early in the day. "Okay, Toby. I'll get up. Give me a few minutes and I'll be downstairs," he told the boy gently, trying not to take his bad mood out on his nephew.

"Okay, Uncle Willy! Mommy's making pancakes for breakfast. Hurry up or I might eat them all by myself," he informed his uncle as he left the room.

William forced himself from his bed and went to the bathroom to clean up before joining his family in the kitchen. He dreaded facing his sister, feeling ashamed and guilty again at the memory of her reaction to his confession the evening before. He eventually went down to the kitchen and poured himself a hot cup of coffee. Sarah was busy flipping the pancakes she was preparing so he quietly took his seat at the table next to his nephew.

He sat quietly watching his sister as she served them all pancakes. She sat down and ate her pancakes in silence not looking at him which made him feel even worse. He felt he would choke on the pancakes he was trying to force down his throat. He managed to swallow only a few pieces when he had to excuse himself to get some fresh air. William stepped through the sliding glass door to the screened porch and sat on the bench swing trying to control his emotions. He didn't know how to handle his sister's silence and obvious disappointment in him.

A few moments later his sister joined him on the porch, after telling Toby to go watch some cartoons when he finished his breakfast so she could talk to his uncle. She stood in front of her brother noticing how pale and awful he looked. She realized he was torturing himself much more than she ever could and took pity on him. She took a seat next to her brother putting a reassuring arm around his shoulder. "What are we going to do to fix this William?" she asked him softly. He looked up at her with pain in his eyes to find forgiveness and understanding staring back at him. He hugged his sister tight, relieved he hadn't lost her. They sat together on their swing discussing the situation, trying to figure out how to fix the damage he caused. Sarah couldn't help but feel sorry for her brother once she understood he truly loved Elizabeth. Sarah decided she would do whatever she could to help him.

The weeks slowly passed for Elizabeth as she felt more tired and run down after weeks of barely eating. As time passed she became more depressed, sleeping later into each morning and taking naps in the afternoons. When Susan noticed Elizabeth's continuing delicate state and mentioned her concern to her husband. Richard dismissed his wife's concerns with a simple wave of his hand. "She brought this upon herself. She'll get over it eventually," he said coldly. Susan was irritated with his lack of concern for his younger sister but didn't pursue the issue further, busy planning the annual barbeque they held every summer for a select group of friends and business associates. They've had the party every summer for the past six years for over a hundred of the most prestigious people they knew, each guest selected carefully for their social standing or for their position in business. Many of the guests would be executives from banks and brokerage firms that Richard dealt with or wanted to deal with.

The party was thrown in full fashion with delicate outdoor lighting and an orchestra playing music for dancing. There would be no sparing of expense, serving only the highest quality of food and beverages which would include lobster, shrimp, caviar and the best champagne money could buy. The party would be held on the following Saturday evening outside in the large elaborately landscaped back yard. Elizabeth, of course was expected to play the gracious hostess entertaining all of the guests, which included the Parkers.

Elizabeth filled her days with reading books on various subjects and sleeping. The few days prior to the big party Susan began assigning her duties which she accepted gratefully to keep her mind occupied. On the Friday before the party she joined Susan at the salon to have a manicure and pedicure so she would be perfectly groomed as expected. Normally, Elizabeth would have enjoyed the pampering but this time it only reminded her of the last day she had spent with William. The day he made her so completely happy to only break her heart in a million pieces by the end of that wonderful day.

Sarah Blake was sipping her coffee and reading the paper when she came across an article about Richard Marks. In the society section of the newspaper there was a picture of Richard Marks' home and a blurb regarding the upcoming annual barbeque he was throwing that weekend, describing the elaborate food and entertainment that was provided at the past events. Sarah no longer cared about Richard Marks and what he had done to her and her child. She let go of the hatred she had felt for him a long time ago. She took interest in the event only because of the new situation with her brother. After reading the story which detailed everything down to which caterer was lucky enough to land the job, Sarah had a thought. She went over and over things in her mind finally deciding what she needed to do. She went over a list of things she would need to do to prepare, then went in search of her brother.

She found him without any trouble, playing with Toby in the back yard. "William, do you think you could do me a favor and stay with Toby tomorrow? I have an invitation to visit with friends. I would be leaving early and I'm unsure of what time I'll return in the evening," she decided not to fill her brother in on her true intent for the next day, figuring he wouldn't want her to go anywhere near Richard Marks.

"Sure sis. No problem," he responded.

William and Sarah had been brain storming every night after Toby went to bed but couldn't figure out a way around Richard's security so he could approach Elizabeth and explain. William had paid a private detective he had used in the past who he trusted completely to watch Elizabeth only to be disappointed, but not surprised when he was informed that she was constantly escorted by bodyguards. After reading the article in the paper Sarah realized she may be able to approach Elizabeth herself on his behalf. It had been a long time since she saw Richard Marks and doubted he would even recognize her.

She went to her room to find a proper outfit for the following day and found the only elegant gown she owned which had been purchased the year before to attend a charity event with William. She picked out some shoes and appropriate jewelry, packing them in a small bag. She made an appointment at the salon for early the next morning. She planned to have her hair and nails done in preparation for the evening knowing if she was to go unnoticed she must appear as if she belonged there. The weather was expected to be perfect for the outdoor dinner party which would provide her with the perfect access to the party. She planned to park at the marina that wasn't far from Richard's house, walk up the beach and into the party by the access way she noticed in the picture of his home, hoping he wouldn't have security at the back of the house.

If she was successful she would manage to get to Elizabeth and only hoped she would allow her to explain on behalf of her brother. She went to bed that evening filled with nervous energy. Sarah woke early, quietly taking her dress and overnight bag out to her car. She forced herself to eat some toast and drank a hot cup of coffee before leaving for her salon appointment. She started her car determined to help her brother and repay him for the years of hard work and sacrifice he endured to care for her and her son. She arrived at the salon promptly at nine o'clock. She expected to be done at the salon around noon and then would have to find a place to stay the night in Stamford which would provide a place to dress for the party.

Sarah had plenty of time to work out the details of her plan and rehearse what she wanted to say to Elizabeth while she was at the salon and on the drive to Stamford. She checked into a hotel located approximately thirty minutes from Richard's home. The party was said to start at six o'clock however, Sarah thought it best to let some other guests arrive before she tried to enter the party. She had about three hours to kill before getting dressed and making the drive to the marina. She decided to go downstairs to the hotel restaurant and have an early dinner, doubting she would have the stomach or the time to eat later at the party. She took her time eating her meal, attempting to calm her nerves with a glass of wine.

After her meal she took a short walk to kill some time and gather her courage before returning to the hotel to dress for the evening. As she looked at herself in the mirror, looking sophisticated and elegant, her courage grew knowing she looked nothing like the innocent young girl Richard had taken advantage of years ago. Sarah was still beautiful with a nice figure despite having a child. She looked just as she needed and left the hotel with her chin held high determined to accomplish what she set out to do.

She arrived at the marina shortly after six o'clock and parked her car. She took her time walking down the beach with her shoes and handbag in her hand, going over and over what she would say to Elizabeth should she manage to get her alone. When she came close to the house she could hear the sound of the orchestra playing mingling with the sound of people talking and laughing. She stood at the bottom of the stone stairway, taking a deep breath before beginning the climb that would take her to Elizabeth. To Sarah's relief, there was no guard at the stairway and she managed to walk right into the party. She did her best to appear to mingle with the other guests saying hello and smiling as she slowly headed in the direction of the house, scanning the crowd along the way in an attempt to spot Elizabeth.

She spotted Richard at the bar talking with some of his guests, as she pretended to mingle, strolling through the crowd. Sarah was surprised when she realized she no longer saw Richard the same way. She felt nothing for him except pity. Sarah was pleased to realize she didn't fear him at all. She was tempted to go straight up to him and say hello just to see the look on his arrogant face but knew she needed to focus on her purpose for being there. She continued to scan the crowd and after an hour or so, finally spotted Elizabeth talking to a handsome young man with brown hair. She knew immediately it was Elizabeth by the long auburn hair and petite physique, just as William had described.

She scanned the crowd of guests that surrounded Elizabeth to be sure Richard wasn't nearby and decided it was time to make her move. She approached Elizabeth with a wide smile on her face, "Elizabeth Marks! Oh my goodness! I haven't seen you in ages. How are you?" she exclaimed hugging Elizabeth gently. Elizabeth awkwardly hugged Sarah in return trying not to let on that she didn't remember the woman suddenly embracing her. Sarah had been counting on Elizabeth's etiquette and upbringing to allow her this opening. Her manners would not allow her to embarrass anyone.

"I'm fine. Thank you," Elizabeth answered as she searched her mind for a name that never came.

"Well, you just look absolutely stunning! Like a beautiful flower blooming right in front of me! Speaking of flowers, I understand you have a wonderful garden on the grounds. Would it be too much to ask for a quick tour of the garden everyone has been talking so much about?"

Elizabeth had no desire to escort one of her brother's guests through the garden but would be considered rude if she refused. "Of course," she returned kindly. "Jonathan would you excuse me for a few minutes?" she asked her escort politely.

"Don't be too long," he responded as Elizabeth walked off with Sarah towards the garden. Sarah babbled cheerfully along the way for appearance sake. Once they were out of the sight and earshot of the guests, Sarah stopped and turned to face Elizabeth.

"Is something wrong?" Elizabeth inquired noticing the woman's sudden change of expression.

"I know you have no idea who I am because you've never met me before. I have something I need to talk to you about and hope you will give me a few minutes of your time."

Elizabeth was annoyed by the intrusion of this stranger. "What's this about?" she demanded firmly.

"William." Sarah said bluntly. Elizabeth's face grew pale and she immediately turned to leave.

"Elizabeth, please hear me out. I'll never bother you again. Please listen to what I have to say!" she begged as Elizabeth was walking away.

Something in the woman's voice made Elizabeth stop. She slowly turned back to the stranger. "Who are you?"

"Sarah Blake. William is my brother," she explained.

"You're Sarah Blake?" Elizabeth looked pale as she responded.

"Please Elizabeth. Hear me out?" Elizabeth looked around to be sure no one else was coming.

"You have my full attention," she said and sat on the bench feeling a little shaky.

"Thank you, Elizabeth. I want you to know that what my brother did was inexcusable however things are not as your brother makes them out to be." Sarah began telling her about her relationship with Richard years before and what caused her brother to do what he did. She told Elizabeth about the lab technician that had been bribed and all William's attempts to make Richard take responsibility. "I have a son, Elizabeth, your nephew. An adorable eight year old boy named Toby."

Elizabeth sat listening in disbelief as she described the cold and cruel actions of her brother. "What he tried to do was wrong but he realized that well before your brother came and found you. William loves you Elizabeth but couldn't tell you the truth for fear of losing you. He sincerely wanted to marry you Elizabeth. Believe me, my brother's actions had nothing to do with money, he has more than enough of his own, revenge was his only desire. William is a very kind person who made the mistake of believing he could be cold and cruel like Richard. He feels awful for what he has done to you and has been trying to find a way to talk to you ever since."

"Why should I believe any of this?" she asked angrily.

"I understand how you feel Elizabeth. You gave your heart to a man who deceived you but your brother is the evil one. Did you know that he had William beaten outside the restaurant that day? He was in the hospital for days with a concussion and broken ribs."

Elizabeth didn't want to believe her brother would be so cruel. "I want you to leave Sarah," Elizabeth ordered. "I have listened to all I want to hear."

Sarah Blake looked at her with regret. "I am leaving Elizabeth but I wanted you to know that William loves you and regrets the pain he has caused you. He doesn't know I'm here and he would never have allowed me to come if I told him, but he's so miserable I had to try," she said as she stood to leave. "I understand more than you know the heartache your suffering after putting your trust in a man so freely. I apologize that your pain resulted because of my mistakes years ago." Sarah pulled a slip of paper from her purse and handed it to Elizabeth. "Please take this. It's my telephone number and address. Please contact me should you ever need any-thing...Anything," she stressed as she left Elizabeth alone, walking back in the direction of the party.

Sarah walked directly to the bar and ordered a shot of bourbon. She thanked the bartender, pouring the amber fluid down her throat in one fluid motion. As she turned to leave Sarah heard a man's voice next to her. "Can I order you another?" Richard Marks asked her softly. Sarah turned, looking Richard straight in the eye. "No. Thank you," she said coldly and disappeared into the crowd of guests. It took Richard only a moment to realize who she was and felt the color drain from his face as he turned and scanned the crowd.

Elizabeth stopped dead in her tracks as she watched her brother speaking to Sarah Blake at the bar. She watched her brother's expression change upon recognition of the uninvited guest. Elizabeth knew what Sarah had told her was true when she saw the flicker of panic on her brother's face. She was glued to that spot as everything started to spin slowly around her. "Elizabeth? Are you alright?" she heard Jonathan ask her but couldn't respond as everything began to spin faster around, fading to black as she fainted. Jonathan managed to catch her before she hit the ground, immediately picking her up and carried her frantically towards the house.

Jonathan walked through the crowd of guests into the living room depositing Elizabeth gently on the couch. Susan had noticed Jonathan carrying Elizabeth and quickly followed him into the house. "What happened?" she asked.

"She fainted. Please call a doctor," he told her. One of the servants provided a wet towel so Jonathan wiped her forehead, trying to revive her. "Elizabeth," he said softly with concern. A moment later Susan returned with the family doctor who happened to be one of the guests.

"Jonathan, would you mind carrying Elizabeth upstairs to her room so the doctor can examine her privately?" Susan requested quietly. Without a reply Jonathan lifted Elizabeth gently and carried her up the stairs with the doctor following closely behind. He gently put her on the bed and told the doctor that she had fainted. He asked Susan and Jonathan to wait outside while he examined Elizabeth.

As the door shut behind them Elizabeth began to stir. She slowly looked around as if she didn't know where she was, trying to sit up in a panic. The doctor gently comforted Elizabeth and asked her to stay still. "What happened?" Elizabeth asked confused.

"Apparently you fainted," the doctor explained. "How do you feel now?" he asked her kindly.

"A little shaky," she admitted.

The doctor asked her several questions and checked her pulse. "Elizabeth, I must ask you... under the circumstances... when was your last menstrual cycle?" Elizabeth tried to remember as she realized the reason for his question. She frantically tried to remember but couldn't.

"Last week," she lied.

"Good. How have you been feeling lately?" he inquired further.

"Not real well actually. I have had some kind of bug and haven't been eating that much," she told him honestly.

"Well that explains it then. You need to start taking better care of yourself. I'm ordering you to stay in bed the rest of the evening. I'll have some food sent up to you shortly. Be sure to eat something so you don't faint again," he told her firmly.

"Yes doctor," she replied. "Thank you."

She watched as the doctor exited the room then heard some voices in the hall. A moment later there was a soft knock at the door as Jonathan appeared in the doorway. "May I come in?" he asked. Elizabeth nodded her consent embarrassed by the scene she must have caused. "Are you feeling better?" he asked as he sat on the side of the bed.

"Yes, thank you. I'm sorry for the trouble," she told him.

"You're never any trouble," he responded kindly.

"Tell that to my brother," she said bitterly before she could stop herself.

"What do you mean Elizabeth? I thought you and your brother got along well," he asked surprised at her angry comment.

Elizabeth regretted making the comment, "I don't know what I'm saying Jonathan. I guess I'm just cranky. I'm sorry."

"Stop apologizing Elizabeth. You have nothing to be sorry about," he told her with concern. "I'm just happy you're alright. The doctor says you're to eat something and remain in bed the rest of the evening."

Relieved to have an excuse to get away from the party she nodded. "So he tells me."

"I'll let you rest and make sure someone sends something up for you to eat. I'll call you tomorrow." he said as he stood to leave.

"Okay," she replied as he kissed her on the forehead and left the room. Before long a servant appeared with a platter of food for Elizabeth. She thanked the young maid and forced herself to eat as much as possible despite her lack of appetite.

Sarah disappeared into the crowd, making her way to the stone stairway and down to the beach. She didn't care if Richard recognized her. She had accomplished what she came to do. Even if Elizabeth never forgave William, at least she heard the truth, whether she chose to believe it or not. She looked at the clock when she arrived at her car in the marina parking lot, deciding she would check out of the hotel and drive home since she was still wound up from her escapade. She drove to the hotel where she changed her clothes, packed her things then went to the lobby to pay the bill. Toby would be asleep well before she got home but she knew William would probably be waiting up for her. She took the time on the drive home to decide if she would tell William that she had spoken with Elizabeth.

Elizabeth rested her head against the pillow feeling exhausted. The meeting with Sarah Blake had shaken her up and she wasn't sure how to feel about everything she said. She knew her brother had recognized Sarah at the bar so there had to be some truth to what she said. She knew first hand how cold Richard could be. She suddenly remembered the slip of paper Sarah had given her and checked her brazier to see if it was still there. Having no pockets in an evening dress it was the only place she could think to put it. She stared at the paper and wondered what William was doing at that moment. She wondered if he truly loved her as Sarah claimed, then recalled the doctor's question.

"When was your last menstrual cycle?" he had asked her bluntly. Elizabeth thought back trying to establish when her last cycle had been. She knew she had gotten it a week before graduation because she was worried about having cramps the day of the ceremony. After that she just didn't remember. She had gone on the boat trip with William shortly after graduation. "Oh my god. It's not possible! William said…." and her thoughts trailed off as she realized that the story of the vasectomy was probably a lie as well. "Oh my god!" she said out loud in the empty room. Fear gripped her as she realized she was probably pregnant. The fainting spell and the nausea she had been experiencing for the past several weeks were symptoms. What was she going to do? Tears filled Elizabeth's eyes as she realized the gravity of her situation.

If Sarah Blake's speech had softened Elizabeth's anger towards William, this new situation had certainly ruined any hopes of forgiveness. "How could he lie about something so important?" she cried into her pillow. She had to know for sure but couldn't think of how to get a test done without her brother finding out. She could make an appointment with the doctor but was afraid of her brother's influence. Elizabeth concluded that the only way to keep this a secret was to purchase a home pregnancy kit but had to figure out how to get past her brother's body guards that were constantly watching her.

She took a deep breath, wiping the tears from her face. She went to the bathroom to prepare for bed, brushing her teeth and her hair then changing out of the gown she still wore. She went to her closet and pulled out the small wooden chest that she had hidden behind some shoe boxes. She kept some money in the box that she had saved over the years so she wouldn't always have to ask her brother. She placed the slip of paper with Sarah's information in the box then took out cash in an amount she thought she would need and then some extra just in case. She placed the box back in her hiding spot and shut her closet door. Elizabeth only had to figure out how to get what she needed without anyone knowing. She thought about it for a while, forming her plan. She set her alarm clock to be sure not to over sleep then went to bed. Elizabeth was awake for quite awhile, crying until she finally fell asleep.

Chapter Ten

Sarah pulled into her drive way at almost midnight quietly taking her bags into the house trying not to wake William or her son. She tip toed into the house, putting her bags in the foyer so she could take them up on her way to bed. She went to the kitchen after deciding she could use a cocktail, still feeling wide awake. She wasn't surprised to find her brother waiting for her in the kitchen looking tired and depressed. Her heart went out to him as she looked at his pale unshaven face.

"Was everything alright with Toby today?" she asked him as she made herself a drink. "Yeah, everything was fine. I guess you had a good time since you're home so late," he commented.

Sarah looked at her brother and found it impossible to lie to him. "Not exactly. But I did what I set out to do," she replied honestly.

"What do you mean? You didn't have fun with your friends?" he asked confused by her answer. She sat across from her brother with her cocktail in hand, taking a large sip before answering.

"I didn't go to see my friends today," she told him honestly.

He looked at his sister surprised by her reply. "Then where were you all day? Are you dating someone and didn't want to tell me?"

"Nope. I'm not dating anyone at the moment," she stalled. "Would you like a drink?"

He waited for her to make his drink and continue only to find himself repeating his question as she handed him the glass. "Well, are you going to tell me where you were?" he asked impatiently.

Sarah took a deep breath and looked her brother in the eye. "I went to see Elizabeth, William," she replied.

For a moment he looked as if he misunderstood what she said. "You did what?!" he exclaimed.

"I went to see Elizabeth," she repeated calmly.

"I heard you the first time Sarah. What in the hell were you thinking going anywhere near there!?" he demanded angrily.

"Calm down William. I was reading the paper the other day about some huge party Richard was having. I thought I might be able to get to Elizabeth and speak to her."

He absorbed what she said still angry at her for going anywhere near Richard Marks. "Well what happened?" he asked beginning to calm down, wondering if she actually spoke to Elizabeth.

"I walked into the party right off the beach without notice. After about an hour I finally spotted Elizabeth and approached her. I pretended to be someone she met in the past hoping her manners wouldn't allow her to admit she didn't know who I was. I asked her to show me the garden to get her away from the other guests so I could talk to her. It worked," she told him, intentionally leaving out that she had also bumped into Richard.

Sarah told him about their conversation and how things had ended. "I'm sorry I couldn't come home with better news. She is understandably very angry. On a positive note, she didn't have me arrested for trespassing and she kept the paper with my number on it," she told him trying to lift his spirits.

"How did she look? Was she well?" William asked concerned.

"Never having seen her before she looked fine to me," she answered not wanting him to worry. Even though they had never met, Sarah thought Elizabeth appeared tired and pale. "I would give her some time. Maybe she will come around and try to call eventually."

"Maybe," he said sadly. "Why didn't you tell me what you wanted to do?" he asked upset she had taken such a risk.

Sarah looked at him and laughed, "If I had told you, would you have tried to stop me?"

"You better believe it!" understanding his sister's reason the moment the words left his mouth. He forgot that his sister could be just as stubborn as he was sometimes.

"I'm going up to bed sis. Please don't do anything foolish like this again. Stay away from Richard Marks, Sarah. I wouldn't be able to live with myself if something happened to you because of what I did," he stated firmly.

"Okay William. Good night."

Elizabeth woke up early the next morning to the sound of her alarm clock quickly turning off the machine and jumping out of bed, ignoring the all too familiar nauseous feeling she had every morning. Elizabeth quickly but quietly dressed and packed her beach bag with her money, a blanket and a book. She quietly opened her bedroom door, peeking around to be sure no one was around. She was relieved when she managed to sneak out of the house without notice and quickly made her way down to the beach. Elizabeth had dressed warmly knowing it would be chilly on the beach before sunrise. She walked quickly at first until she was a safe distance from the house then slowed her pace, knowing she would arrive at the marina a little early. She watched the sun rise as she made her way down the beach but found little comfort or joy in the scene. She had remembered the store in the marina opened early and hoped they stocked what she needed.

She had noticed on her various trips that marina stores often kept a wide variety of items for the convenience of the boaters. If they didn't stock what she needed then she would have to call a cab to take her to the nearest drug store. She arrived at the marina a half an hour early as anticipated. She sat on the beach nearby trying to read her book to pass the time. She was having a terrible time concentrating, feeling nervous that someone would come looking for her before she could purchase the item she required. Each minute that passed seemed like an eternity but finally the store opened. She went to the section with the feminine products and was relieved to find they had what she needed. Their selection was slim, only carrying one brand but she was willing to take what she could get. She took the item to the cashier and quickly paid as she blushed profusely.

She left the store and quickly ran back down to the beach stopping only once to hide the purchased item at the bottom of the bag. She walked back down the beach until she was close to the house. Elizabeth stopped, taking the blanket from her bag and spread it out flat on the sand. She sat down on the blanket pulling out her book trying to appear as if nothing was any different from any other day. Elizabeth knew they would be bringing breakfast to her empty room and would immediately notify Richard of her absence. She knew timing would be imperative if she wanted them to believe she had gone nowhere but down to the beach.

It didn't take long before she heard the body guards yelling in the yard above her. Elizabeth couldn't help but smile thinking about everyone franticly looking for her, assuming she had run away again. Elizabeth wished she had the courage to do just that. Just leave, never to endure her brother's cold and cruel ways again. "One day," she thought to herself.

"She's down here!" she heard the guard yell up to the house. He walked down the stairs and she turned towards the man with a questioning look on her face.

"Something wrong?" she asked innocently.

The man scowled at her, resenting his babysitting assignment even more now than before. "Your brother would like to see you," he told her gruffly. Elizabeth sighed as if he were interrupting something important then stood up, gathering her blanket and book placing them both in her beach bag before walking back up the stairs to the house.

She walked into the dining room to face her brother. "You wanted to see me Richard?" she asked pretending not to know why.

"Where were you?" he demanded angrily.

"I woke up early so I decided to go to the beach, watch the sun come up, and read for a while," she explained as if she didn't understand why he was making such a fuss.

"How many times have I told you not to leave without telling someone where you were going?!" he yelled as he slammed his fist on the table.

Knowing his anger didn't come from concern for her well being, she yelled back at him. "Next time, I'll be sure to wake the entire house before dawn if that will make you happy Richard! After all, I know just how much you really care and worry about me," she sneered as she left the dining room.

She was caught off guard when her brother grabbed her arm and swung her around to face him. "Don't ever walk away from me when I'm talking to you!" he said angrily.

Elizabeth tore her arm from his grip and glared at Richard with hatred, standing up to her brother for the first time in her life. "Don't touch me!" she said looking him straight in the eye, standing her ground but her brother swiftly slapped her face. He was surprised then angry at his sister's new found courage. Elizabeth stumbled back not expecting the blow and held her cheek in shock.

Despite the sting, she stood up again and faced her brother. She glared at him angrily and without another word walked away from him heading straight for her room.

"Don't you walk away from me! Elizabeth! Come back here this instant!" Elizabeth heard his bellowing but never bothered to look back. She went straight to her room and locked the door behind her. Shaking, she took the purchased item from her bag and quickly hid it in her bathroom behind all the other female products, fearing her brother may come after her. She threw the bag and its remaining contents in the corner and sat on the edge of her bed, bracing herself, just in case Richard chose to pursue their argument any further. She waited a while then realized he wasn't coming after her.

Relieved, she walked to the mirror and looked at her stinging cheek. There was a bright red hand mark on the side of her face which made her temper flare. She was proud that she had stood up to her brother, showing him she was not afraid of him but was not prepared for the slap in the face she received for her bravery. She began to calm down after a few moments then ran to the bathroom, bending over the commode, heaving violently. Once her stomach calmed she brushed her teeth then shut and locked the bathroom door. She retrieved her package, reading the instructions carefully. She did everything the directions told her to do and paced the bathroom floor as she waited the two minutes for the results. Two minutes that felt like an eternity, each second utter torture.

When two minutes finally passed she looked at the little plastic stick that would decide her future. Elizabeth calmly took the plastic stick and shoved it back into its box along with the instructions and all the wrappers. Not knowing what else to do with the evidence of her pregnancy, she went to her closet and placed the trash into her wooden box hidden in her closet. She made sure to bury it even deeper below the stack of shoe boxes, fearing someone would find it. She looked around the empty room through tears as she slowly made her way out to the balcony.

Elizabeth felt all kinds of emotions all at the same time. Shame, fear, and heartache were the first to arrive, followed by happiness and pride at the thought of having a child. Pride and happiness were soon overtaken by heartache again as she realized she was alone and her brother wouldn't be happy. She sat and cried completely confused not knowing what to do. She knew she couldn't tell anyone but also knew it wasn't a secret she could keep for long. Elizabeth knew with her family's social status that it would be considered a scandal and her brother would be publicly humiliated. She considered having an abortion but couldn't bear the thought. She sat on the balcony feeling tired and exhausted by her plight. She had no idea what to do and soon felt numb as she sat looking out at the oversized and lavishly landscaped yard. She laughed out loud at how ironic life seemed to be. All the money in the world, all the expensive furnishings, all the servants, but not one friend she could count on or talk to. Elizabeth felt completely lost and alone.

Elizabeth went to take a shower, hoping the spray of hot water would sooth and comfort her. She was disappointed when once undressed she found herself caressing her stomach wondering what sex the child would be. She let the hot water run down her body, trying to picture herself as a mother and experienced her first motherly instinct. She suddenly wanted to protect her child. She wanted to take care of her child no matter what. She decided that she would have her baby, determined to find a way to provide for her child.

Elizabeth got out of the shower with new spirit and drive. The first thing she needed to do for her unborn child was eat, something she hadn't done yet that day. She dressed and went downstairs to get something to eat, only to be intercepted by one of the servants on her way. "You have a phone call, Miss Elizabeth."

She went to the foyer and picked up the receiver. "Hello," she said into the phone, wondering who could be calling.

"Elizabeth, its Jonathan. How are you feeling today?" he asked, still concerned about the episode the evening before.

"Much better. Thank you for asking," she replied politely.

"Glad to hear it. Listen... I was wondering.... if you're feeling up to it that is... could I take you to dinner tonight?" he asked hopefully.

Elizabeth's first instinct was to decline but after a moment decided otherwise. "That would be lovely, Jonathan."

"Great! How about I pick you up around six?" he asked happily.

"That would be fine. I'll see you then," she said before saying good bye and hanging up the phone.

"We just might have a father for you after all," she said silently to her unborn baby as she went in search of food.

William was sitting at the desk in his den, trying to concentrate on some paperwork when his cell phone rang. "Hello," he answered gruffly frustrated that he couldn't seem to accomplish any work recently.

"Are we a little grumpy today?" asked his friend on the other end.

"Mike? Hey, I'm sorry. I'm just having a bad day. What's up?"

"Actually, I have some very interesting information for you," he stated proudly.

"Oh really? Then let's hear it!" William replied impatiently.

"Remember when we talked a couple of weeks ago about the death of your friend's parents?"

"Yeah I remember. What about it?" William asked, giving his friend his full attention. "Remember the cop I told you I spoke with? The one that got transferred?" asked Zimmerman, trying to refresh his friend's memory.

"Yeah, I remember," William replied feeling impatient again.

"Well, a couple of days ago I received a package from an "anonymous" source. It contained some copies of police reports and such regarding the investigation into the murder of Mr. and Mrs. Marks," Mike told him then paused to take a sip of the coffee he was drinking.

"Anyway, the final report written by the cop that was originally in charge of the case had named Richard Marks III as the prime suspect!"

William stood up and began pacing after his friend's last statement. "Did the report say why he was naming him the prime suspect?" he asked Mike.

"He put in his report that Richard Marks III had motive, which was of course money and since it was a professional hit no alibi would matter. The other evidence used in naming him a prime suspect was financial records showing that there had been two large cash withdrawals from his accounts. The first withdrawal dated a couple of days before his parents died and the other a couple of days after."

The thought that the man could have hired someone to murder his own parents enraged William. "What a son of a bitch! Let me guess, that's when the cop got transferred?" he asked trying to confirm his suspicions.

"Exactly two days after by the looks of the paper work in front of me. But William, that's not the worst part," he told his friend with concern.

"What else could be worse?" William asked.

"The source sent a copy of a letter he received in the mail. It contained a photograph of his wife and child. The letter simply said 'back off or else'. The envelope that was enclosed was post marked the same day of his transfer. It is obvious the cop that sent me the information understandably doesn't want to be considered a formal source," Mike informed him worried that this information was too hot to handle.

William absorbed all the information Mike Zimmerman provided and was amazed at the lengths Richard Marks III had gone to in order to get his own parents' money. "Mike, could you fax me a copy of the papers you received?" he asked, suddenly worried for Elizabeth's safety. "What if Elizabeth got in his way as well?" he asked himself.

"To tell you the truth, I'm not sure I want this stuff on my desk, if you know what I mean. Even if we didn't already have an agreement I'm not sure I would want this kind of heat on my shoulders. I'll overnight the originals to you for safe keeping if you want them. Just remember, if this ever comes to a head, I get first dibs on the story," Mike replied always thinking like a reporter.

"You got it. Send me the papers at my home address. Thanks for everything Mike," he said then hung up the phone. William sat down then stood back up and began pacing his office. Thoughts whirled through his mind leaving only questions without answers. The one question most important to him was if Richard would hurt Elizabeth. "If Richard Marks III was mean enough to have his own parents killed why would he hesitate to do the same to Elizabeth? Why would he bother to come after Elizabeth and have his thugs beat me nearly to death if he cared so little? Kill off your parents but keep the nuisance of a sister around? Something just doesn't make sense. Maybe Richard didn't have his parents killed and it was all done just to save himself from a public scandal?"

William knew full well that money and power is what drove Richard Marks but was he that money hungry.....? Unless.... there was something in his parents' Will that made him need Elizabeth? At this thought, William decided to call his attorney to make some inquiries. He explained to his attorney what he was trying to find out but didn't explain why. His attorney said he would make some inquiries and would get back to him.

He remembered the articles that had been faxed to him that he had left on his boat and made a mental note to drive out and retrieve them so he could keep them with the other papers that were expected to arrive the next day. He was sure Elizabeth had no idea of her brother's actions. He was determined to make sure nothing happened to Elizabeth but knew he would have to have some kind of proof before he would ever get her to listen to anything he had to say. He wasn't sure if he should share the new information with Sarah, afraid of upsetting her any further.

Elizabeth forced herself to eat something healthy and then took a short walk outside through the garden with her shadow in tow. The only place she had any privacy these days was in her room. She walked around thinking about her child and Jonathan. It hadn't occurred to her until his call that he could be her only solution. He was a kind and gentle man. She thought that he would make a wonderful father. She could just marry him and everyone would be happy. Could she actually marry him knowing she was carrying another man's child? This is the part that concerned her. Elizabeth was not a deceitful person by nature, but how else would she care for her child and avoid a scandal? Her inheritance would not be hers for another three years and she had no way to provide for her child without that money. Richard would probably throw her out and disown her if he knew.

She tried to picture herself married to Jonathan. It wasn't a bad picture. He was handsome and was very fond of her. "He would make a good husband," she thought to herself, again unsure if she would be able to lie to him. She knew if she chose to marry him she would need to find some reason to do it quickly so no one would suspect she was already pregnant. She was trying desperately to convince herself that she should marry Jonathan but her heart wasn't being agreeable. Despite everything, she still loved William or loved the man she thought of as William, the man he had pretended to be.

She walked back to the house to get ready for her dinner date with Jonathan. Jonathan appeared promptly at six as promised, complimenting Elizabeth immediately on how lovely she looked. Elizabeth always appreciated Jonathan's sincere attempts to win her affection. They left the house shortly after six, allowing a few minutes for Jonathan to properly greet Richard before taking Elizabeth to dinner. He had made a reservation at a nearby restaurant for six thirty. He escorted Elizabeth to his car, making sure to open her door in the traditional fashion. They drove to the restaurant, chatting about different subjects they both had interest in. She always enjoyed the conversations she had with Jonathan. He always seemed to take sincere interest in what she had to say and always took her opinions seriously unlike her brother and his friends. Most of the women she spoke to were happy discussing fashion and their children, always appearing bored if she talked of any other subjects.

They entered the restaurant and were seated on the patio overlooking the ocean. Jonathan had asked for this seating when he made the reservation, knowing Elizabeth would enjoy the view. Elizabeth felt more relaxed in his company. She looked at Jonathan intently, again considering her situation. He noticed the strange way she was looking at him and asked if anything was wrong.

"No Jonathan," she said smiling. He liked the way she smiled at him and decided to take advantage of her good mood. Jonathan leaned toward Elizabeth taking her hand and gently pulled her towards him. He kissed her softly enjoying her response to his affections, glad that he had managed to soften the resistance their families had caused.

She looked into his eyes with admiration as he pulled away. They finished their meal shortly after the band began to play soft music in the background. Jonathan asked her to dance then spent the next hour twirling her around the dance floor enjoying every smile he managed to put on her beautiful face, glad to see she was enjoying herself. Their date felt more like the last evening they went dancing. She had been happy and relaxed in his company, laughing and flirting with him as they danced. They returned to their table smiling as they quenched their thirst. Jonathan asked the waiter for their bill looking at her sadly not wanting the evening to end.

"What's wrong?" she asked when his expression changed.

"I don't want the evening to end," he explained to her with a pout on his face. She laughed at his exaggeration of his disappointment.

"Well…who says it has to end?" she asked playfully.

"What do you have in mind?" he asked with a mischievous grin.

"How about a walk on the beach?" she suggested.

"That sounds wonderful!" he said with enthusiasm. They drove back to the house and she quickly went to her room to retrieve her beach blanket. They went through the backyard and down the stone stairway that took them to the beach. They walked for a while, again discussing various topics with surprising ease. After a while they realized the sun was going down and decided to sit and watch the sun set. They managed to find a quiet little spot, spreading the blanket out on the beach. Jonathan had already discarded his jacket and tie in the car after dinner, then removed his shoes and socks, cuffing up his pants when they reached the beach.

She thought he looked more handsome without the stuffy jacket. The top buttons of his shirt were undone and he was barefoot with wind blown hair. She sat next to him on the blanket, admiring the beautiful sunset. Jonathan took her hand as she turned to him with a smile. Jonathan kissed her, this time more passionately, having more privacy in their secluded spot. She responded to his kiss relieved to be in his arms, needing to be in his arms. His passion grew with her response as they kissed, enjoying each other. Jonathan began caressing her hips and legs as he kissed her. His passion was inflamed to another level when Elizabeth began to caress him in response. "Oh Elizabeth!" he moaned softly in her ear as he kissed her neck.

Jonathan was extremely aroused and tried to pull away in an attempt to stop before things went too far. Elizabeth pulled him back to the ground on top of her. She had been feeling so alone that his sincere affection for her had inflamed a passionate response that she wasn't ready to extinguish. This response made Jonathan lose his head completely forgetting where they were. He began to caress her again this time running his hands down the length of her dress and back up again to access the bare flesh underneath. When she did nothing to stop his advances, he couldn't help but continue. Soon he felt as though he could barely breathe, wanting her desperately. He slowly lowered the shoulder straps on her dress to allow better access to the curves near her breasts while he kissed her everywhere. He wanted her desperately. "Elizabeth?" he asked looking into her eyes wondering if she wanted him to stop. She looked at him without reserve, wrapping the blanket around them in answer to his unspoken question.

Later they walked silently back to the house hand in hand. When they reached the stairway that would take them back to the house, they both sat down and put their shoes on, taking a moment to examine the other to be sure they both looked presentable in case they ran into anyone at the house. It was almost eleven and Elizabeth hoped her brother would be in bed. She walked Jonathan to his car, kissing him good night. They decided he would come see her the next day even though he had to work. He told her he would take a half day and arrive sometime in the late afternoon. Elizabeth went to her room, relieved that she didn't run into anyone on the way.

She took a shower then decided to sit on the balcony not quite feeling tired enough for bed. She thought about Jonathan and couldn't help but feel guilty. She hadn't planned to make love to him, especially on the beach, but had been so lonely and broken hearted she desperately needed the affection. She was surprised that she had enjoyed it so much under the circumstances. This confirmed her assumption that Jonathan would be a good husband but still wondered if she could live with the guilt if she lied to him. She went to bed that evening fighting with her conscience and her desire to provide a good life for her child.

Chapter Eleven

William felt like a wild cat, trapped, unable to pounce on his prey. He received the package containing the papers he was waiting for and after reviewing them up close, was certain Richard had something to do with his parents' death. Unable to sit still, William decided to drive out to his boat to retrieve the articles he had left there. He needed to check on his boat anyway, not having bothered to go there since it was delivered. He packed a small suitcase and let Sarah know where he would be. He told her he didn't know for sure if he would return immediately or not.

He drove towards Stamford, which did nothing to calm his spirit, thinking of Elizabeth and regretting again the mess he had made. He was determined to try to get to her some how and tell her the truth, if only to protect her. He wished for nothing more than her forgiveness and to hold her in his arms again but knew it was unlikely to ever happen.

William had been thinking of how to get around Richard's security for weeks but kept coming up empty. His private detective reported to him again that the security surrounding Elizabeth hadn't yet been decreased. He knew he would be recognized immediately by any security around her and was not willing to take the risk of causing her further friction with her brother. He knew if he tried to call her or mail her a letter they would be intercepted and immediately reported to Richard. His main problem seemed to be his identity and wished there was a way to change it.

Elizabeth had made her decision after determining it was the only feasible option available to her. She went about her day rehearsing in her mind what she wanted to say to Jonathan when he arrived later that afternoon. She dressed making sure to take extra time grooming, needing all the confidence she could muster. She already had a run in with her brother that morning before he left for the office.

"You and Jonathan must have had a nice time last evening since you returned so late," he said being more pleasant than usual.

"We had a nice time," she answered not bothering to provide him with any details.

"When do you plan to see him again?" he inquired.

"He will be visiting this afternoon," she told him.

"Well, well. Already have the man skipping out on work? You must have shown him a really good time last evening," he sneered before leaving the room. Lately, whenever they were alone, Richard always made a snide comment that left her fuming. She could only imagine how angry he would be and the treatment she would receive if she told him she was pregnant.

She awkwardly greeted Jonathan, feeling nervous and shy. Jonathan assumed her sudden awkwardness was due to the intimacy they shared the evening before, not realizing the true source of her nervousness. They decided to go out on the back patio to enjoy the brilliant, sunny afternoon. He pulled out a chair for her then leaned down and kissed her softly before taking his own seat. One of the servants appeared with two glasses and a pitcher of iced tea, placing it before them on the table before disappearing back into the house. Once their privacy was established, Jonathan took her hand in his and smiled. "I had a wonderful time last night Elizabeth. I hope you haven't found you regret it."

She saw the concern in his eyes and only felt guilty again for her deception. "No, not really," she answered shyly.

"Elizabeth, I love you. I am crazy about you. My only regret about last evening is that I had left you unprotected. I should have taken the responsibility and stopped before things went too far. For that, I apologize."

"You can't blame yourself, Jonathan. I was there too and could have stopped you at anytime," she told him honestly.

"But Elizabeth, what if you get pregnant?" he asked her with concern. She shrugged her shoulders not able to lie outright. She wasn't able to look at him as she tried to fight the tears now welling up in her eyes. He put his finger under her chin and lifted her face so he could see her. Jonathan was unable to stand seeing the worry and tears in her eyes. "Marry me, Elizabeth," he said without hesitation.

Stunned by his sudden proposal, Elizabeth couldn't speak. "Marry me? Be my wife?" he repeated as he bent down on one knee. He patiently waited for her reply, hoping she would say yes.

Jonathan had confused her tears with fear that she would be shamed by an unexpected pregnancy. He was making everything too easy for her and was unable to decline. "Are you sure you want to marry me Jonathan? We haven't known each other that long," she said giving him an honest opportunity to withdrawal his proposal.

"I love you and that's what matters to me. I am crazy about you and would be proud to be your husband," he told her softly.

She answered him without further hesitation, "Okay, I'll marry you Jonathan."

He stood up and lifted her out of the chair, hugging her tightly. "You won't regret this Elizabeth. I'll do whatever I can to make you happy!" he told her kissing her softly. "Now, what do you say we go shopping and pick you out an engagement ring!" he said happily pulling her by the hand towards the house. "Go get your things!" he said as he patted her on the behind. She couldn't help but laugh at his enthusiasm and obediently went to retrieve her hand bag, avoiding looking at herself in the mirror when she went to her room.

He drove to the local jeweler where they showed them dozens of different rings in all shapes and sizes. "Anything you want Elizabeth." Tears welled up in her eyes again as she remembered the ring William had given her. Jonathan put his arm around her proudly, assuming they were tears of happiness. She managed to finally pick out a ring that was completely different than the one William gave her. She chose one that held one single one-karat diamond cut in the shape of a circle. She kissed him softly on the lips as the jeweler wrapped up the ring for them.

Jonathan was so happy she agreed to marry him, he didn't notice Elizabeth was being so quiet. "Are you hungry? We could stop and get something to eat?" he asked her happily.

"Sure," she replied, knowing she needed to eat whether she was hungry or not. Elizabeth's heart jumped into her throat as he pulled into the marina located near the house. She desperately tried to hide her surprise as he pulled into a parking spot. He jumped out and went around the car to open her door. He escorted her into the restaurant where they were seated in a quiet corner he requested. Once they sat down he took the ring from the box and gently put it on her figure with a big grin on his face.

Elizabeth did her best to appear happy, slowly forcing herself to eat her dinner and concentrate on what Jonathan was saying. "We'll tell your brother tonight, if it's okay with you," he said and continued as she nodded in response, having a mouth full of food she found difficult to swallow. "Elizabeth, would you mind if we got married quickly? I mean just in case?" he asked quietly hoping she understood his meaning. She understood him more than he knew and couldn't believe that he had been the one to suggest it.

"It would probably be a good idea," she responded forcing herself to smile at him.

They finished their meal then walked to the car hand in hand. She smiled at him warmly as he opened the car door for her. Elizabeth tried to concentrate on Jonathan's excited rambling as he made suggestion after suggestion for their upcoming wedding as they drove back to the house. "Where would you like to go on our honeymoon? Florida?" he suggested.

"No, not Florida," she responded bluntly. Realizing her answer was too rough, she softened her voice, "I would like to go somewhere I've never been before," she explained.

"Okay… How about Hawaii?"

Elizabeth didn't really care where they went except that Florida held memories she didn't want to relive, especially on her honeymoon. "That would be wonderful," she said trying to sound enthusiastic.

William had arrived at the marina hours earlier and found the papers he wanted, immediately placing them in his briefcase with the others. He decided to go get some dinner and froze as he saw Elizabeth coming out of the restaurant. He was about to call her name when he saw a man take her hand, directing her towards the parking lot. Jealousy immediately flooded through William's veins, burning a whole through his heart. He watched helplessly as Elizabeth left with the man and got into his car. His appetite gone, replaced with jealous rage, he went to the bar instead and quickly drank a double shot of bourbon.

He went back to his boat raging with jealousy. He didn't like seeing Elizabeth smiling at another man. His anger festered as he poured himself another glass of bourbon and paced the boat like a caged animal. As he drank more and more William's thoughts became more unreasonable. "I can't believe I actually thought she was heart broken over me! Hugh! Cold like her brother!" he raged. "Already prancing around with another man!" William continued his drunken rage until his rage eventually turned to grief, no longer able to fight his broken heart. He stumbled into his bed sobbing like a child until finally passing out from the large amounts of bourbon he had consumed in such a short span of time.

Elizabeth and Jonathan arrived back at the house shortly after seven. Jonathan took her by the hand, pulling her into his arms as he helped her out of the car, kissing her hard on the lips. They went into the house heading straight for the library, assuming her brother would be there enjoying his after dinner cigar and bourbon. To Jonathan's delight their assumption was correct and shook his soon to be brother-in-law's hand with great enthusiasm.

"Have a good time?" Richard asked Jonathan, ignoring his sister.

"Very good actually," Jonathan said motioning for Elizabeth to join him. He proudly put his arm around Elizabeth's shoulder and told Richard their news. "Elizabeth has agreed to be my wife!" he told Richard happily.

"Smart girl," he responded looking at his sister with approval and shook Jonathan's hand. After Richard handed him a celebratory drink, Jonathan informed him of their plans for a quick wedding. Richard was happy to hear the plans for a quick wedding and asked if they had a date in mind.

"I was thinking in about four or six weeks? Do you think we'll have enough time to plan a proper wedding?" he asked Richard.

"I'm sure we can pull it off. I'll have Susan put an announcement in the papers tomorrow and start working on the arrangements right away," he told Jonathan confidently, completely ignoring Elizabeth again. Jonathan thanked him and said he would see him soon.

Elizabeth walked Jonathan to the door and kissed him good night. "I can't wait to see you again but I can't make it back until the weekend. I have meetings the rest of the week. I'll call you tomorrow night," he informed her before giving her one last quick kiss good night.

Elizabeth felt exhausted and wanted nothing more than to crawl into bed but her brother called her as she passed the library on her way to her room. With a sigh, she went into the library to see what her brother could possibly want. After all, he should be happy she agreed to marry Jonathan. "What is it?" she asked impatiently.

"What, may I ask, made you change your mind about marrying Jonathan?" Richard asked snidely.

"What does it matter? You're getting what you want regardless of the reason," she snapped back at him, again holding her ground, no longer willing to let her brother intimidate her.

"You had better watch your tone, Elizabeth!" he yelled as he slammed his glass down on the side table and stood to his full height.

She glared at him then found herself challenging him further. "My lord," she gracefully bowed, "If you do not need my services any longer I will retire for the evening," she mocked, sarcastically imitating the tone and manner of an old-fashioned servant.

As expected her response angered him further but when he swung his hand to slap her face she was ready and quickly dogged the blow. She grabbed the poker from the fire place and turned to him with rage in her eyes. Richard stunned by her quickness and attempt to defend herself was unsure how to react. Elizabeth glared at him with the poker in one hand warning her brother to back off. "Should you ever put your hands on me again, you will regret it!" she exclaimed.

He laughed at her as if her threat held no power. His amusement was soon replaced by anger at her next reply. "Funny it will be when I leave here, never to return, breaking my engagement to Jonathan you so desperately want!" she threatened. Richard knew she was serious by the look in her eyes. He had never seen this kind of spirit in his sister before. Richard waved his hand in the air as if suddenly bored with the scene trying to appear unmoved by her threat.

"Off to bed with you," he ordered, as if nothing had happened between him. Elizabeth laughed as she set the poker down in its stand and left the room, amazed at his arrogance.

Although he would never show it, Richard had taken his sister's threat seriously. Her sudden engagement to Jonathan was just what he wanted admitting only to himself that his sister was right. He didn't care why she changed her mind. Soon she would be married, no longer standing in his way. He poured himself a last drink before retiring for the evening, attempting to calm the blood racing through his veins.

Elizabeth closed the door behind her, still amazed at her brother's arrogance and thought of Sarah Blake. If Richard could treat her, his own flesh and blood so coldly, what made her think he wouldn't treat someone else even more cruelly? She thought about all the things Sarah Blake had told her about her brother, remembering the accusation that her brother's hired thugs had nearly beaten William to death. After Richard's second attempt to subdue her awakened spirit with force, she sadly admitted that Sarah's story was probably true. After this realization, she pictured Sarah Blake's heartache and humiliation she must have suffered at the hands of her brother. Now in a similar position, she understood all too clearly how she must have felt. Sarah only had her brother and no money, relying on her own labor and her brother's assistance to provide for her child.

Feeling the protectiveness again for her unborn child, Elizabeth better understood how William must have felt, unable to better assist his sister and the anger he must have felt at Richard's coldness. She understood the protective instinct that must have driven William's need for revenge when he was unable to force Richard to take proper responsibility for the child through legal channels. Her sympathy for William's feelings was quickly extinguished remembering again he had done to her exactly what his brother did to Sarah. Elizabeth wouldn't give him the chance to deny his child's existence, intending never to tell him the child existed. Her unborn child was conceived with love even if that love was one-sided. She would love that child without condition for the rest of her life.

William woke late the next morning with a pounding headache. Its only purpose was to punish him for the large quantity of bourbon he consumed the evening before. William groaned as he rolled over and looked at the clock. He climbed out of bed in search of some aspirin then deciding to take a shower hoping it would soothe his aching head. The shower revived him a little but did nothing to soothe his aching heart caused by the vision of Elizabeth with another man. He knew he had no right to be jealous after what he had done to her but found he couldn't help himself. He dressed feeling frustrated, knowing that he was the only one to blame.

He packed his things, took his belongings then locked up the boat. He deposited the suitcase along with his briefcase in his car then went to the restaurant for something to eat before making the drive home. Although his stomach wasn't being very agreeable, he forced himself to eat, knowing it would settle his stomach and his aching head. He drove home wondering about the man he had seen with Elizabeth, wondering if he treated her with kindness. He wondered if she had allowed him access to her luscious lips. He was unable to stop the jealousy that raged in him at the thought. He wondered if the man she had been with was the same man she had told him about. The man her brother wanted her to marry. William realized with regret that his deceit probably pushed Elizabeth right into the other man's arms, again concluding he had only himself to blame.

He arrived home with a heavy heart. Even Toby's enthusiastic greeting did little to numb his pain. Sarah greeted her brother, looking at him with great concern, certain something must have happened on his short trip. She quickly gave Toby a suggestion she knew would keep him busy for a short time so she could speak to her brother privately. "You look awful," she told her brother once Toby was a safe distance away. "What happened?" she asked with concern as she sat across from him at the kitchen table.

"I saw Elizabeth," he stated without further explanation.

"Did you speak to her?" she asked after a moment.

"No. I went to the boat to check on things and saw her coming out of the restaurant," he explained.

"But you weren't able to speak to her?"

He looked at his sister with torture in his eyes, "She was with another man." His sister understood his renewed misery at this explanation and tried to comfort him.

"Maybe they're just friends?" she suggested simply.

"They were holding hands," he told her flatly.

"Oh." Sarah searched her mind for a response that would comfort William without result.

"It's my own fault. I have only myself to blame. I have to accept that I have lost her forever," he said expressing his defeat as he lowered his head down onto the table.

"I'm sorry, William," his sister said, trying to comfort him again. She hated to see him so depressed. He had always been so full of energy and drive. She had no idea what to do to take away his pain.

William tried to distract himself from his grief for the remainder of the day by playing with Toby and burying himself in his work. He didn't sleep well that evening, again haunted by dreams of Elizabeth. This time he saw her with the other man, laughing with him, flirting with him, and kissing him. He woke up several times covered with sweat when his dreams took him to a more intimate level. William had been making love to Elizabeth in his dream only to have the other man appear in his place. William tried desperately to remove the images from his mind when he finally climbed out of bed at dawn, afraid to sleep. His dreams had served to only deepen his grief.

He attempted to erase the images from his mind as he stood in the shower under the scalding hot stream of water. Afterwards, he went downstairs to the kitchen to brew a pot of hot coffee. He took his mug into his office and tried to bury himself again in his work. A couple of hours later he heard Sarah and Toby moving about the house but didn't bother to leave his work to join them for breakfast. A short time later his sister knocked softly on the office door. She hadn't realized he was up and had gone up to his empty room in search of him before trying the office. "Come in."

His sister opened the door, approaching slowly with a strange look on her face. William immediately thought something was wrong with Toby. "Is something wrong? Toby?" he asked feeling a moment of panic that his nephew was hurt.

"Toby's fine," she said without changing her expression. She knew how much he was suffering and regretted that she had to add to his grief. She found she could not speak and gently placed the newspaper down on the desk in front of him. He looked at her questioningly then looked down at the paper. He sat in shock looking at the picture before him as he slowly read the paragraph below it. The small article served to confirm his suspicion that the man he had seen Elizabeth with was indeed the man her brother had wanted her to marry. The engagement announcement stated they were to be married in only five short weeks leaving William feeling completely dejected.

"I'm sorry William," was all Sarah could manage to say as she saw the misery in his eyes.

His misery was quickly replaced with jealous rage as he paced angrily in his office. "How can she marry him? She told me herself she didn't want to marry that guy. She said that it was her brother's wish!"

"It wasn't that long ago that she accepted my marriage proposal and now she is going to marry him in only five weeks? Why would she agree to marry him and marry him so quickly? I bet Richard is forcing her into it!" he continued to pace and rage as his sister sat watching him silently. "It doesn't make sense!"

Sarah watched her brother as he suddenly froze, turning white right before her eyes. For a moment she thought he was going to faint and fall to the floor in front of her. "Oh my god...." he said putting his hand to his mouth. "Oh my god," he repeated again then looked at his sister with fear in his eyes.

"What is it?" she asked, now standing in front of him concerned at the fear she saw on his face.

"She's pregnant," he said simply. Sarah was stunned by his statement wondering if he could be right. That would certainly explain her sudden change of heart and short engagement. William was sure she was pregnant and began to pace again. "How could she marry another man and not tell me she's pregnant?!" he yelled, feeling helpless.

"William, you don't know for sure that she's pregnant," she told him attempting to calm his rage.

"Why else would she change her mind and agree to marry him so quickly?" he responded, waiting for some other explanation from his sister that never came. "I will not stand by while some other man marries the woman I love and raises my child!" he screamed in a fit of rage, throwing his coffee mug against the wall smashing it to pieces.

Sarah had never seen her brother this angry. The last time she saw him lose his temper was after he found out Richard had bribed the lab technician years ago. Toby came running, after hearing the loud noise of the mug smashing into the wall. Toby stood in the doorway of the office, afraid by the expression on their faces. Even at eight years old he knew something was wrong. "What's wrong Mommy?" Toby asked with a quiver in his voice.

Sarah and William quickly adjusted their expressions in an effort to console the boy. "Nothing sweetheart," Sarah said forcing a smile.

"But I heard a loud noise," he said, unconvinced.

"I was a little clumsy this morning and knocked the coffee mug off the desk by accident," William told his nephew, feeling guilty for scaring his nephew. He smiled at his nephew trying to convince him nothing was wrong. This explanation seemed to satisfy Toby and his fear was soon forgotten.

"Uncle Willy, do you want to play ball with me?" he asked hopefully.

William's guilt for scaring his nephew wouldn't allow him to decline. "Sure, Toby. Can you give me a few minutes so I can clean up my mess?"

"Sure, Uncle Willy," he said then tugged his uncle's sleeve and waved him closer. William went down on one knee so Toby could whisper in his ear. "Be sure to do a good job or Mommy will be mad!" he said seriously. William couldn't help but laugh and ruffled the boy's hair before he left the office.

"I'll take care of the mug William. Go play with Toby. We'll talk more later when he goes to bed," his sister said kindly. William left the room glad for the distraction Toby was about to provide.

The days began to pass more quickly for Elizabeth, caught up in the wave of duties and plans she had to attend to for her upcoming wedding. Susan assisted her in making the necessary arrangements. They picked a date based on availability at the church and decided to have the reception at the house since the preferred reception halls were unavailable at such short notice. They picked out invitations and began to put together the guest list. Although Elizabeth stated she wanted to keep it small the list easily included more than two hundred guests once Jonathan's list was added. Her brother insisted on inviting his many business associates regardless of her objections. They would be renting some tents arranged through their favorite caterer. The tents would be decorated with tables covered with fine linens, candles and flowers. The caterer would light the tents with delicate strings of white twinkle lights. They also arranged for a band to come in and play music for dancing.

After all the initial plans were in order Susan took Elizabeth in search of a wedding gown. Elizabeth found no joy in the search, feeling guilty for deceiving Jonathan. As the days passed, she was becoming increasingly nervous, feeling worse each day. She no longer suffered the nausea in the morning that had caused her so much grief and found her appetite growing despite her stress and tension. She was starting to gain a little bit of weight so she was careful not to over eat taking the time to choose outfits that were not quite as tapered, afraid someone may take notice of her slowly changing figure. She needed to find a gown that would allow for some weight gain in the waist area without causing suspicion. She tried on numerous gowns in several different stores before finding one that fit her needs yet still looked elegant on her little frame. She left the store with an appointment set for the following week for another fitting after the seamstress made the initial alterations.

Jonathan had come to visit each weekend but they didn't share anymore intimate moments. He said he wanted to wait until after their wedding, regretting his lack of control despite the fact that he had enjoyed that exquisite moment immensely. Elizabeth was relieved when he told her this, agreeing that it was the right thing. Although she was fond of Jonathan, she was beginning to feel very nervous about the wedding, doubting her decision. Not having to worry about satisfying Jonathan's manly needs between now and the wedding relieved some of the stress beginning to feel like a large weight on her shoulders.

After Sarah had put her son to bed that evening, she joined her brother on the back patio carrying a tray containing a pitcher of their favorite cocktail. William thanked his sister as he took his glass. Sarah couldn't stand seeing him so unhappy. He had begun to lose weight and was looking like a ball of yarn beginning to fray and unravel with his unshaven face and old summer clothes he had thrown on, not caring what he looked like in his grief. William had always been a tower of strength and energy, never letting anything or anyone beat him or stop him from getting what he wanted. She was unsure what to do for him now.

"Are you feeling any better?" Sarah asked him with concern. William simply shrugged his shoulders sadly, not intending to cause his sister any worry but could not hide his grief. His earlier rage had faded replaced by despair and helplessness.

"I can't let this wedding happen Sarah, but I don't know how to stop it either. I have all of this proof that her brother is a lying bastard but can't get close to Elizabeth!"

Sarah felt horrible for her brother and made the only suggestion she could think of, "Maybe I should try to get to her again for you?" Her brother stood up suddenly and towered over his sister.

"If you dare go anywhere near Richard Marks III again I will take you over my knee! I'll not have you putting yourself at risk again! This was my mistake and I will figure out a way to fix it!" he said firmly, angry at her suggestion.

"Okay, William. It was just a thought," she responded regretting making the suggestion after seeing the anger and fear on her brother's face.

"Promise me, Sarah. Promise me you won't go near Richard or Elizabeth!" he demanded.

"I promise, William. Calm down."

He looked at his sister, taking a deep breath to relieve the tension in his body. "Even if Elizabeth never forgives me she should be told the truth about her parents and her brother. If he is trying to force her to marry this man it is for his own selfish reasons and would have nothing at all to do with her well being."

"You're probably right William but how can you get to her undetected without putting either one of you at risk?" she asked agreeing with his previous statement and feeling the same frustration as he.

William shrugged his shoulders. "I have no idea," he admitted again, feeling beaten but unwilling to admit defeat. They sat and discussed the possibilities over and over for the rest of the evening always coming back to the same conclusion. He had to get to Elizabeth without alerting anyone to his presence which required being invisible. They both went to bed that evening just as frustrated as when they began their discussion several hours earlier.

William woke the next morning feeling no better than the night before. He went to his study in an attempt to bury himself in his work. After an hour of managing to accomplish nothing, his cell phone rang. "Hello."

"William? This is Jack. How are you?" his trusted attorney asked him in greeting. In his grief and misery, William had forgotten the request for information regarding Elizabeth's parents' Will. William trusted his attorney completely, having met Jack in his college years and had taken all his legal business to him ever since.

"I'm fine," William lied, "How are you?" he asked politely.

"Very well. I'm sorry it took me so long to get back to you but it wasn't so easy getting the information you requested. I had to pull some strings and call in a few favors to get it," he informed William in an attempt to explain his slow response.

"Believe me, I understand. What did you find out?" William asked impatiently.

"It appears that Richard Marks III and his sister both inherited a specific amount of money which is accessible to them upon their twenty-first birthday. The

Will stipulated Richard as his sister's guardian if he was over eighteen and both parents died at the same time. The other stipulations involved the remaining assets. Should Elizabeth marry before her twenty-first birthday, Richard will inherit the remainder of the assets, his sister only receiving the initial specified funds. If she doesn't marry by then the remaining assets would be divided equally between them," he informed his friend.

William wasn't surprised at the information. He had suspected there was a reason for her brother to push her into marriage. The quicker he married her off, the faster he would get the rest of the family fortune.

"May I ask what your interest is in this particular Will?" his attorney asked with concern.

"It's complicated," he stated. "You could say that Elizabeth Marks is a friend of mine and I had a feeling her brother may be up to no good."

"I see," replied his friend with obviously concern in his voice.

"What is it, Jack? Is there something else I should know?" William asked anxiously hearing the concern in his friend's voice.

"Yes. There is one more thing that bothered me but not so much until you told me your concerns about Richard Marks III." Jack paused a moment trying to find the best way to tell his friend the next piece of information without alarming him.

"Go on, Jack. Tell me now," he demanded impatiently.

"The stipulation that concerns me states that if Elizabeth should not marry before her twenty-first birthday and never inherits any of the money under the terms of any of the other stipulations first...." his friend paused to take a breath dreading telling his friend the next, "Basically, should she suffer an untimely death prior to receiving any of the inheritance, Richard gets it all. Once she inherits any portion of the money it is hers and would be up to her to leave the money to whomever she wishes."

"Oh, god," William said, now understanding the full meaning of Elizabeth's situation. "So what you're saying is Richard profits greatly from either her death or her marriage before her twenty-first birthday, which ever comes first?" he asked his attorney irritably.

"It appears that would be the simplest way to say it," his friend regrettably informed him. William's mind raced with thoughts of Elizabeth and the danger she didn't know she was in. "If Richard failed to see her marry soon, would he then try to have her killed as he did his parents?" he asked himself as a chill ran down his spine.

"William? Are you there?" his friend asked, wondering if William had already hung up.

"Yes. I'm here. Sorry." William's instinct for financial situations kicked in. "Listen carefully, Jack. I need you to do a few things for me and right away."

"Okay. What do you need?" his friend asked, concerned at the tone in William's voice. Was that fear he heard or just concern? Jack listened carefully as William gave him a list of instructions and information he would need. "I'll get on it immediately," he said before hanging up.

William was disappointed his friend was unable to obtain a copy of the Will to provide him proof of Elizabeth's brother's true intentions. He was determined to find a way to warn her and paced his office in frustration. How could Elizabeth's parents be so careless? He suspected they had no idea of the evil they had brought into this world when Richard Marks III was born, therefore would never suspect that the stipulations in their Will would have put Elizabeth in harms way. They had named him her guardian, obviously having full trust and faith in their son.

William stopped to look at the pictures of his parents that hung on the wall in his study. He had about ten photos enlarged and framed shortly after he had purchased the home years before. The wall was like his tribute to them. There to remind him of their love and the sacrifices they had made for their children. Feeling guilty again at the mess he had created, thought how disappointed his mother would be in him now.

He stared at one picture of his parents and grand-parents as they all sat around the dinner table smiling one Christmas years ago. He looked closely at the picture, focusing his attention on his late grandmother. Suddenly knowing what he needed to do, he looked up at the ceiling and said hoping she could hear, "Thanks Grams!! You are a god send!" William left his office to talk to his sister. She would be able to help him get the items that he would need to pull-off his newly forming plan.

Chapter Twelve

"Sarah!" William hollered anxiously looking about the house for his sister. His sister came in the front door, surprised when her brother hugged her hard. "There you are!" he exclaimed releasing her from his embrace.

"What's going on?" she asked her brother curious about his sudden change of mood.

"Where's Toby?" he asked. "I just dropped him off at a friend's house. They invited him to go to the beach with their family. Why?"

"Perfect. Let's go. We have to go shopping!" Sarah didn't question him as she followed him out the door seeing a new light in his eyes. On the way, William told his sister about the Will and the information his attorney had provided.

"Oh my god. William, what are you going to do?" she asked knowing this new information was the reason she saw the fight back in her brother's eyes. He filled her in on his plan on the way to the store. Sarah happily assisted her brother in his efforts, helping him pick out the items he would need. She couldn't help laughing when she saw him in the disguise they had put together.

"Hush!" he demanded turning bright red with embarrassment.

He looked in the mirror, understanding his sister's amusement. Ironically he thought to himself, "If I make it through this in one piece, I'll never live this down." He pictured his sister telling stories years later at dinner parties while everyone laughed at his expense.

He practiced his intended movements and asked his sister her opinion. "I think you could pull it off," she said trying to control her giggles. He looked at her seriously which only served to make his sister laugh harder.

"Sarah, this is serious! Please!" he pleaded.

"I'm sorry," she said reminding herself how serious the situation was. She walked around him carefully examining his chosen disguise. "Yes. This should do fine with a few minor touches."

"Good." He said anxious to remove the articles as his sister left the fitting room. He took the items to his sister as she picked out the few remaining items he would need. William paid for the items and they returned home to further discuss the details of his plan. His sister gave him a few suggestions later that afternoon to help him make his appearance more genuine.

Before he went to bed, he hugged his sister again and thanked her for all her help. He was anxious to get things going but still had some things to do before he could put his plan into action. He was waiting for a package from his attorney that was due to arrive the next morning. He had already packed his suitcase, making sure to include the items for his disguise, praying his plan worked. He knew it could take days to pull it off but he would wait forever if necessary but unfortunately he didn't have that long. There was only a few weeks left to warn Elizabeth before the wedding.

The next morning William impatiently waited for the package from his attorney. He had put his luggage in his car along with copies of the all the papers he had compiled as proof of Richard's wrong doing. He had also attached a letter to Elizabeth, explaining things in case he was unable to do anything except pass her the papers discreetly. He hoped to have at least a few minutes to explain things to her before he gave her the proof but wasn't sure how she would react to his intrusion.

The package finally arrived around eleven and he quickly ripped it open. He scanned the pages of his revised Will and once confident that it was as he instructed, quickly signed the papers. He put the signed Will in another envelope he had already addressed to his attorney along with the original papers that provided proof of Richard's offenses. He had enclosed a letter to Jack explaining the enclosed papers and his instructions of what to do with the contents should anything happen to him or Elizabeth. He had also included specific instructions for the delivery of another enclosed letter that was sealed in a smaller envelope addressed to Elizabeth, to be delivered to her directly should something happen to him. He sealed the envelope, making sure to drop it in a nearby mailbox before making the drive to the marina in Stamford.

After her brother left, Sarah sat on the back porch watching Toby play in the back yard. She worried about her brother, hoping everything would work out. She had her doubts that Elizabeth would ever forgive him, especially if she was pregnant as her brother suspected. Knowing how she had felt when Richard had thrust her aside like an old blanket denying his first born son the care of his biological father. Her brother, she admitted, had acted out of love for her but had intentionally deceived Elizabeth. She hoped he was able to warn her and save her from any harm but forgiveness would only come in the form of a true miracle. She prayed to god to take mercy on her brother and help him through the ordeal. Surely all the good things he had done have earned him some kindness after his one mistake which he desperately wanted to take back. He was doing all within his power to make amends, even if it meant his life.

Sarah had expressed her concern that he would be hurt or worse after Richard's previously brutal warning. William told her bluntly, without hesitation, that he would suffer any fate including death to protect Elizabeth from any further harm. She had understood that he had to do this or he would never be able to live with himself or the guilt that would eat at him everyday for the rest of his life. She only hoped that she would see her brother succeed, returning to her and Toby safe and sound. She made him promise to call her everyday while he was away so she would know he was alright. She knew the next few days would be difficult for both of them but knew she couldn't let her imagination and fear get the best of her.

Elizabeth grew more nervous with each passing day. She went for her last fitting for her wedding gown the day before and had felt dizzy as she looked at herself in the white flowing dress. Every time she saw Jonathan she felt fresh guilt but his visits reassured her at the same time. She was convinced she was making the right decision, because of his sincere affections and her ease in his company. In some ways he felt more like the loveable brother she never had, her only true friend in the world.

Responses to the invitations for the wedding were flooding in daily with only a few regrets. Elizabeth had wanted a small wedding but as usual no one cared about her wishes. Her brother was using the opportunity to entertain his various business contacts, trying to strengthen his position through the marriage between Jonathan and Elizabeth. Jonathan's family had strength in the banking industry which Richard felt was very important to the future of his company.

As the wedding approached, now only days away, she began to feel restless. Jonathan would not see her again until the rehearsal dinner the night before the ceremony, now busy with tying up lose ends at work since they would be away for two weeks on their honeymoon. She had to admit she was looking forward to the honeymoon, if only to put some distance between her and her hateful brother. The wedding was to be this coming Saturday and regardless of the body guards still watching her every move, Elizabeth began taking daily walks on the beach, usually bringing her beach bag with a blanket and a book to help pass the time, distracting her from her thoughts.

On the Tuesday before the wedding she went down to the beach, stretching out on her blanket with her newest book. The body guard stood watching her, scanning the area. Whenever she was still as she was today the guard would pull back some allowing her a modest amount of privacy. The guards had been ordered not to let her get out of their sight and not to allow any men to approach her. They were aware of Elizabeth's prior disappearance and understood that they were there to prevent her from doing it again. They weren't there to protect her from anyone but herself which allowed the guards to feel more relaxed when she was sitting still, reading on the beach.

Elizabeth was unaware that she was being watched by someone other than her assigned escort, content for the moment as she concentrated on her book, trying not to think of her wedding, her guilt, or William who was still haunting her dreams. The dreams seem to be occurring more often with the wedding fast approaching. She had woken up several nights in the last week covered with sweat as a result of the sultry dreams of William, making passionate love to her while whispering promises of love now lost to her because of his deception.

Everyday William walked down the length of the beach, sat under an umbrella and watched the area of sandy beach near Elizabeth's house, hoping to spot her through the binoculars he had gotten from his boat. He felt this was safer, not wanting to draw any attention. After several days, he finally watched as Elizabeth walked down from the house and spread out her beach blanket. He watched her for a while as she read, trying to control his breathing and racing heart. After a few moments, he put the binoculars on the chair and picked up the cane he had purchased walking slowly in Elizabeth's direction.

Elizabeth noticed some movement out of the corner of her eye and watched for a moment as an old lady walked slowly in her direction stumbling awkwardly in the sand, trying to maneuver her uncooperative old body through the punishing sand with the assistance of a cane. She watched the old woman make her way slowly down the beach, "Baxter!" she yelled over and over. Elizabeth assumed Baxter was a lost pet, feeling sorry for the woman struggling to walk through the hot sand.

William walked slowly making sure to stumble occasionally and hunch over as an older woman would, hollering the name of his imaginary lost pet he was using, hoping to throw off the security guard. He did his best to use a raspy sounding old lady voice each time he opened his mouth, pretending to look around for the lost animal. As he came closer he watched the guard through the dark oversized sun glasses he had chosen to help hide his face. As he hoped, the guard was thankfully ignoring the approach of the old lady dressed in the ugly floral dress designed to hide every inch of her body from the punishing sun. He wore a silver haired wig and an oversized brim hat, typical of an elderly woman wanting to avoid the sun and the burned skin she would easily suffer if left uncovered.

William turned his attention to Elizabeth who was watching the old lady with concern. He had counted on her kind heart to assist him in his approach and only hoped she didn't scream when he exposed his true identity. He kept yelling the dog's name as he approached Elizabeth. He was careful to turn his back to the guard in an attempt to block his view of Elizabeth's face. Luckily the sun would be his eyes when facing the other direction which provided the perfect excuse for the position he took in front of Elizabeth.

In the same old lady voice he asked, loud enough so the guard would hear, if she had seen a small black dog roaming around. He hoped the guard was still paying him no mind, as he knelt next to her with his knees positioned on her blanket. His heart pounded as he whispered to her softly in his natural voice. "Elizabeth, it's me, William. Please don't scream or attract any attention from your guard. I'm not here to hurt you and only wish to speak to you for a moment."

Elizabeth looked up into his face in shock as she heard his familiar voice. She was stunned and didn't move or speak for a moment unsure how to react. She didn't want the guard or Richard to hurt him so she quietly replied trying to appear as if nothing was amiss. "If you don't leave you will not need to worry about my guard," she threatened under her breath.

William knew he had to explain quickly so proceeded to fuss over the blanket exclaiming its beauty in the raspy female voice for the benefit of the guard. "I don't have much time. You must listen to me. You may be in danger Elizabeth." He swiftly retrieved the papers he had secured to his thigh under the dress with a shoe lace, careful not to draw attention to his action. He let them drop on the blanket between them as he continued to explain. "Your brother has been lying to you for years. Your parents didn't die in a plane crash, they were murdered. The papers in front of me provide proof that your brother may have been involved. I know this is a lot for you to absorb but you must believe me. I only came here to warn you." William paused for a short moment allowing her to absorb what he said. She looked at him with disbelief then looked down at the papers he had put in front of her.

"Elizabeth, I know you have no reason to trust me but please take the papers and look at them later when you're alone. Your parents' Will stipulated that if you marry by age twenty-one Richard will inherit most of your parents' fortune which explains his arrangement you told me about," he hated to hurt or alarm her but she must know the truth and he had to tell her quickly before the guard became suspicious.

"The Will also stated that if you didn't marry by then that you would receive half of everything, something I assume Richard doesn't want to happen. In the event of your death should you not already be married he will get everything. Your brother wants you to marry quickly so he will get just about everything other than the money in your specific trust fund." He looked at her as she started to shake and felt a pang of guilt for bringing her such horrible news.

"If your brother had something to do with your parents' death then he may try to hurt you if you don't marry quickly enough to satisfy his greed. Elizabeth, do you understand what I'm saying to you?" he asked gently.

Elizabeth looked at him as if she didn't hear a word he said, looking pale. "I don't believe you," she said in a whisper he barely heard.

"I know this is difficult for you to hear. You always want to believe the best of people. It's something I love about you," he told her softly fighting the desire to pull her in his arms and comfort her. "Why are you getting married? Did your brother force your hand?" he asked.

She looked at him with anger in her eyes. "None of your business."

"Is it because you're pregnant with my child?" he asked and instantly knew the answer when she stiffened next to him and refused to answer. "Elizabeth, please don't marry him if you're pregnant," he pleaded softly. "I love you and even if you can never forgive me, I'll take care of you and my child."

Elizabeth looked at William dressed in his ridiculous disguise and fumed at his words. "You love me? You lied to me. What makes you think I would ever trust you again?" she spit out trying not to raise her voice.

"I know sweetheart. I understand I don't deserve your trust or your forgiveness but I will provide whatever you need financially or otherwise. Please take the papers and just consider everything I've said. I must go before your guard gets suspicious. If you need anything please call but I'm begging you not to marry because of the child. I will be there for you, I promise you that."

He took a deep breath and sighed, looking into her face longing to touch her. He watched as she took the papers and slipped them into her beach bag, which appeared to have gone unnoticed by the guard since William was still blocking his view. He placed his hand lightly on her hand for a moment then stood to leave, careful to appear unstable as an old woman would using the cane to help him stand.

"Good day, miss," he said once more in raspy old lady voice waving as he turned back the way he came. He began yelling for the dog that didn't exist. It broke his heart to leave her there and took great effort not to look back in her direction. He slowly made his way back to the spot with his binoculars and umbrella. He took the binoculars, wanting to watch Elizabeth but was disappointed to find her already gone.

He only hoped she would read the papers he gave her. He hoped she would call him and allow him to help her. He hoped she would one day forgive him. He wished most of all for her to be safe and happy even if that meant she would be in the arms of someone else. He made his way back to his boat, gladly discarding his disguise into an overnight bag and headed straight for the shower. He would call Sarah later once he had time to collect his emotions and inform her that he would be home the following day.

William dried himself off and went back into the bedroom to dress. He went to the restaurant for something to eat and a much needed drink to help calm his nerves. He returned to his boat intending to call his sister but was surprised when he entered to find several men searching his boat. Before he could demand an explanation for the intrusion he blacked out, hit in the head with his own cane by another man he hadn't seen standing behind him.

Elizabeth smiled and waved good bye to the old lady for the benefit of the guard. Regardless of her anger she had no desire to see William hurt. She did her best to appear as if nothing was wrong, trying to read her book. After a few moments she stood and gathered the blanket, carefully stuffing it into her bag, burying the papers underneath. She made her way in the house and went directly to her room, locking the door behind her. She went into the bathroom with the bag being sure to lock that door as well. In case anyone came looking for her she turned on the shower so they would not bother her. She pulled the papers out of her bag, scanning through them. William had highlighted all the important dates and information he wanted her to pay attention to first. She was stunned as she read the articles describing her parents' death. She was so shocked after reading the reports from the police officer naming her brother a suspect in her parents' murder that she vomited violently.

She didn't want to believe her brother had anything to do with her parents' death but couldn't deny the possibility was real with the proof lying in front of her on the bathroom floor. She picked up the letter written in William's hand explaining everything he had given her in detail. He told her that he wasn't able to get a copy of the Will but was sure she could confirm it by calling the family attorney. He urged her to be cautious if she felt the need, not wanting her to draw Richard's attention.

William ended the letter with another apology, telling her that he truly loved her and his proposal had been sincere. He wrote of his regret at the hurt he has caused her. He listed his telephone number at the bottom should she ever need him, promising he would be there for her. She numbly put all the papers back into the bottom of her bag then undressed for her shower. She sobbed uncontrollably into the spray of the water, feeling fresh grief after finding out the brutal way her parents' had died. She felt more helpless than ever and had no one to turn to for advice. Jonathan was her only friend but she couldn't discuss any of this with him.

She emerged from the bathroom feeling exhausted and confused. She took the beach bag to the closet and quickly retrieved her secret box placing the papers safely within it before putting it back in its hiding place. She knew someone would come in search of her soon, summoning her for dinner. She did her best to control her emotions while blow drying her hair. She looked at herself in the mirror but only saw an empty shell of a person. If it weren't for the child growing within her, she feared she would have chosen death in her despair.

She had made a vow to take good care of her child so she took a deep breath that did nothing to calm her soul then went to the dining room to join her family for dinner. She forced the tasteless food down her throat to keep up her strength and provide the nutrition her child needed to be healthy. Susan commented on her silence, teasing her about having pre-wedding jitters. How would she respond, Elizabeth wondered if she shared her brother's cruel secrets with her sister-in-law? Did she know that her husband had fathered a child with another? Did she know about the Will and its stipulations? Did she care or was she as greedy and selfish as her husband? All kinds of questions flowed through Elizabeth's mind as she sat trying not to show her true feelings.

She excused herself as soon as she felt it was safe to do so without being questioned and returned to her room. She sat on her balcony, letting the tears run down her face without restraint. She sat wondering if her brother would try to hurt her if she chose not to marry Jonathan. If it weren't for the child she carried, she would not care. If it were not for her child, she would confront her brother with the information she received. She must protect her child by protecting herself. She wasn't sure if she should marry Jonathan but now faced with the prospect of her brother's rage if she didn't, felt more confused than ever.

She desperately wanted to stand up to her brother and defy him but couldn't put her child at risk. Exhausted from the day and her emotions, she couldn't think anymore. She told herself the best course would be to continue with her plans to marry Jonathan. She couldn't bring herself to trust William to take care of them after all his deception, feeling fresh anger for having put her in this situation. Her only defense was to satisfy her brother's greed and marry Jonathan, if only to keep her child safe. He would finally be happy once he received his inheritance he felt was so much more important than his own flesh and blood.

Elizabeth resented her brother for his treatment of Sarah Blake that resulted in William's need for revenge, putting her in the position to deceive a good man into marrying her to protect her unborn child. She had never done anything to anyone but was bearing the full brunt of the aftermath Richard and William's war had created. "It's not fair", she cried into her pillow. Elizabeth was haunted by new more disturbing dreams that night. Visions of her parents' bloody, dead bodies flashed through her mind then changed to Richard, laughing at her as he proudly counted the money he so desperately wanted. Then flashes of William calling her name, begging her not to go….begging her to forgive him….

Chapter Thirteen

William woke with a start, moaning when his head began to pound caused by the sudden movement. He looked around trying to adjust his eyes to the darkness. He sat on the cold, hard floor shivering from the dampness of his prison. He recalled the men that appeared unexpectedly on his boat, assuming they had brought him here, no doubt following the orders of Richard Marks III. As his eyes began to adjust to the darkness he was better able to observe his surroundings. It was a small room with a cold cement floor surrounded by cinder block brick walls. There were no windows that he could see but thought he saw a door through the darkness. He slowly stood, fighting the pounding in his head that made him feel as if he would black out again. He tenderly rubbed the back of his head and felt the hard lump left by his assailants.

He walked slowly to the door and felt around it for a door knob. To his dismay there was no latch or doorknob that he could find. "The door must have some type of lock or latch only on the outside," he thought irritably. He ran his fingers along the edges of the doorway, searching for a spot that he could fit his fingers through but the door was tightly sealed all around, even along the floor. There was barely a shadow of light sneaking in from its cracks.

He wondered how they had known about his arrival. Did they spot him on the beach talking to Elizabeth? Did they see through his disguise? Did he make things worse for Elizabeth by coming here to warn her? Panic gripped him at the thought that Elizabeth would be hurt but calmed down at the thought that Richard wouldn't touch her as long as she was set to marry Jonathan Parker. His earlier jealousy towards the man was now replaced with the hope that he would make Elizabeth happy, realizing that he may never see her again.

He sat in the dark room, wondering how long he had been there unconscious. He couldn't tell the time of day in the darkness of his new prison. His assailants had been sure to strip him of all possessions leaving him only the shorts and torn shirt he was wearing. They had even stripped him of his shoes, which left him feeling cold to the bone despite the summer season. He forced himself to keep moving and walking to cut down on the chill but soon tired from the injury to his aching head. William sat with his head leaning against the hard wall as he fell to sleep thinking of Sarah, Toby and Elizabeth and how he had failed them all.

Sarah barely slept the night before, worrying about her brother. He hadn't called her as promised and she was worried something had happened. She had tried to call his phone late last night but received no answer. She tried again before she bothered to brush her teeth. Again she received no answer. She tried to control the panic that was welling up inside, remembering she had a son to care for. She went about her normal routine, feeding Toby his breakfast and watching him play outside. When noon came and she still received no word from William, she found it impossible to sit still any longer. She made a call to one of Toby's friend's mother and arranged for him to stay with her for the day and possibly overnight if necessary, only saying there was a family emergency she needed to attend to.

Sarah packed a quick overnight bag for each of them then drove Toby to his friend's house, telling Toby she was going to visit some friends. Sarah made the drive to the marina, fighting the need to speed along the way. She pulled into the parking lot, jumped out of the car and practically ran to the spot she knew his boat was docked. She climbed over the side, shocked at what she found. The door had been left partly open and a shiver immediately climbed up her spine as she fought back the tears building in her eyes. The contents of the boat were all over, drawers had been over turned and his clothes thrown about. As she looked around at the mess she was sure that something had gone terribly wrong with his plan. She cried as she realized her brother may already be dead.

Sarah slowly pulled the business card from her purse and stared at it sadly. "Should anything happen to me Sarah, call Jack. Here is his card. He will know what to do," he had told her before he left. She took her cell phone from her handbag and slowly dialed the number wishing she had begged him not to go. After receiving a brief greeting from Jack's receptionist, she was quickly connected to William's attorney.

"Hello? Sarah? Is everything all right?" he asked immediately concerned after receiving the package from William a few days before with its morbid instructions. "Uh, no, I..." Sarah tried to fight her emotions and the tears again welling up in her eyes. "William's missing. I drove out to his boat and it's been vandalized!" she said in a shaky voice.

"Oh god...." followed by a brief silence. "Sarah, I want you to get away from the boat incase someone should return. Go to the marina restaurant and wait. I will make a few calls then get back to you in a little bit," he instructed. "Sarah? Did you hear me?" he asked after receiving no response.

"Yes. Okay. Go to the restaurant. Thank you Jack," she said as she hung up. She walked to the shelf on the wall that held several picture frames, taking one with her before she left the boat as instructed. Once she was seated in the restaurant bar and had ordered a shot of bourbon she needed to calm her nerves, she looked at the picture sadly. She stared at William's smiling face having one arm around Sarah and the other around Toby.

The picture had been taken at Toby's last birthday party. She didn't care who saw the tears now streaming uncontrollably down her face. The bartender handed her the bourbon and a box of tissues without saying a word.

After a few minutes her cell phone rang and she greeted Jack as politely as possible. "Sarah?" he asked.

"Yes, Jack," she responded softly.

"I have made some calls. I have called the local police department and they're sending someone over now. When they arrive, take them to the boat and give them any information they require. Alright?" he asked, waiting for confirmation that she had been listening.

"Okay, Jack," she answered sadly, trying her best not to fall apart.

"After they've gotten all they need from you, go home Sarah. Go home and wait to hear from me. William made it clear he didn't want you anywhere near Richard Marks III," he told her.

"Yeah, okay," she said numbly, hanging up before he could press the issue further. She was unsure if she was able to walk back down to the boat let alone drive home again. She saw the police car pull up a few moments later and made her way out to meet the officer as instructed. She walked them down to the boat, answering all their questions and watched as they wrote down everything she said. She watched as they took pictures of the boat and inspected it for clues.

After an hour and a half of answering the same questions over and over, they told her to go home and they would do everything they could to find her brother. She managed a thank you as they walked her to her car. She made the drive home, deciding being with Toby was the best thing for her. She found it hard to concentrate on her driving having to pull over several times over-whelmed by her grief, but finally arrived at home just after dark. She had decided it was too late to pick up Toby so she entered the house alone which now felt empty and cold. Sarah cried herself to sleep, wondering if she would ever see her brother again.

Elizabeth woke up feeling rotten and tired. The nightmares she had kept her from sleeping and left her with a dull headache. She felt angry at the world, everyone in it responsible for her suffering at the hands of her brother. She suddenly wanted to be free of them all, Richard, William, and Jonathan. She wanted to disappear, never to return. She wanted to run away and raise her child somewhere safe and quiet. She never really cared about the money she was supposed to inherit and wondered if it was possible for her to take care of her child alone. She thought about the money in her secret box and wondered how far it would take her.

The wedding was quickly approaching and she knew she had to make up her mind soon. She always found herself thinking in circles that led her back to the fear that she wouldn't be able to provide a proper life for her child. She had no desire to see her brother and try to hide the disgust she felt for him so she stayed in her room until she was sure he would have left for the office. When she finally descended the stairs in search of food for her growing child, she was disappointed to find her brother still there.

Elizabeth did her best to avoid her brother but unfortunately she heard him call her name from the library. She sighed, wondering if she could pretend she didn't hear him until she heard him call her name again, louder this time. She walked into the library trying to keep her emotions in check. "Yes, Richard?" she asked gruffly.

"You're up late this morning. Not feeling well?" he asked icily.

"I have a headache and didn't sleep well," she told him turning away to escape before he questioned her further.

"Really? Maybe it has something to do with the visitor you had yesterday?" he asked casually.

"What are you talking about? I had no visitors yesterday," she lied bravely standing her ground.

"No? Jerald said you had a visitor on the beach yesterday. A little old lady, he said?" he persisted trying to trick her into giving herself away.

"Her? I had forgotten all about her. The lady had lost her dog. What would that have to do with my not sleeping?" she replied acting as if he were out of his mind.

Her brother quickly walked across the room towards her, obviously angry. "You lying little tramp! I know it was William Blake dressed as an old lady and you will tell me what he said to you!" he exclaimed grabbing her arm roughly.

"Careful, Richard," she said calmly looking down at his rough grip on her arm. "You may leave a mark and have to explain to your guests why the bride has your hand print on her arm," she responded coldly.

Richard immediately let go of her but did not back down from his demand. "Tell me what he said!" he repeated angrily.

"Show no fear," she told herself attempting to control her emotions. She took an impatient breath and calmly took a seat nearby, "Honestly Richard. I don't understand why you get yourself in such a tizzy. Do you honestly think I would allow William back in my life after what he did?"

Richard looked at her suspiciously not believing her for a moment. "What did he say?" he repeated.

"He said he was sorry for lying to me. He begged for forgiveness and claimed his undying love," she told him trying to seem amused and untouched by his visit.

"And what did you tell him?" Richard inquired, still suspicious.

"I told him to leave before I have the guard remove him. I told him I had no feelings for him, that I never did and was only having a good time with him," she said, smiling proudly at the look on her brother's face. "He left after that. I doubt he will bother me again," she said as if she could care less.

"It's good to hear that," her brother responded unsure if he should believe her. "If you care so little for him why didn't you tell me?" he challenged.

"I didn't wish to upset you. I wanted everyone in good spirits this week, for the wedding," she lied knowing that the wedding was her brother's weakness.

He thought it best not to press the issue further. She was going to marry Jonathan and that's all he cared about. Elizabeth went in search of some food, fighting back a smile, proud that she had managed to stand up to her brother and not give away the true conversation she had with William. She was glad she was able to hide her true feelings so well. "I'm getting too good at this lying thing," she thought sadly.

William woke to the sound of footsteps and voices. He became instantly alert when he realized someone was opening the door. He quietly moved to the wall along side the doorway waiting to pounce. As the door flung open and a large figure of a man appeared, William ran at him hard throwing all his body weight into him, knocking the man hard to the floor. A second later William collapsed, struck again over the head by a second man. William looked up from the floor into a face he didn't recognize, however he knew the voice that now came from the doorway.

"William Blake.... Do you never learn?" Richard asked as he towered over William's crumpled body.

"I knew you were behind this Richard!" William grumbled through clenched teeth as he tried to ignore the pounding in his head. He took a deep breath and stood to face his enemy.

Richard raised his hand to his men, telling them silently to hold their places. "Well William, I always thought of you as intelligent but by the looks of things, I was wrong. Did you really think you could beat me?" he snarled. "I warned you to stay away from my sister but you don't listen! Now you will remain here until she is safely married and on her honeymoon."

William glared at him trying to control his temper. "You will release me at once!" William demanded.

"I don't think so. You see, despite the fact my sister hates your guts and wants nothing more to do with you, I will not have you interrupting the ceremony and causing our family any further embarrassment. I suggest you behave in the meantime," he told William smiling viscously, "If you cause anymore trouble for me I'm afraid something terrible might happen to your adorable little sister and that bastard son of hers," he sneered.

William lunged at him angrily, only to be knocked to his knees from another swift blow delivered by one of Richard's thugs. William growled with fury as he tried to catch his breath. "I warned you, William. I think it's time you understand just how serious I am," Richard told him laughing as he nodded to his men and left the room. The two men began to beat William repeatedly, not stopping until his body went limp as he passed out again. They left him with no food or water, latching the door securely.

Thomas Banks has known William for most of his life. He grew up with William, attending the same high school and they've been good friends. Thomas had finished school and became a police officer until he resigned after a routine traffic stop went sour, leaving his partner dead, forcing him to shoot down the armed assailant. The assailant ended up being a sixteen year old boy, strung out on drugs. Thomas couldn't bring himself to patrol the streets after that day, failing to save his partner's life and forced to take another, the life of only a child.

After he left the force, he started his own private detective agency doing low profile cases to pay the bills. Things were very slow at first, barely making enough to pay his rent and put food on the table. Shortly after he started the business, his father turned ill and was taken to the hospital. He was told his father needed a kidney transplant but his insurance would only cover half of the expenses. Thomas tried everything he could to find the money but came up empty having no collateral, only an apartment and a business not yet making any profit. His father had sold his house years before when his only son moved out and moved into a smaller, more affordable apartment. He remembered his father telling him there was no sense keeping it for just him, his wife having passed years before.

William had come to visit Thomas's father in the hospital and overheard Thomas arguing with the doctor about money. In utter frustration, Thomas confided in William, telling him they just found a kidney they thought would be compatible but were unable to perform the surgery without some guarantee of payment. William had stormed out of the room and wrote a check handing it to the doctor without hesitation.

The doctors performed the operation the same day. Thomas's father lived with his new kidney for almost a month before his body rejected the organ and infection got the best of him. Without bothering to ask his permission, William paid for the funeral as well, knowing Thomas was broke. Thomas was grateful to his friend, promising to pay him back one day. William told him not to worry about it and has never mentioned it since. Thomas still felt he owed William so much for his generosity. His father may have lived for years afterwards had the kidney been a better match.

William had thrown a lot of work his way over the years. He used him to run general back ground checks on associates or do research on any subject or person. This time when he received a call from William requesting him to keep an eye on the wealthy Elizabeth Marks, Thomas was both concerned and curious. He knew William asked him to do it because he could trust him to keep things confidential.

His concern grew after watching Elizabeth Marks for weeks as she was followed everywhere by very large security guards. He had found a spot on the beach not far from her home that was perfect to keep a watchful eye on Elizabeth without being noticed. The spot he picked was at the bottom of a small cliff and provided shade and privacy with its tall, thick trees and shrubs. Each morning before dawn, he climbed into the small hiding place feeling like a small boy in the woods, sitting in his special hiding spot from the world.

He had watched Elizabeth Marks for weeks, noticing the sadness that she didn't bother to hide when she thought no one was watching. He sat fascinated, watching her cry on several occasions as she tried to pretend to read one of her books. He never before imagined someone of her wealth and status being as unhappy as she obviously was. One morning just after he reached his special hiding place, he watched as Elizabeth quickly walked down the beach just before dawn. Thomas had followed her, watching through binoculars so he could remain unseen at a safe distance behind. He had watched her purchase a pregnancy test through the window of the marina store, stuffing it safely in her bag. At this point he was very concerned and even after William told him he no longer needed his services in the matter, Thomas had returned to his spot each day not having a family of his own to worry about.

He watched with interest as an old woman approached Elizabeth only to realize after a few moments that it was his friend William in disguise. "What the hell is going on?" he asked himself watching his friend and the guard closely, ready to defend William if needed. The guard appeared completely fooled by his friend's disguise. Thomas may have been fooled as well except the very expensive binoculars he used in his line of work predominantly displayed William's hairy fingers and five o'clock shadow.

He watched his friend intently until he safely walked away. Elizabeth went back to her reading immediately but he had seen her hands shaking through his binoculars. She smiled as she gathered up her blanket and returned to the house. Thomas was alarmed when he watched the guard say something into his head set and point in the direction that William had left. Obviously not fooled by William's disguise after all, Thomas watched a man emerge from the stairway a moment later and sprint down the beach in William's direction. He realized that William could be in danger but couldn't move from his spot until the other guard had left. Finally the guard went up to the house and Thomas ran from his spot back to where his car was parked.

Thomas started his car and began to pull out of the parking spot when he heard a strange noise. He stopped the car, realizing he had a flat tire. He looked around in a panic but no one was around to assist him. He quickly removed the spare tire and jack from the trunk, changing the tire as fast as he could. It took him almost an hour to change the tire since the lug nuts were on so tight. He cursed as he looked at his watch and sped down the road in the direction of the marina. He pulled into the parking lot and parked his car cautiously looking around for any sign of William or the man that had followed him. He got out of the car and walked in the direction of the restaurant when he spotted William walking down the dock in the direction of his boat.

Thomas was about to yell his friend's name when he noticed someone following him. Thomas immediately recognized the man from the beach, instinctively blending in with the people sitting outside the restaurant enjoying cocktails in the summer sun. He scanned the crowd of people, trying to spot anymore of Richard's thugs that may be close by then waited until the man was out of sight. Thomas casually strolled along the dock in the same direction. He came to the corner that led to the slip where William's boat was docked and peeked cautiously around the corner. One man came off the boat barking an order at the other man he had recognized from the beach. That man started back in his direction, forcing Thomas to sprint back the way he came so he wouldn't be discovered.

Knowing there was no where to go besides up the docks, unless they drove the boat out of the slip Thomas sat at one of the outdoor tables and watched the man go to the parking lot and return a few moments later with a small toolbox in his hands. He sat nervously as it became dark, hoping his friend wasn't already dead. His hopes quickly sank as he watched the men leave in a group with a large piece of rolled up carpet slung across two of the men's shoulders. He knew immediately his friend was wrapped within the carpet, praying he was still alive. He waited a few moments allowing the men to walk around the side of the building towards the parking lot, watching as they tossed the bundle into the back of a pick up truck.

Thomas casually made his way back to his car following the men in the dark as they drove away, careful to keep his distance but careful not to lose them. He followed the men for almost an hour before they pulled off onto a side road. Thomas turned off his head lights and slowly followed until he could tell that the cars had stopped. He backed up his car finding a spot off the side of the road where no one would spot it. He quietly got out of his car and made his way up the road following the sound of the men's voices. He watched as they entered an old farm house with their large bundle in hand. Thomas sat watching and listening but was unable to do anything as two of the men stood guard outside. He watched as the other men left, leaving only two men remaining with the old pick up truck parked outside.

Thomas knew that his friend was still alive. They wouldn't have brought him here and put guards at the house if he were dead. He breathed a sigh of relief and thanked god he wasn't too late. He sat quietly all night waiting for a chance to help his friend but no such opening appeared. He nodded off leaning against a tree trunk sometime in the middle of the night after watching one of the guards relieve the other as they took turns sleeping in the old house.

He woke in the early hours to the sound of the two men arguing. He listened as the first man scolded the other for falling asleep during his watch. Thomas watched patiently, hour after hour but the men didn't move from their assigned position, always leaving one man standing guard as the other went for food or took a bathroom break. Frustrated, Thomas was considering fetching the police when he heard a car coming up the road. Thomas ducked deeper into the brush to be sure he wasn't spotted. The limousine approached the front of the old, rickety farmhouse and he watched as Richard Marks III got out looking around in disgust.

Richard Marks followed his men inside as Thomas sat alert straining to hear anything to indicate his friend was still alive. Unfortunately he couldn't hear anything being so far from the house. It wasn't long before Richard returned to his vehicle, disappearing back down the dirt road. Thomas was concerned when the two guards didn't appear with Richard. "What are they doing?" Just as Thomas was about to leave his spot and try to find out what was going on in the farmhouse, the two men appeared, laughing and patting each other on the back. They jumped into the pick-up truck spitting rocks and dust everywhere as they sped down the dirt road. Panicked at the thought that his friend was now dead, Thomas forced himself to wait a few moments before leaving his spot, fearing someone may return.

After what felt like an eternity, he carefully stepped out of his hiding place and ran across the yard into the old farm house. He looked around the darkened barn scanning the area for his friend but only found a lot of dust, dirt, spider webs and piles of old hay. He knew his friend was in there somewhere and began walking around carefully scanning the floors. He was poking at the piles of hay when he noticed a metal ring on the floor. Thomas cleared the area with his foot realizing it was a hatch to a basement built below. He opened the hatch to find a stairway that faded into the darkness. Thomas climbed carefully down the stairs into a much darker hallway. He could barely make out the two doors, one of which was left open and one that was latched from the outside. Thomas assumed William was inside the one that was closed, quickly unlatching the door, scanning the dark room for his friend. Once his eyes adjusted to the darkness he was able to see the crumbled body on the floor. He hurried to him checking to see if he was alive. To his relief, he was breathing but could tell he was hurt badly. Thomas knew from his days as a policeman that he shouldn't move him but was unwilling to leave him there should the men return. He lifted William over his shoulder as gently as he could and slowly made his way back up the stairs. He finally made it back to his car having to stop several times along the way to catch his breath. William had always been the larger of the two men, being a few inches taller with a much broader build than Thomas.

He gently put William in the car across the back seat then quickly drove him to the closest hospital. He ran into the emergency room calling for someone to come help his friend. He watched as the nurses wheeled his friend down the hall, feeling helpless. He sat in the waiting room anxious to hear news of William's condition, praying he had gotten to him in time.

After what felt like an eternity, a doctor finally emerged with a very serious look on his face. "Are you the gentleman who brought in the injured man?" the doctor inquired.

"Yes, how is he?" Thomas asked.

"Your friend has some internal bleeding and a nasty head injury. We're going to have to operate to try to stop the bleeding. Do you know how this happened?"

"Yes. He was beaten by two large men and then left to die!" he answered angrily.

"We'll need any information you can provide. If he was assaulted we'll need to notify the police," the doctor informed him.

Thomas shook his head, "No. You can't do that yet. The men that assaulted him will try again if they find out he is still alive." He showed the doctor his identification and explained that his friend's life was still in danger. "You must keep his identity a secret. Keep him listed as a John Doe. I'll take care of the rest." The doctor argued with him for a few moments pointing out he had a legal obligation to contact the police but finally agreed after Thomas pointed out that he would only be putting his friend's life in danger.

"I know who is responsible for this and believe me, he will pay for it!" he promised, giving the doctor his business card. "Please call me anytime if his condition changes. I'll stay until the surgery is over and I'm sure he is okay," he told the doctor.

"We're prepping him for surgery now. I'll let you know how he is as soon as possible," the doctor told him, leaving to prepare for surgery. Several hours later the doctor returned and informed Thomas that he had made it through the surgery. "We have managed to stop the bleeding and his vitals are stable. He is still unconscious and we are concerned about the head injury. We'll be taking some x-rays and closely monitoring his progress for the next day or so. We won't know for sure the extent of the damage he may have suffered from the head injury until he wakes up. I'll call you immediately should his condition change."

Thomas thanked the doctor, relieved his friend was still alive and hoped he would recover fully. He left the hospital vowing that Richard Marks III would pay for what he has done. He would repay William for his past kindness by assuring Richard Marks III was held responsible for his actions.

Chapter Fourteen

Sarah sat watching her son playing in the yard, sadly thinking of her brother. Although there was no proof that her brother was dead she feared the worst after seeing the condition of his boat. She had fought off the nausea that threatened when she had seen the spot where a large piece of carpet had been sliced and removed from the floor in the salon. She assumed the piece was removed in an attempt to conceal any evidence of her brother's death, possibly to hide the blood she feared had been spilt.

She tried to tell herself he may still be alive but her grieving heart told her otherwise. She wondered if he had managed to speak to Elizabeth or if he had been spotted too soon. She had to find out if there was a chance he could be alive. She called information, writing the numbers down on a scrap piece of paper. Sarah dialed the number and took a deep breath. "Marks' residence."

"Hello. Is Elizabeth available?" Sarah asked sweetly into the phone trying to sound younger than her years.

"May I ask who is calling?" asked the man on the other end that she assumed was the butler.

"Yes, this is Sally Jensen. We went to school to-gether," she lied hoping this would get her through to Elizabeth. She held her breath waiting for the man's response and was happy when he didn't ask her anymore questions.

"One moment please."

She waited impatiently with her heart beating in her throat, jumping when she heard the female voice on the other end. "Hello?"

"Elizabeth?" she asked trying to confirm who she was talking to before continuing.

"Yes, this is Elizabeth."

"Elizabeth, please listen carefully. I told the man that answered that I was a friend from school named Sally Jensen. Please don't give me away. This is Sarah Blake."

Elizabeth paused for only a moment before replying. "Sally, dear, how are you?"

"Thank you, Elizabeth," Sarah said quietly. "My brother's missing for a couple of days now and I needed to know if you had seen him."

"Yes, Yes. I'm doing well," Elizabeth responded kindly trying not to draw the suspicion of the butler lingering nearby.

"You did? He has been missing for two days now. Was it before that you saw him?" Sarah asked quietly into the receiver.

"Of course, Sally. That would be wonderful!" Sarah understood Elizabeth's answer to be yes.

"Have you seen or heard from him since?" Sarah asked hoping she would again say yes.

"No, of course I understand," Elizabeth responded, wondering what had happened to William.

"Do you have any idea where he might be?" she asked Elizabeth as a last shot in the dark.

"I'm sorry to hear that, Sally. I'll call you when I get back from the honeymoon and we'll meet for lunch." Sarah's heart sank at her last response.

"Thank you Elizabeth," she said in a quivering voice.

"Please let me know how your mother is feeling. I wish her well. Goodbye," Elizabeth said hanging up the phone. Sarah understood what Elizabeth had meant with her last statement. She was trying to tell her she hoped

William was alright and to send her word when she knew more.

Sarah cried again, sure that William had fallen into the ruthless hands of Richard Marks III. Elizabeth confirmed she had seen William right around the time he disappeared. Sarah felt completely helpless and didn't know what to do. She had made a promise to William that she wouldn't go anywhere near the Marks if anything happened to him. She would keep her promise but found it difficult as she envisioned her fingers around Richard Marks' throat, slowly depriving him of air.

Elizabeth returned to her room and sat on her bed shaking uncontrollably. The horrible thoughts that entered her mind now left her paralyzed with fear. Richard had already let her know he was aware that William had visited her on the beach. Had his guards followed him? Where was he now? Was he injured? Was he alive? Elizabeth ran to the bathroom as nausea and grief rocked her body, thinking him dead, killed the same way as her parents.

She cried without caring if someone should find her, curled up in a ball on the cold tiled bathroom floor. Elizabeth hated her brother now more than ever and would like nothing more than to strangle him with her bare hands. She reminded herself that she must concentrate on her child. The only thing left for her to care about. She no longer cared about her brother and no longer pictured herself happily married to Jonathan. She felt it would be a betrayal to William and their unborn child to marry Jonathan. His last request, "Please don't marry because of the child. I will take care of you both." William had risked his own safety to warn her of her brother's evil intentions and let her know he would take care of her and her child. She now believed that he truly loved her despite his cruel intentions when they met. She no longer doubted Sarah Blake's story and that her son was truly Richard's.

She realized that Richard was truly evil and cruel. She knew she couldn't marry Jonathan but had to find a way to break free and protect herself in the process. The wedding was tomorrow and she had to attend the rehearsal dinner in a few short hours. She remembered the papers that William had given her that were safely tucked away in her precious little box, hidden at the back of her closet. She began to form a plan of escape and a way to ensure her own safety and the safety of her unborn child.

Elizabeth took a shower in preparation of the upcoming dinner while continuing to play out her plan in her mind. She knew she had to get control of her emotions and pretend that nothing was wrong. She had to convince everyone that she was happy and excited about the wedding scheduled for the next morning. She finalized her plan in her mind and with an hour left before she was expected to join everyone down stairs, she locked her door and pulled out the personalized stationary given to her by her sister-in-law as a Christmas gift.

She wrote two letters, the first to Jonathan apologizing for hurting him. She sealed the envelope, regretting that she would have to hurt such a good man. The second letter was to her brother and would secure her safety. When she was done and read over the letter satisfied that it was clear and concise, she went to her closet in search of her special box. She removed the papers William had given her and put them in the envelope with the letter. She carefully sealed the envelope, writing in large bold letters 'Richard' on the front. She tucked both letters safely under her mattress and took a deep calming breath. "You must be strong. You can do this," Elizabeth told herself as she opened the door and went downstairs to greet her guests.

Elizabeth walked slowly down the stairs determined to put on a fabulous performance. She walked into the library joining the others with a wide grin on her face.

When she saw Jonathan in the corner talking to her brother, she hurried to him throwing her arms around his neck, kissing him on the lips. "Jonathan! I missed you!"

Jonathan was delighted with her greeting and hugged her tightly. "I missed you too," he told her sincerely. He put an arm around her proudly as Elizabeth smiled from ear to ear. "Are you ready to go?" he asked to the group. They all departed in high spirits, climbing into two limousines that would take them to the church for the rehearsal. Afterwards they would all return to the house and have the traditional celebration dinner.

Elizabeth went about her expected duties, sure to appear excited, fidgeting as would be expected of any young bride. She constantly smiled, showing plenty of affection to her husband-to-be. She hated showing such false affection, knowing how hurt Jonathan would be the next day but knew she had no other choice.

They went through the motions of the mock ceremony, taking their places as instructed by the priest. Everyone thought Elizabeth was an excited young bride as she hoped, which was confirmed when Elizabeth overheard Susan commenting how glad she was that Elizabeth was so happy. Elizabeth was proud of her performance so far and confidently climbed back into the limousine with the group, making sure to cuddle close to Jonathan when he held her hand.

Although Richard didn't say much to her directly, which wasn't different than any other day, he managed to stand up at dinner and propose a toast to his sister and welcome Jonathan to the family. He smiled at the group, spouting what appeared to be a heartfelt wish for their future happiness. It took all of Elizabeth's strength not to throw her champagne glass at his arrogant head. She smiled and thanked him, doing her best to appear touched by his speech then kissed Jonathan, smiling at him fondly.

Elizabeth was relieved when the guests began to leave. She spent a few moments alone with Jonathan on the front step before he left for the evening. Once they were alone, he kissed her several times pulling her close. "I can't wait for tomorrow," he whispered in her ear.

"Jonathan, you've been so good to me! You will make a wonderful husband," she told him truthfully, feeling guilty again for the pain she would cause him. She kissed him hard and hugged him tightly knowing she wouldn't be seeing him again. He kissed her one last time and turned to leave. "Get some sleep darling. We have a long day a head of us." She watched him go sadly, thinking one day he would make someone very happy.

She went back into the house smiling as she said good night to her brother and his wife. As Elizabeth left the room, they looked at each other happy that things had gone so well. They both believed she was excited to marry Jonathan. Richard was feeling very confident, especially with William tucked safely away. Soon his sister would be married and out of his hair forever. Richard had pleasant dreams that evening confident he would soon obtain the rest of his fortune.

Elizabeth shut and locked her door collapsing onto her bed. She was exhausted by her performance but was confident that it had worked as she planned. She took a few minutes to relax then found a small bag in her closet, packing only two changes of clothes and her special box containing the money she had saved along with some pictures of her parents. She stuffed the bag under her bed hidden behind the decorative skirt. She took out a pair of jeans and a warm shirt also stuffing them under her bed with a comfortable pair of sneakers. She changed her alarm clock to the desired time being sure to lower the volume as much as possible so no one else would hear it. She climbed into bed trying to get some sleep. Jonathan was right when he said she had a long day in front of her.

Elizabeth found it impossible to sleep, watching the minutes tick slowly by. When it was almost time for her alarm to ring and found herself still awake, she turned off the alarm, quietly climbing out of bed. She moved about the room as quietly as possible pulling on the jeans and tying the shoelaces of her sneakers in the dark. She pulled out the bag she had packed and felt underneath her mattress for the envelopes she placed there earlier that day. She stuffed her pillows under the comforter forming a mound that would appear to be her sleeping body should someone check on her in the middle of the night. She took the letters from underneath her mattress, placing the first letter to Jonathan on the night stand propping it up against the lamp. She looked down at her hand as she removed the engagement ring Jonathan had given her, gently placing it next to the envelope, again feeling guilty at the pain she would cause him when he found her gone the next day.

The second letter she put flat on her dresser and her anger swelled providing her the courage she needed to go forward with her plan to escape her brother forever. She took a deep breath hanging the bag over her head and shoulder leaving her hands free to climb over the balcony and shimmy down the pillar that supported the balcony above. She managed to make the climb without breaking her neck and crouched quietly in the darkness, listening for any indication that someone was aware of her movement. After a moment of pure silence, she dashed quickly across the backyard and down to the beach. She made her way down the beach in the darkness using only the stars to light her way.

It was three o'clock in the morning when she left the house. She knew she must put as much distance as possible between her and Richard in the next four hours. She arrived at the marina in no time and made her way to the main road. She knew there were public buses that ran along the main road and hoped that she would be able to catch one of them before she was discovered missing. She didn't care what direction she went, caring only to escape the borders of Stamford as soon as possible. Once she was out of Stamford, she could make her way to any destination.

She walked along the main road for an hour before she finally found a bus stop. She wasn't sure when the first bus would arrive but sat on the bench glad to rest her tired feet. It was still dark with very little traffic. Elizabeth was relieved when a bus pulled up only an hour later. She was safely on the bus heading away from Stamford before the sun appeared to start a new day, arriving in the next town shortly after sunrise.

Elizabeth went into the diner located a few blocks from the bus stop, inquiring about the closest bus terminal or train station. She used the pay phone to call a cab after they gave her the information. She quickly used the bathroom then sipped a hot cup of coffee as she waited, making sure to sit with a view of the front parking lot. She waited twenty minutes before the yellow cab pulled up in front of the diner. She went out to the cab and gave the driver the address.

Another twenty minutes later she handed the driver his money and exited the vehicle, happy that she had managed to get away unnoticed. She entered the bus terminal and studied the signs listing the destinations she had to choose from. She had no idea where she wanted to go until she saw the listing for Atlantic City, New Jersey leaving in a convenient fifteen minutes. Without further hesitation she purchased the ticket and made her way to the assigned platform. She climbed onto the bus feeling free for the first time in her life. She could easily get a job in Atlantic City at one of the restaurants or hotels, she thought confidently. After another hour had passed Elizabeth permitted herself a nap, feeling confident she had successfully escaped.

Susan was finishing her breakfast of grapefruit and toast, wondering why Elizabeth hadn't come down for breakfast. She assumed she had the pre-wedding night jitters and had a hard time falling asleep as she herself had the evening before her wedding. She finished her breakfast then went in search of the bride-to-be. She knocked softly on her door several times. After receiving no answer she slowly opened the door and poked her head inside. She immediately saw the lump on the bed. Walking towards the bed smiling she went to gently shake the bride attempting to wake her. Surprised when she realized the lump were only pillows she naively went to Elizabeth's bathroom calling her name.

It took Susan a few minutes to realize that Elizabeth wasn't there and to notice the envelope propped on the bedside table. "Jonathan" was written in large letters on the front of the envelope. Susan sadly walked over to the table and found the engagement ring placed beside the envelope. "Oh my," Susan sighed, knowing that her husband would be furious. She folded the envelope and placed it in the pocket of her bathrobe along with the ring intending to give it to Jonathan later. She turned to leave the room but noticed the second envelope on the other dresser with "Richard" written boldly on the front. Susan picked up the envelope not looking forward to telling her husband that Elizabeth was missing.

"Better get this over with," she thought miserably, knowing the miserable day she now had to face. Having to tell the groom and their guests that the wedding was cancelled wasn't something she had expected. She slowly descended the stairs with the envelope in her hand walking silently into the dining room where Richard was sipping his coffee and reading the paper. He looked up at her, "Is she getting up?" he asked completely unaware of the situation.

"Well…." Susan found it impossible to say the words so she simply handed him the envelope and took a seat a safe distant from her husband. He looked questioningly at his wife as she handed him the letter. He opened the envelope, the color draining from his face as he read his sister's letter. He slammed an angry fist against the table. "Leave me!" he yelled at his wife not willing to share the contents of the letter. Susan quickly exited the room, all too willing to escape and avoid being subjected to his nasty temper.

Dear Richard,

As you are aware by now I have left and will not marry Jonathan as you wished. I realize that you can no longer hurt me. I can't hurt a good man and deceive him to satisfy your greed. My only regret is the pain I will cause Jonathan by my decision.

I want you to be aware that I know everything. I am ashamed that you are family. I know about our parents' death and their Will. I want you to know that if money is what you love than consider this my dying wish since I now consider myself dead to you and you are dead to me. I have no brother. Take the money, I don't want or need any of it.

I am warning you, should you try to find me you'll do so at your own peril. The enclosed papers provide proof of your involvement in our parents' death. The money will no longer protect you Richard. If I so much as suspect you're looking for me, even in error, copies of the enclosed papers will be sent to every newspaper and news station in the area. You would never escape the scandal and doubt in the minds of your associates and stock holders even if you managed to once again dodge the law.

Come – try to find me. I would take great pleasure in watching you squirm as your entire life crumbled around your cold heart. I am not being kind for your sake but for the sake of your naïve wife and those innocent children. Realize, Richard, if I get wind of any further 'misbehavior' on your part, I will reveal the real Richard Marks, III, without hesitation to your wife, your children and the rest of the world.

Your dearly departed sister,
Elizabeth

Richard scanned the papers that were enclosed and began to shake violently when he realized she could do as she threatened. He would be ruined by the scandal alone, causing the company stock to plummet and then he would lose everything. "Damn her and damn William Blake!" he said angrily lying his head on the table as he realized his defeat. After a few moments Richard tossed the papers into the fireplace and watched as they burned.

After hurrying away from her enraged husband, Susan dressed then summoned the limousine driver. She gave him instructions on where to take her as she climbed into the limo, not looking forward to the responsibilities that haven fallen on her shoulders. She made the ride to the Parker's house thinking how hurt Jonathan was going to be. Susan still couldn't believe Elizabeth ran out on the wedding. She had appeared so happy and excited the night before.

The limousine pulled up in front of the house and Susan climbed out with the ring and letter tucked safely in her handbag. She rang the bell and waited a moment for someone to answer. She was greeted by Jonathan's mother. "Susan? What are you doing here? Is something wrong?" she asked, instantly concerned since she should be at the house helping the bride-to-be.

"May I come in?" Susan asked softly, entering their home after Mrs. Parker moved aside. "Is Jonathan here?"

"Of course. What's going on?" Mrs. Parker asked growing impatient.

"Please ask Jonathan to come down. I need to speak with him," she replied avoiding her question. Mrs. Parker looked as if she was about to say something then silently went in search of her son. A moment later she was joined by both Jonathan and his mother.

Jonathan took one look at Susan's face and knew something was wrong. "What's wrong? Is Elizabeth hurt?" he asked with concern which made Susan feel worse. Without answering she reached into her purse, retrieving the ring and envelope then slowly handed it to him. Jonathan looked at her questioningly which quickly turned to dismay as he saw the engagement ring in his hand. Susan took Mrs. Parker by the hand and led her into another room to allow Jonathan some privacy.

Jonathan sat down looking at the ring, knowing instantly the wedding was off. He placed the ring in his shirt pocket and slowly opened the envelope.

Dear Jonathan,
I am truly sorry for the pain I am about to cause you. I can't marry you. It wouldn't be fair to you. You're truly a good man and have been a true friend. I want you to know that this has nothing to do with you. I only hope that you can one day forgive me for the pain I have caused you. I hope that one day I will be able to explain things so you can better understand my decision.
Please take good care of yourself. I do care deeply for you and will always cherish the friendship we shared.

With sincere regret,
Elizabeth

Jonathan folded the letter and placed it gently back into its envelope then went in search of Susan. "Where is she? I want to speak to her now!" he stated firmly.

Susan looked at him sadly, "Jonathan, she's disappeared. We have no idea where she is. I'm very sorry."

Jonathan stared at her surprised by her statement. "Gone?.... Gone?" he said numbly. He had been determined to convince her to marry him assuming she had simply gotten nervous. He knew now that there would be no wedding. She was gone, lost to him. Jonathan slowly walked away feeling his heart breaking. "She had been so happy yesterday," he thought which only confused him further.

Susan spoke with Mrs. Parker for a few moments and expressed her regret for the situation. "We are all surprised by Elizabeth's decision and disappearance. Please let me know if you need anything. I'll call the church and the reception hall. I'll take care of everything. Please concentrate on Jonathan. I'm sure he's broken hearted."

Susan left and began making calls to notify the minister and caterer that the wedding has been canceled. They told her they would take care of notifying the guests as they arrive, since it was now too late to call them all individually. She thanked them and returned home feeling truly sorry for Jonathan. He had looked so upset when she told him Elizabeth was gone.

Elizabeth arrived in Atlantic City just after dark and hailed a cab. She gave the driver an address of a small hotel she found in the phone book located on the outskirts of the city which was less expensive than the larger casino hotels. She looked around at the city shining brightly in the darkness. Elizabeth was feeling free and happy, excited to take on the new life she had chosen. She checked into her hotel, looking forward to a hot shower and a good night's sleep before looking for a job in the morning.

She hoped to find a job quickly knowing that her meager funds wouldn't last long. She curled up in bed trying not to think of William. She ignored the dull ache in her heart as she fell asleep, exhausted from her journey.

Chapter Fifteen

With each passing day, the little bit of hope that Sarah had left was fading. Each day, more convinced that her brother was dead. She called the attorney daily to see if he had found out anything only to be disappointed. On Sunday morning Sarah was reading the paper in an effort to distract herself from her morbid thoughts and was shocked by what she read.

'Bride Disappears' read the headline with a large photo of Elizabeth. Sarah read the article describing how the sister of Richard Marks III had disappeared the morning of her wedding. Although she had left a note of explanation, the family had no idea of her location and wished she would come home. This statement was surely for appearance sake, Sarah thought bitterly. "Good for her!" she said out loud in the empty room. "Good for her!"

This news lifted her spirits a little knowing William would be happy she hadn't married Jonathan Parker. At that moment the phone rang, making her jump, "Hello," she answered.

"Sarah?" replied a scratchy weak male voice making Sarah jump out of her chair. "William? Is it really you?!" she exclaimed.

"Yes, Sarah, it's me. Please calm down," he said as he could hear his sister crying on the other end. "Listen to me," he commanded. "I called because I wanted you to know I'm alright but I don't want you to tell anyone that I called. Is that clear?"

"Why? What's going on? Are you really okay?" she asked concerned by his gruffness.

"I'll explain later. Promise?" he asked insisting on her silence.

"Promise," she responded. "I'm just glad you're alright. I thought you were dead," she said, starting to cry again. "I even called your lawyer as instructed!"

"I know. I just got off the phone with him. That's why I called. He said you were very upset. Just don't tell anyone you've heard from me. As far as you're concerned I'm still missing. I'll get back to you in a couple of days."

"Okay William, whatever you want. Please be careful!" she told him firmly. Sarah hung up the phone relieved that her brother was safe. She wondered if he knew about Elizabeth running out on the wedding then realized she had forgotten to ask William where he was.

William was resting in his hospital bed with Thomas sitting in the chair nearby, discussing everything that had happened and the plan Thomas had already put into action while William was recovering from the surgery. After being unconscious for nearly two days and the doctors had began to fear the worst, William regained consciousness. William was very tired but forced himself to concentrate on what Thomas was saying.

"He will pay! I'm making sure of that!" he told him angrily as he filled William in on all the details. William smiled at his friend's determination to make Richard pay for all he has done, remembering that feeling all too well. The pain he felt knowing that Elizabeth was married only yesterday while he was unconscious overwhelmed any other feelings he may have otherwise had at that moment.

"You take care of it. I trust you. Just make sure my sister and nephew are alright," he told him sleepily, trying to fight the fatigue overtaking him.

"Okay. I get it. I can see you're tired. I'll let you rest. I'll try to stop in tomorrow but if I can't then I'll call and check in on you," he said as he stood to leave.

"Thomas......Thanks....Thanks for everything," William said seriously. Thomas simply smiled, nodded then left the hospital to continue with his plans.

Elizabeth woke feeling refreshed and excited, ready to start her new life. She took a shower and dressed before going down to the restaurant for breakfast. She sipped her coffee and ate the bagel and fruit that was provided at no additional cost. When she was finished, she began making inquiries about employment. First she approached the hotel receptionist who informed her that at the moment they weren't hiring. She thanked the receptionist then made her way outside to visit the various hotels and restaurants hoping she would find something quickly.

After a long day of filling out applications Elizabeth returned to her hotel with aching feet. So far she had no luck but hoped to hear from one of the hotels where she had left an application. She was exhausted and hungry. She went to the restaurant and ordered the least expensive item on the menu. She ordered only water and a BLT sandwich, trying to stretch her funds as long as possible. The hotel she was staying in was reasonably priced but would only provide her with a few weeks lodging before her funds would be depleted.

She had purchased a newspaper in the lobby and read over the employment ads, circling the ones she thought she would look into. Elizabeth fell asleep quickly after the hours of walking in search of a job. She woke the next morning following the same routine as the day before. She was determined to find a job as quickly as possible. This routine continued for the next week without success and Elizabeth began to worry.

"What will I do if I can't find a job?" she asked herself, beginning to feel desperate. She went downstairs for her usual breakfast when she was stopped by the receptionist on her way to the restaurant. "Miss Marks?" she called from behind the counter.

Elizabeth turned and walked towards the counter, "Yes?" she replied politely.

"Are you still in need of employment?" she asked Elizabeth. Elizabeth nodded in response as her heart did a flip. "We just had someone quit without notice. Would you be interested in a position as a maid? Basically you would be cleaning the rooms after customers check out and it doesn't pay much."

"Yes. I would be interested. Frankly I need a job right away," she explained.

"Okay. Fill out this application and bring it back to me as soon as possible. I'll see what I can do." Elizabeth took the paperwork and thanked the receptionist. She took the application into the restaurant and filled it out as she ate breakfast. Afterwards, she brought the paperwork back to the receptionist completely filled out and signed. The receptionist scanned the paperwork then asked her about references and emergency contacts which she had left blank.

"I have no family or references," she informed her sadly. The receptionist felt sorry for the young girl. "Could you take a seat for a few moments?" she asked.

"Sure," Elizabeth took a seat and watched the receptionist disappear into the back office. She sat anxiously waiting for their decision. The receptionist went to the manager's office and argued with him to give the girl a try. "She has no family and desperately needs a job. We need a maid immediately and if she doesn't work out we'll be no worse for it," she pointed out to her manager.

"Alright, Kelly. Have her fill-out all the required paperwork. See if she can start tomorrow."

Kelly grabbed the papers for Elizabeth to fill out and returned to the desk smiling. She waved at Elizabeth to come over to the desk. "Can you start tomorrow?" she asked smiling brightly.

Elizabeth smiled widely as she responded, "Yes! Thank you!"

Kelly began to go over the paperwork and the details of her new job informing her of the time she would need to report for work. "Can I ask you a personal question?" she asked quietly. After Elizabeth nodded in response, Kelly continued, "I noticed you listed the hotel as your address. Does this mean you have no place to stay?"

"Yes. I'm new to the area," she explained not willing to provide any further explanation.

"Well, I assume you will not be able to afford to stay here on this salary?" she asked politely keeping her voice low so their conversation would be private.

"Probably not," Elizabeth agreed.

"Well, if you're interested, my mother is trying to rent a room in her house. It's not too far from here and there's a bus that runs conveniently between here and the house," Kelly offered, trying to help the young girl who was obviously alone.

"Really? That would be wonderful." Elizabeth smiled at her sudden change of luck.

"If you'd like to see it, I could take you over when I get off of work at four o'clock?" Kelly offered.

"That would be great, if it's not too much trouble," Elizabeth responded feeling guilty but grateful for all this woman was doing for her.

"No problem at all. Meet me here at four o'clock. Finish up the paperwork and leave it with me before you go about your day. If you have any questions just let me know."

"Thank you so much for all your help," Elizabeth said gratefully then set to work filling out the numerous papers she was required to complete. She left the papers with Kelly, promising to be back at four. She went back to her room relieved that she had found a job and may have an affordable place to live.

She was happy but restless deciding to take a walk and enjoy the rest of the day. She wandered around the area and found a small second hand shop that sold various things including clothes. She browsed the selection of clothes they had in the maternity section and was pleased to find they had some very nice things that were in good condition. The clothes she purchased were styled and designed to expand with an expectant mother's figure while not appearing to be maternity apparel. She purchased several pairs of pants and blouses along with a comfortable pair of walking shoes for a small amount of money. She was extremely pleased she wouldn't have to wear the same two outfits again.

She enjoyed a light lunch at a deli before returning to the hotel with her new clothes, looking forward to a shower before her outing with Kelly. She changed into one of the new outfits and joined Kelly promptly at four o'clock in the lobby as promised.

She greeted Kelly happily, grateful for her kindness. She climbed into the passenger seat of Kelly's car, chatting happily along the way. Twenty minutes later they pulled up in front of a small green and white Cape Cod style home. It was a friendly looking house although was in need of some paint after years of wear caused by the weather. They went up the stairs to the covered front porch that contained a wooden bench swing, hung by chains, and two rocking chairs with a small table in between.

Kelly opened the door, knocking and calling for her mother as she entered. Kelly's mother appeared in a doorway and her face brightened at the sight of her daughter. "Kelly!" she exclaimed immediately embracing her daughter. Elizabeth was touched by the immediate show of affection between Kelly and her mother, making her long for the affections of her own mother.

"Mom, this is Elizabeth. She's interested in renting the room." Kelly explained.

"Elizabeth?" she asked, making sure she had heard the name correctly. Kelly nodded in response to her mother's question. "You're interested in renting the room? Well, I guess you should see it first. Come this way," she commanded as she walked towards the stairs. They both followed Kelly's mother slowly up the stairs. When they reached the top, Elizabeth noticed that the elderly woman was a little out of breath. "I don't use the upper floor anymore," she explained. "I don't do stairs very well. I use the bedroom on the first floor that used to be my late husband's office. There is a bathroom down stairs as well so I never have the need to come up here anymore," she explained in more detail.

"This is the room and there is a full bathroom up here in the hall that you would have all to yourself," she told her allowing Elizabeth to step into the room so she could look around. The room was simply decorated with white walls and soft blue curtains. It contained a full size bed covered with a fluffy, blue comforter that matched the curtains. The floors were hardwood and there was with a thick, blue throw rug on the floor. The room also had a small closet, two dressers and a rocking chair set nearby the window. The room was very welcoming and Elizabeth was thrilled with her luck.

"It's wonderful!" she said happily to them both. They showed her the bathroom that was more than adequate for her needs and then returned downstairs.

"My name is Angie. If you want to rent the room it's yours," she told Elizabeth. "Would you like some tea?" Elizabeth nodded and thanked her gratefully. Angie placed a small plate of cookies in the middle of the table then poured each of them a cup of tea. They chatted for a few moments and agreed on the amount of rent Angie required.

"When would you like to move in?" Angie inquired.

"As soon as possible," she replied. "When is convenient for you?"

"For all I care you can move in tonight or whenever you'd like," she told Elizabeth kindly.

"Tonight? Really? That would be great actually. I start my job at the hotel in the morning. I don't have many clothes so it wouldn't take long to pack up and check out. I can give you two weeks rent in advance and by then I should have my first paycheck. Is that alright?" Elizabeth asked, hoping Angie would be agreeable.

"That's fine with me," Angie replied, already deciding she liked this young lady, thinking she should make a good tenant. Elizabeth pulled the promised bills from her handbag handing them to Angie.

"I guess I should get to it then. I should be back in about two hours."

"Do you want me to give you a ride back to the hotel?" Kelly offered.

"Thank you for the offer but it may be better if I took the bus you told me about so I can familiarize myself with the schedule. I want to make sure I get to work on time. Thanks for everything, Kelly. I appreciate all of your help," she said sincerely.

Kelly smiled at the young woman, "You're welcome. If you need anything just give me a call." Angie handed her a key and directed her to the closest bus stop. Elizabeth thanked them both again and happily made her way down the street. She was so thrilled with the room she had found and how affordable it was. She would be able to afford to start saving some money to help pay for the many things she would need once her baby was born. She hadn't told her new friends that she was pregnant but that would come later when they all got to know each other better.

Two and a half hours later, Elizabeth arrived at her new home with her meager belongings stuffed into her one small bag. She settled into her room then realized she never ate dinner. She went back downstairs intending to ask Angie if there was a diner or deli nearby and was surprised when she was shuffled into the kitchen and ordered to sit. A moment later there was a full plate piled high with roast beef, potatoes, carrots, gravy and biscuits.

"You must be hungry," Angie told her as she placed the plate in front of her. "Eat."

The scent of the food made Elizabeth's mouth water as she thanked Angie for the meal as her stomach rumbled. She ate the food gratefully, thinking it the best meal she had since she left Connecticut. The dish was so tasty and she had been so hungry, she ate the food in complete silence enjoying every bite.

"That was so wonderful!" she told Angie gratefully. They sat at the table and chatted, drinking tea and nibbling on some cookies that Angie had put out for dessert. She listened as the little old lady with grey curly hair told her stories about her family and her younger years. Elizabeth was smiling as she climbed the stairs to retire, tired from the long day. She found she liked Angie immediately and was glad that she had come here. She knew everything was going to be alright.

Richard quickly recovered from Elizabeth's departure, telling his wife she was no longer his concern. "Don't you care at all about Elizabeth? What if something happens to her?" Susan was offended as he simply shrugged his shoulders continuing to read the newspaper and drink his coffee. She left the room angered at his lack of concern for his sister. Knowing there was nothing she could do about it, she busied herself with the duties of running the house.

Richard had managed to dodge the press who were constantly trying to interview him the week following the botched wedding. He refused to answer any questions. "No comment," he would say, walking away as if they didn't exist. He went to the office everyday as usual and conducted his business as if nothing happened. He had decided not to risk the scandal and allow Elizabeth to do whatever she wanted. He was relieved not to have the burden of taking care of his younger sister and was more than happy to pretend she was dead.

Richard was sitting at his desk, going over some papers he needed to sign when the door to his office swung open. "What the hell?" he yelled as he stood offended by the sudden intrusion as six men entered his office at once.

"Richard Marks?" the first man asked.

"Yes? Who are you?" Richard demanded angrily.

"Richard Marks you are under arrest," the man said as he showed Richard his badge. Richard's mouth fell open when he saw the badge that read 'FBI'.

"What's this about?!" Richard demanded.

Two of the other men walked around his desk, pulling his arms behind his back to handcuff him. "Richard Marks III, you are charged with attempted murder and conspiracy to commit murder," the officer told him as he began to read him his rights. "You have the right to remain silent…."

"What are you talking about!? This is absurd! Do you have any idea who I am?" he ranted as he was escorted out of his office. "Call my lawyer!" he yelled to his secretary as they forced him towards the elevator.

Richard ranted angrily all the way to FBI head-quarters where they intended to question him before locking him in a jail cell to wait for his bail hearing. The officers looked at each other and smiled at the arrogance of the man in the back seat. "This is a mistake. You will regret this! You have no idea who you're messing with!" The agents knew there would be no escape for this guy. The evidence and testimony they had from two different witnesses was enough to put him away for a very long time.

Richard sat in an empty room for an hour before the agents came in to question him. They had allowed him one phone call in order to contact his attorney. They didn't want to take the chance that this man would get away on a technicality. Richard refused to answer any questions without his lawyer as they expected. They left him in the locked room for another hour until his attorney arrived. They provided his attorney with information on the charges and the evidence that supported the charges.

"I would like to speak to my client privately," he told the agents. They escorted the attorney to the room where Richard was waiting.

"What the hell took you so long? I have been here for hours! Get me out of here now!" Richard growled.

"I'm afraid it's not that easy this time, Richard. It appears they have some very strong evidence against you," he informed Richard calmly.

"What do you mean strong evidence?" Richard asked impatiently.

"They have two witnesses that have given written statements accusing you of attempted murder. They say you had thugs kidnap, beat up and leave a....... William Blake, to die in the cellar of an old farmhouse," his attorney informed him.

"William Blake?" he fumed, angry that the man had somehow escaped.

"Richard, there's more. They have two men in custody. They said you ordered them to lock Blake up. They said you paid them to watch him, beat him and leave him there to die in that farmhouse. Those two men have cut themselves a deal and agreed to testify against you. I doubt you'll be able to get out of this one," his attorney told him bluntly.

Richard's face turned white as he realized he was probably going to jail. "I have requested bail but I doubt they'll allow it Richard. The press has already gathered outside the building. You've created quite a mess," his attorney informed him. "I will do what I can but the evidence is extremely damaging. Even if you got off on a technicality your reputation will still be ruined forever."

He allowed Richard to absorb what he said before he continued. "There is one more thing Richard. The charge of Conspiracy to Commit Murder is a separate charge naming you suspect in the death of your parents. They're reopening the case. That makes two separate charges for two separate crimes."

Richard couldn't believe what his attorney was telling him. This time he would not be able to buy his way out. The public was already aware of the charges, his name tainted forever. He sat numbly across from his lawyer in shock not knowing what to say or do. His attorney rose and knocked on the door signaling the guard to open the door. "I'll do my best Richard but it doesn't look good. I'll be in touch," he said then left Richard sitting in the cold room all alone.

Susan was stunned and confused when she received the call from her husband's secretary, saying he had been arrested. She called his attorney but was told he was already on his way to see Richard. She left a message for him to call her as soon as he returned to the office. She paced nervously, waiting for the lawyer to call her and explain what was happening.

A couple of hours later Susan spoke to the attorney and began to cry as he explained the charges and the evidence they had against her husband. "Oh my god!" she cried wondering if her husband was truly guilty. "It's not possible!"

"I saw the evidence myself, Susan. Richard never even bothered to deny that he had done it. Never once said he was innocent. My advice to you, is start preparing for the fact your husband is probably going to jail for a long time. Your husband will be in the spot light in a very bad way. Prepare your children so they aren't surprised by the press. I'm sorry," he felt sorry for Susan as he hung up the phone. She was just another innocent victim of Richard's. The attorney had no doubt that Richard was guilty, knowing him for years and the lengths he would go to get what he wanted.

Susan crumbled to the floor, sobbing uncontrollably as she wondered what she was going to do without her husband. How could she tell her children about their father? She went to her room trying to collect herself, so she could speak to her children later that afternoon when they came home for dinner. Susan felt helpless and betrayed by a man who had promised to take care of her. Now her and her children would be publicly humiliated.

Thomas and William sat impatiently in the hospital room waiting for the call. When they finally received the call that Richard Marks was safely in the custody of the FBI, Thomas took William home. William was getting stronger each day and was released with instructions to take it easy for the next several weeks. William was just happy to be going home, anxious to see his sister and his nephew. They made the drive, discussing everything Thomas had accomplished in such a short time. He had contacted a trusted friend in the FBI, providing him everything he had as evidence. It didn't take the FBI long to track down the thugs that Richard had hired and they had quickly offered up Richard in exchange for a shorter sentence. They gathered further evidence at the farmhouse, taking blood samples that had been left by William as a result of the beating.

They had taken statements from William and Thomas which provided an unbreakable case against Richard Marks. William still assumed Elizabeth was safely married and on her honeymoon, glad that she was at least safe. He arrived home to a mixture of screams of delight from his nephew and hugs combined with tears of joy from his sister. He had a lot to tell his sister, not wanting her to hear everything on the news. They all sat together with Thomas chatting as Sarah prepared dinner for them all. After she put Toby to bed, they made their way to the back porch to share a pitcher of their favorite cocktail.

William told Sarah everything that had happened and how Thomas had saved his life. Sarah hugged Thomas firmly, thanking him for all he had done for her brother. She remembered Thomas from the neighborhood where they grew up and that her brother had mentioned him a couple of times over the years. After a while William grew tired and decided he needed to go to bed. Sarah invited Thomas to spend the night instead of driving so late at night. He graciously accepted and continued to enjoy Sarah's company, sharing another pitcher of her favorite cocktail as they talked on the porch. Thomas was surprised to realize he was really enjoying her company. She was easy to talk to showing interest in various subjects. She asked him a lot of questions about his work and about things that had happened while he had been watching Elizabeth. They laughed together when he told her the story of William dressed as an old lady and how he had recognized him immediately by his hairy fingers and five o'clock shadow.

They suddenly grew serious, thinking about Elizabeth, "It's a shame she went and married that guy," Thomas said, thinking how much William had obviously cared about her.

"She didn't marry him Thomas! The papers said she disappeared before the wedding!" she told him, realizing her brother hadn't known after all.

"What? Are you sure?" Sarah nodded and went inside to retrieve the article she had kept. He scanned over the article.

"The article said no one knows where she is."

"Oh god. What if Richard Marks did something to her too?" Thomas thought out loud.

"I didn't think of that. I just assumed she took off, not wanting to marry that guy," she said concerned. "William will be broken hearted if anything has happened to her!"

"I know. I know. He thinks she's safely on her honeymoon," he said, trying to decide how he should handle this newest information. "If William finds out, he will assume Richard did something and go after him. I'll talk to my friend at the FBI and see if he can find out anything about where she might be. Let's not say anything to William just yet."

Sarah agreed it may be the best way to handle the situation for the moment. "Okay, but try to find something out quickly. I hate lying to my brother." She carefully hid the article in her handbag, hoping she would be found safe and sound. They both retired for the evening, praying Elizabeth was alive and well for William's sake.

Elizabeth woke in her new home, feeling well rested and ready to start her new job. She showered and dressed then made her way downstairs, ready to catch the bus. Angie was there waiting with a warm plate of scrambled eggs and toast. She ordered her to sit and eat then poured her a cup of coffee. "You don't have to keep feeding me, Angie," she said feeling as though she was taking advantage of her friend's kindness.

"We both have to eat don't we? Just as easy to make for two as it is for one. If it makes you feel better, you can chip in on groceries after you get a paycheck," she responded, understanding and respecting the young lady's need to provide for herself.

"That sounds like a great idea. Thank you Angie." Elizabeth finished her plate and her coffee then made her way to the bus stop. She arrived at the hotel on time and reported to the manager for training and instruction. She was given a uniform so the guests would be able to identify her as part of the housekeeping staff and went about her duties, doing her best to do a good job. She wasn't used to the manual labor involved in her new job, always having servants that did the cleaning for her but she did her best, taking pride in her work. "If this is the cost of freedom I'll surely pay it without regret," she thought to herself.

Elizabeth found herself exhausted at the end of each day, finding little energy to do more than eat and go to bed. She enjoyed her days off by walking the beach and reading a book that Angie had given her. She soon found the labor easier, adjusting to her new routine. Elizabeth was content working and going home to spend time with Angie. She was great company, always having a funny story to tell. She admired the elderly woman and her determination to stay independent despite her seventy-five years. Kelly had told her that she had invited her mother to live with her a couple of times but she had refused, wanting to maintain her freedom and not become a burden to her family until absolutely necessary.

As hard as Elizabeth tried not to think of William, concentrating on her job and enjoying Angie's company, it became increasingly difficult as she noticed her belly begin to grow. At night and on her days off, she always found her thoughts wandering back to William, grief taking of hold of her heart. Sometimes she would cry herself to sleep and other times she was haunted by dreams reminding her of the time they had spent together. In her heart she had forgiven him for his deceit and often wondered what it would be like if he was with her to watch their child grow.

She hadn't seen a doctor yet but planned to make an appointment with an obstetrician as soon as she could afford it. She had considered calling William's sister and meeting her nephew but couldn't bring herself to call or visit until she had established her independence. She would have a hard time facing them knowing William died because of her and her brother. For the time being, she would continue living a simple life, renting a room from a little old lady and cleaning in the hotel.

Chapter Sixteen

Richard was in a foul mood when Susan arrived to visit him in jail, having just been told he was denied bail. The judge ruled he was only to be permitted supervised visits and phone calls with his attorney, his wife and his children due to the harshness of the charges and his illegal use of his power and money. He sat across from his wife as she cried, begging him to tell her he was innocent. "Richard, please tell me you didn't do what they say you did! Please!"

Richard didn't bother to reply and looked at his wife coldly across the table. "Richard?" she said astonished by his cold expression. "Talk to me damn it!" she exclaimed, frustrated by his silence.

"Take care of the kids, Susan," was all he said as he motioned to the guard to return him to his cell. Susan watched in shock as her husband walked away as if she meant nothing to him. She left in tears, not understanding why he had treated her that way.

Richard returned to his cell and sat numbly on the bed, cursing the day he had met Sarah Blake. A few minutes later a guard came to his cell and motioned for him to come out. "What now?" Richard asked, not wishing to be bothered by anyone.

"Just go," the guard ordered as he shoved him along. He was escorted to a small room and told to sit down. The door was closed and locked behind him. He sat alone for a while until the FBI agent that arrested him came into the room and sat in the chair across from him.

"Where's your sister, Elizabeth?" he asked Richard bluntly.

"My sister? She took off the morning of her wedding. I have no idea where she is nor do I care," he told the agent coldly.

"How do we know she left of her own free will? Maybe you locked her up somewhere like you did William Blake?" the agent said trying to provoke Richard into admitting something.

"She left a note stating she didn't want to get married and I haven't seen her since," was the only comment he made.

"A note? Really? Can you produce this note?" he asked Richard, not believing him for a second.

"No," he said without further explanation.

"Why not?" the agent persisted.

"I burnt it. I was angry," Richard replied.

"How convenient. I suggest you come clean and tell us what you did to your sister!" the agent yelled in an attempt to provoke Richard into a confession. Richard didn't even twitch in response to the agent's badgering.

"My wife found the note and gave it to me. I'm sure she will confirm that it existed. Can I go now?" he asked as if he had better things to do. The agent motioned to the guard to return Richard to his cell.

The agent exited the room and joined his partner in the hall. "We need to go speak to his wife. Let's go."

Susan was in tears all the way home, shocked by her husband's coldness towards her. He had never treated her so harshly before and it left her feeling confused. She realized he'd never told her he was innocent either as the attorney had warned. She didn't want to believe her husband would have done such horrible things but knew after the way he treated her, he probably did and would go to jail, leaving her and the children alone.

She sat sipping a glass of whiskey to calm her nerves when she heard the door bell ring. The butler escorted two men inside and introduced them to Susan. "Miss Susan, these gentlemen are from the FBI and wish to speak with you." Susan thanked the butler and stood wondering what the visit was about.

"What can I do for you?" she asked in her practiced hostess voice.

"We have a few questions. Do you know where your sister-in-law Elizabeth is?"

"No. She left the morning of her wedding and we haven't heard from her since. Why?" Susan asked, curious why they would be asking her about Elizabeth.

"We were made aware of her disappearance and understand your husband stood to inherit a great deal of money upon her death. Under the circumstances and the nature of the charges against him, we want to investigate her disappearance to make sure your husband hasn't harmed her."

Susan was dismayed at the agent's explanation, suddenly felt faint and was forced to sit to maintain her composure. "I...."

"Mrs. Marks, when did you last see Elizabeth?"

"It was the night before her wedding. She seemed so happy and excited to get married. It came as a great shock when we found she had taken off," she said sadly.

"Did she leave any word of where she was going?"

"She left two envelopes and the engagement ring in her room. One was addressed to my husband and the other to her fiancé," she said crying softly.

"Did you read either of the letters?" Susan only shook her head. "Do you still have either of the letters?" Susan shook her head again.

"I gave my husband his letter and never saw it again. I delivered the other directly to her fiancé."

"I see. Can you give me his name and address please. We'll have to question him as well." Susan wrote down the information he requested and handed it to him. "Here is my card. Please be sure to call me immediately should you hear from Elizabeth." Susan nodded again and escorted them to the door.

Could Richard have hurt his own sister, she wondered, sobbing at the thought. Susan ran to her room,
horrified and angry at her husband.

Jonathan Parker was in his office, going over some
paperwork when his secretary buzzed him. "There are
two gentlemen here to see you, Mr. Parker."

"Send them in," he told her through the speaker
phone. Jonathan rose to greet the visitors assuming they
were there for business reasons. As the two men entered
his office he shook each of the men's hands and
introduced himself, "What can I do for you gentlemen?"

The two men introduced themselves, showing
their FBI badges in the process. A little surprised by a
visit from the FBI, he assumed they were investigating
something to do with the bank. "We need to ask you
some questions."

"Please have a seat," Jonathan motioned, wondering what they needed to know from him.

"Thank you. We are here to ask you about Elizabeth Marks and her recent disappearance," the first man
told him bluntly. "When was the last time you saw or
heard from her?"

Jonathan's face clouded over with obvious grief at
the mention of his fiancé's unexpected departure. "The
night before the wedding at the rehearsal was the last
time I saw her. I haven't heard from her since," he said
sadly. "Is she in some kind of trouble?" he asked with
concern.

"We don't really know. We are trying to make sure
she's alright. We spoke to Susan Marks earlier and she
mentioned a letter she delivered to you that was left by
Elizabeth. Do you have this letter she spoke of?"

"No. I was so angry when she left I ripped it up
and threw it away," he explained.

"Did the letter say where she was going?" the
agent asked, looking for any real evidence that Elizabeth
Marks had actually left on her own.

"No. She just apologized for hurting me, blah, blah, blah…" he said, angry again for her leaving the day of their wedding.

"You haven't heard anything from her since?" the second agent asked again.

"No. What's this about?" Jonathan asked getting frustrated.

"Mr. Parker, are you aware of the charges against Richard Marks?" Jonathan nodded in response and the agent continued explaining. "Well, Mr. Marks stood to inherit a great deal of money should his sister die before she married. Our concern is that Mr. Marks may have done something to her. So far we have no evidence either way but considering the charges against him along with the inheritance and the timing of her disappearance, we are trying to find out for sure if she's alright."

Jonathan was appalled by what they told him. Could Richard have hurt his own sister? "That doesn't make sense. Richard is the one who pushed her into marrying me in the first place. Why would he then decide to kill her?" Jonathan's stomach turned to knots as he heard himself say the words.

"Mr. Marks would also inherit a certain amount of money if she married by a certain age. Maybe he decided that wasn't enough for him?" the agent suggested. Jonathan was stunned into silence as the agent handed him a business card. "Thank you for your help. If you think of anything or hear from Elizabeth please let me know immediately."

Jonathan escorted the gentlemen to the door and returned to his chair trying to absorb what they had just told him. The thought that Elizabeth could be dead sent a wave of nausea through his abdomen. For the first time since he received her note, he wished she had left him by her own choice.

Thomas wasn't happy about the news he received regarding Elizabeth's disappearance. They couldn't find evidence to prove either way that she was safe and had left on her own accord, the alleged letters having been destroyed. The agents felt it was most likely true that the letters existed since they had three different people confirm their existence, however they knew the letters could have been a fabrication by Richard. The only thing they could do was put a trace on her social security number and hope, if she was alright, she would require employment. This could take some time, they told Thomas, knowing he was hoping for better news.

Thomas went back to William and Sarah's to deliver the news personally, knowing they couldn't keep the information from William any longer. He had called Sarah to tell her he was coming and she invited him for dinner which he eagerly accepted. He arrived at Sarah's surprised at how anxious he felt. She greeted him at the door smiling which caused his heart to do a strange flip flop in his chest. He smiled in return and chatted with them over the dinner Sarah had prepared.

He waited until Toby was in bed and they were all on the back porch sharing cocktails before he approached the subject. Sarah suspected he had something to tell them, waiting until he felt it was the right time. "Sarah, could you fetch that article?" he asked bluntly. She nodded and went to retrieve the article she had hidden from her brother.

"What article?" William asked looking at them both wondering what they were talking about. Sarah returned a moment later and handed the article to William after Thomas motioned for her to do so. William scanned the article and they watched recognition, relief, and then worry cross his face. "She didn't marry him?... They say here she's missing... Where is she?"

Thomas cleared his throat then began to tell William all the information they had regarding her disappearance. "They just can't be certain yet if she actually left on her own or if Richard was somehow involved. They're tracing her social security number hoping it will pop up somewhere if she gets a job. I'm sorry William."

"Oh, god. That bastard! If he has hurt her!..... Oh god! I should have stayed away! This is all my fault!" William exclaimed as he cradled his face in his hands. A moment later he was pacing trying to think of anything he could do to find out if she was okay.

"William, try to stay calm. We don't know if anything is wrong. She may have just taken off on her own. You just need to be patient and hope for the best," Thomas said, trying to soothe his friend's worry and guilt.

"Thomas is right. Give it some time. I know it's hard. Believe me I know. I was sure you were dead and now you're here sitting with me," Sarah said joining in with Thomas in an effort to make William feel better.

"But, she's pregnant. I'm sure of it. She didn't deny it when I asked her on the beach that day! If he hurt her she may have lost the baby, if she is alive at all!" William moaned in obvious agony.

"That could very well explain her sudden decision to leave and not marry that guy. Please try not to think the worst. Hopefully something will pop up on the FBI's trace and we'll know something soon." Thomas said, trying to comfort him. After their experience with Richard Marks, he doubted anything he said would comfort William now. He could only hope they found out something soon.

Angie was enjoying Elizabeth's company immensely and was glad she had found such a wonderful tenant. She was always considerate, making sure to clean up after herself and always showed appreciation for even the smallest meal Angie prepared. Although Angie enjoyed her company, she sensed sadness behind the proud and polite smile of the young girl. She wondered what had happened to her that left her alone but figured she would tell her when she was ready.

It was Elizabeth's day off but the stormy weather kept her from taking her normal walk down to the beach. The thunder and lighting was explosive and shook the little house as the rain poured down heavily on the roof.

Wondering when the storm would pass, they both sat in the living room and turned on the television to watch the news, trying to catch the weather report. Except the newspaper she had purchased when she was looking for a job, Elizabeth had not read the paper or watched the news since she left home. Elizabeth had always preferred reading to television but sat quietly without complaint while they watched the latest sports news flash across the screen.

They chatted through the commercials and stories that they had no interest in, patiently waiting for the weather report. They reported on the latest fire that had taken the lives of two people overnight. Elizabeth and Angie both felt awful when they flashed the picture of the crying children who had just lost their parents to the fire. She thought about her parents for a moment then forced the sad thoughts from her mind.

"The big story today is the incarceration of Richard Marks III of Richard Marks Corporation. Richard Marks III has been charged with attempted murder and conspiracy to commit murder. We have just been told that he was denied bail. Richard Marks' parents died years ago after being brutally murdered in their hotel room. We have just been told the case will be reopened. Richard Marks III has been named the prime suspect in the murder....."

The color drained from her face as she listened and saw a picture of Richard then her parents flash across the screen. "The police are also investigating the disappearance of his sister, Elizabeth Marks...." Elizabeth heard nothing more the reporter said as her own picture flashed across the television screen. "....should anyone have any information on the where-a-bouts of Elizabeth Marks contact the police immediately."

Angie was stunned by the story as she looked at Elizabeth's pale face. "Oh my!" Angie said. "Elizabeth? Are you alright?" she asked concerned by the paleness of her skin. Elizabeth looked at Angie and nodded still shocked at the story on the news.

"Elizabeth, you need to call someone. They think you're dead!" Angie said trying to pull her out of her daze.

"Good. Let them think it!" Elizabeth exclaimed, suddenly lively again.

Angie was astounded at the anger she saw on her young face. "Elizabeth, do you want to talk about this? Do you want to tell me why you prefer that people think you're dead?"

"It doesn't matter anymore. Promise me you won't contact anyone! I'm better off if no one knows where I am." She pleaded, hoping Angie wouldn't press the issue. She was comfortable in her new home and her job. She didn't want to have to pick up and leave after such a short time.

"It's your decision Elizabeth, but I don't understand. Did your brother really do those horrible things?" Angie asked, wondering if she was afraid of her brother and that's why she fled a life obviously full of wealth and material comforts.

"Probably... yes. Just let it go. Please." Elizabeth said firmly as she rose and went to her room, seeking solitude so she could think. The picture she saw of her parents brought her grief freshly to the surface and she cried into her pillow to muffle the sound of her anguish.

The next week passed with some awkward tension between Elizabeth and Angie. Angie was afraid to bring up the subject and upset Elizabeth further. Elizabeth was quiet and withdrawn caught up in her own thoughts and emotions. She hadn't been sleeping well which Angie noticed when she saw the dark circles under her eyes. Her appetite wasn't as good either which made Angie feel sorry for Elizabeth.

Angie didn't press the issue further but made sure to watch the news daily when Elizabeth wasn't around in case something happened that Elizabeth should be made aware of. If anyone at her job had seen the news they certainly hadn't said anything to her. Kelly had seen the news report, watching at her house but decided to keep it to herself. If Elizabeth didn't want to be found, that was her business. She understood why she hadn't listed any references or family when she applied for the job at the hotel. She thought her very brave to have given up the comforts of wealth for freedom from her brother who was obviously not a very nice man.

Susan answered the door to find a policeman standing outside with a serious look on his face. She assumed he had more questions for her since she had been questioned several times over the last several weeks. She had tried several times to visit her husband but he had refused to see her. The policeman entered the house looking very stern. "Mrs. Marks. I regret to inform you that your husband is dead. He took his own life last night. I'm sorry." The officer watched the color drain from her face and managed to catch her as she fainted, falling into his arms.

William and Sarah were sitting on the back porch, watching Toby play and listening to some music on the radio. William was recovering nicely but stress, worry and fatigue which resulted in a lack of sleep and no appetite, left him thin and pale. They listened as the music was cut off and an announcer came on the radio. "This just in….. Richard Marks III of Richard Marks Corporation who had recently been incarcerated on charges of attempted murder and conspiracy to commit murder was found dead in his cell this morning…." William and Sarah looked at each other in shock as they listened. "Sources say they found a metal butter knife grinded down to a sharp angle which may have been used by Richard Marks to cut his own wrists late last night some time after the guards called lights out…." William and Sarah both felt relieved at the news. Richard Marks could no longer hurt them. Sarah felt sorry for Richard's wife and children but was sure they would be alright. They would probably inherit quite a lot of money, allowing them to live quite comfortably.

Angie sat watching the news as she had done for the past week and was shocked by the update she was listening to. She was unsure how Elizabeth would react to the news but knew she would have to tell her when she came home. She sat for the rest of the day, rehearsing in her mind what to say to Elizabeth when she came home. She had been so withdrawn and sad this past week. Angie didn't wish to add to her grief.

Finally when Elizabeth walked through the front door, she went to greet her. Elizabeth immediately saw the look on Angie's face and wondered what was wrong. "Is something wrong?" she asked concerned her friend may be sick.

"Come sit with me," Angie asked softly. She waited for her new young friend to sit at the table across from her and took a deep breath before beginning. "I was watching the news today.... Elizabeth.... There is something you should know."

Elizabeth began to panic, "Do they know where I am?"

"No. That's not it. It's your brother. He committed suicide. Your brother is dead," she told her gently waiting for Elizabeth to absorb the news, ready to comfort her.

"Richard is dead?" she said surprised. "Dead? Are you sure?" Angie nodded. "Dead?" Elizabeth repeated again. Angie walked over to her and put her hand on Elizabeth's shoulder in an attempt to comfort her.

"I'm sorry," she told Elizabeth sadly. Elizabeth stood and went to the living room, turning on the television. She needed to see it for herself. She sat for an hour flipping channels until she finally found one that reported the news. "Richard Marks III of Richard Marks Corporation took his own life......" Elizabeth was unsure how to feel. She watched as they showed her sister-in-law crying as she tried to dodge the media as she left the funeral home where arrangements were being made. "Poor Susan," Elizabeth thought, then made a decision.

Angie had been sitting with her for support as she scanned the channels for news. "I'm going home," she said simply. "Thank you for everything, Angie. You have been a true friend." Elizabeth went to the phone and called Kelly, letting her know she wouldn't be coming back to work. She told her that Angie would explain things to her in more detail but she would be taking the first bus home in the morning. She went upstairs to pack her things and prepare to return to Connecticut. She felt some grief about her brother's death but found she was more relieved that she would no longer have to worry about him trying to find her. She would return home to support Susan and the children in their grief and handle any family matters that may need her attention. She slept quite well that night finding a great weight had been lifted from her shoulders.

She woke early to find Angie waiting for her in the kitchen with fresh hot coffee and scrambled eggs with toast. "Please eat something before you leave," she begged, not wanting her to grow weak on the journey home.

"Thank you Angie. I want you to know I appreciate everything you've done for me since I moved in. I'll miss you," she said and hugged her tightly. They chatted while they ate breakfast then Elizabeth made her way to the bus stop to begin her journey home. She climbed on the bus, thinking how everything had changed so quickly, in only a few short months her life was completely different and would never be the same. Her brother was dead and all threat of harm to her and her unborn child died with him. She would now be able to raise her child in comfort even if she couldn't provide a proper father. William was gone and she ached as she remembered their last meeting. "I will take care of you," he had promised. He couldn't keep his promise because of her brother.

She arrived in Connecticut and took a cab to the house. She climbed out of the cab, taking a long look at her childhood home. She felt like a stranger as she walked up the steps to the house, realizing how much she had changed in the last several months. She was no longer a naïve child. She knocked on the door and was greeted by the butler who was surprised but happy by her unexpected appearance. "Miss Elizabeth! You're okay! Come in!" he took her bags and went to fetch Susan.

Elizabeth sat in the library looking about the room as if it was the first time she had ever been there. The room and the house seemed very cold to her now after living in the warm and caring atmosphere at Angie's. "Elizabeth!?" Susan came into the room crying, immediately hugging her sister-in-law. "Oh, Elizabeth! It's just awful! I don't know what to say!"

Elizabeth patted Susan gently on the back. "Don't worry, Susan. Everything will be alright. I'm sure you're in shock with all that's happened. Richard had us all fooled for a very long time."

Susan sobbed harder as Elizabeth spoke of her brother's deceit openly without reserve. "Where are the kids?"

"They're with their friends today. I had to make the funeral arrangements and thought it would be better for all of us if they weren't around for that." Elizabeth nodded her agreement and asked Susan if she had the number for the family attorney. Susan retrieved the number and suddenly wondering where she had gone. "Elizabeth, where did you go? The police thought Richard had done something to you too."

"I went to Atlantic City. I was working in a hotel there and had rented a room from a little old lady," she explained. "Tomorrow I'll call the attorney and find out what we all need to do to straighten out the finances. I want to be sure that you and the boys are provided for properly. I should also pay a visit to Jonathan. I owe him an explanation. I'm exhausted and I'd like to go to bed unless you need anything else?" she asked Susan kindly.

"I'll be okay. Thank you for coming home, Elizabeth," she said sadly as they both climbed the stairs to retire for the evening. Elizabeth woke the next morning, feeling strangely happy despite the grief stricken household. She ate her breakfast then called the attorney who was shocked and relieved to hear from her. He gave her a brief explanation of what would happen now, letting her know what she would inherit as well as what Susan would receive.

"There is a delicate situation I need to speak to you about so I would like to come in and see you," she told him. He made an appointment for her to come in the day after the funeral. She thanked him and hung up the phone. The viewing and funeral were scheduled for the next day and she was sure there would be a lot of press to deal with. She summoned the driver and gave him the address where she needed to go. She quietly made the drive to Jonathan's office, wondering if he would throw her out immediately. She walked into the office and asked the secretary if he was in. Once she confirmed that Jonathan was in his office, she thanked the woman and walked into the office without waiting for permission.

Jonathan was on the phone, looking shocked as she walked unannounced into his office. "I'll call you back," he said into the phone and hung up without waiting for a reply. He stood slowly walking around the desk. He walked towards Elizabeth, who was surprised when he hugged her tightly. "Thank god you're alright! We all thought Richard had done something to you!"

"I'm alright, Jonathan. I left on my own. I returned after hearing the news of my brother's suicide."

"I heard. How horrible! How is Susan?" Jonathan asked sincerely, reminding Elizabeth why she was so fond of him.

"As well as can be expected. Do you have some time Jonathan? I wanted to talk to you and explain why I left as I did. I owe you that much. I'm sorry that I hurt you that way."

"Uh, well, I guess we could go for a walk and talk," he said stiffly, remembering that he was supposed to be angry with her.

"Thank you, Jonathan," she said as they left his office. They left the building and walked silently along the street ending up in a nearby park. They sat on a park bench as she explained in detail all that had happened. She told him about William, Sarah, Toby and the child she now carried. "I couldn't bring myself to trick you into to marrying me, Jonathan. You're too good a person. I left to protect myself and my child from my brother. I'm truly sorry for the hurt I caused you."

"I had no idea Elizabeth. I'm stunned. I don't know what to say. All of this because of your brother!" he said upset now, realizing all Elizabeth had gone through. "What about William? Does he know about the child?"

"He's dead. He disappeared right after I saw him last. His sister called me and told me he was missing. We're sure Richard killed him too." Elizabeth said as tears ran down her face.

"Elizabeth, William Blake is alive. Richard was charged with attempted murder because he didn't succeed. At least that's what was on the news," he told her surprised she didn't know.

"Are you sure?" she asked afraid to let her heart believe it. Jonathan nodded, sad to know by the look on her face, that she obviously still loved the guy despite what he had done. Her heart thumped in her chest at the thought that William was alive. They walked back to his office and she hugged him tightly. "Thank you for being so understanding, Jonathan. You'll always have a special place in my heart."

She drove back to the house, thinking about William, thankful that he was alright. Knowing that he was okay, she had to decide if she would go see him. She had to deal with the funeral and the attorney first which gave her a couple of days to figure out what she wanted to do.

Elizabeth stood next to her sister-in-law at the viewing, greeting the masses of people that had showed up to pay their respects. Most of them were business associates and came out of obligation. Some were Susan's friends and family that came to support her and the children. It was a horribly gloomy and morbid day with a cloud of shame and embarrassment that hovered in the air, due to the circumstances that surrounded Richard's death and the charges he would have faced had he not taken his own life. No one mentioned it directly to the grieving Marks family but Elizabeth was sure they would be talking about it for sometime.

She did her best to be strong and comfort her sister-in-law but as she watched her niece and nephew cry, she couldn't help but allow her own tears to flow. She cried for her family and their lost husband and father. She cried for her parents who had died at the hands of their only son. She cried for the brother she never had. She cried for her niece and nephew, knowing all too well how it felt to lose their father at such a young age.

There seemed to be an unending flow of people coming in to pay their respects. A few of her friends from school whose parents had known her brother also came to comfort Elizabeth. She looked around at the faces surrounding her, sadly realizing there was not one person there she felt close to. The Parkers came with Jonathan which touched her heart as he squeezed her hand. She was grateful for his kindness after what she had done to him. She wouldn't have blamed him if he hated her forever after breaking his heart. He was the closest thing she had to a true friend in the mass of people that attended the funeral that day and she thanked him sincerely for coming.

By the end of the viewing and burial that followed they were all exhausted and quietly returned to the house. They had been met by reporters all day long and all avoided watching the news knowing there would be an unending amount of reports on Richard's funeral and the scandal that surrounded his death. She was sorry that Susan and the children had to go through all that attention and fuss while mourning the death of her husband and their father. It wasn't fair of Richard to have done this to them but then Richard had always been selfish, right to the end.

They all retired to their rooms exhausted from the day. Elizabeth took a hot bath, needing to relax her aching muscles, tight from the tension of the day. She was in the tub, gently rubbing her swelling belly and thought of William. She still hadn't told anyone except Jonathan that she was pregnant. Tomorrow she would meet with the attorney to take care of the specifics of the estate. She decided she would write a letter to Kelly and Angie to thank them again for their kindness. Elizabeth slept peacefully that night, having no night mares to haunt her.

Harry Finch opened the envelope with a big smile on his face, thinking he had never made so much money at one time. Richard had paid his bill but once the scandal hit and he heard of Richard's death, he sold the pictures he had taken as an insurance policy to the highest bidder. He locked his office door behind him thinking it was time to take a vacation. Looking at the check in his hand he decided Atlantic City would be the perfect place to visit.

William, Sarah and Thomas sat watching the news coverage of the Richard Marks funeral. Thomas found himself constantly finding little excuses to visit just so he could see Sarah. They hadn't heard anything on Elizabeth's disappearance and watched the news constantly in case there was any word. They all felt sorry for the children and the widow Richard had left with the burden of shame and scandal. They watched with interest at the masses of people flowing in and out of the funeral home. William grabbed his sister's hand suddenly as he saw Elizabeth emerge with Susan Marks from the funeral home and climb into the limousine which would take them to the cemetery for the burial. They all looked at each other, hugging each other happily. The reporter commented on the sudden appearance of the missing sister, Elizabeth Marks, stating they have been unable to obtain an interview with Ms. Marks to confirm where she had been for the last several weeks.

William was smiling ear to ear and began to pace about the room. "Should I go see her?" he asked Sarah and Thomas, needing their advice.

"I think you should give her some time to deal with everything going on before you approach her, William. I'm sure you would like nothing more than to hop in the car now but given the circumstances…" Sarah advised while Thomas nodded his agreement.

"I agree with Sarah. Give her a few days. She has a lot on her plate right now," Thomas told him, understanding his need to see her all too well. He had quickly grown quite fond of Sarah and thought about her all the time. He was hesitant to approach her directly with everything that had gone on and respected that she was his friend's sister. He wanted to be sure he had William's approval before he asked her on a date. He wasn't even sure if Sarah had the same feelings or if she was simply grateful to him for helping her brother. He was waiting for the right time to approach William on the subject.

William had noticed the way Thomas kept looking at Sarah and how he made little excuses to come around, coming personally to deliver some paperwork that easily could have been sent in the mail. He was fond of his friend and thought he would be a good match for his sister. He watched his sister closely and thought she had the same feelings for Thomas but didn't approach her on the subject.

William agreed with them both that he should give Elizabeth some time but found it difficult to stay away. William was in good spirits, happy that Elizabeth was alright. He sat on the porch with Thomas as Sarah put Toby to bed and noticed his friend seemed suddenly nervous. He figured he was trying to work up the courage to ask him about Sarah and decided to put him out of his misery.

"So Thomas, when do you plan on asking Sarah out?" he asked with a smile on his face.

Thomas looked surprised at his friend's blunt question and turned slightly pink in the face. "Is it that obvious?" Thomas said laughing.

William nodded then smacked his friend on the back. "Unless you're blind!" William responded.

"Are you okay with it? I didn't want to ask her unless I knew it was okay with you first."

"Yes, man. It's okay with me. I couldn't think of a better guy for my sister," he told him sincerely. William was very fond of Thomas for many reasons. He was honest, kind and knew without a doubt he would be good to his sister. Toby liked him as well which of course made a world of difference.

Thomas smiled like a kid who just got his first bike at Christmas. Sarah joined them, curious to know why they were smiling and laughing. "Did I miss something?" she asked.

Her question sent both Thomas and William into a fit of laughter which made Sarah wonder if they had lost their minds. "What's so funny?"

"Just an inside joke between us men," her brother said in an exaggerated macho voice. "I have some calls to make. I'll be back in a little while," he said patting Thomas on the shoulder as he left him alone with his sister. William couldn't help but smile as he went to his office. He had no calls to make but he looked over some papers he had to sign and busied himself for a while to allow his friend an opportunity to be alone with Sarah.

Thomas sat quietly next to Sarah trying to work up the courage to ask her out. "What was so funny?" she asked, curious to know what had tickled them both. Thomas hesitated for a moment then took a deep breath.

"We were talking about you," he said turning slightly in his seat so he could see her beautiful face.

"Me? What did I do that was that funny?" she asked innocently.

"Nothing really. It was just your timing. I was just asking William if it was okay to ask you out," he explained nervously, watching her face for a reaction.

Sarah blushed at his admission but was happy he wanted to take her out. She had become very fond of him and found herself thinking about him quite often when she was alone. More than once she wondered what it would be like to kiss him. "Really? What did he say?" she asked teasing him.

"He thought it was a great idea. Do you agree?" he asked, still nervous that his affection may be unwelcome.

Sarah smiled at him touched by his obvious shyness. "I think I do, although I don't require my brother's permission."

Thomas was thrilled she wanted to go out with him. "I'm sure you don't but I didn't want to disrespect William if he didn't approve," he explained, hoping she understood.

Sarah appreciated his respect for her brother and wondered again what it would be like to kiss him. "I understand," she said smiling. "So when would you like to go out?"

"When is good for you? I realize you have Toby to think about," he said grinning.

Surprised yet again by his thoughtfulness, she couldn't help herself any longer. She looked into his eyes, leaning in to kiss him. He didn't hesitate to respond, returning her kiss as he pulled her close. Sarah felt flustered when he pulled away, not having desired a man in a very long time. "Saturday good for you?" she said huskily.

He nodded and kissed her again. "Seven o'clock?" he asked softly.

"Fine," she said wanting more.

William appeared, clearing his throat with a wicked grin on his face as he joined them on the porch. "Am I interrupting something?" he said trying not to laugh. "Toby's calling for you sis."

Sarah smiled at Thomas and smacked her brother on the arm as she went to attend to her son. "I guess that went well," William said laughing at his friend who was now turning bright red. Thomas laughed like a teenager in response to his friend's question.

Chapter Seventeen

Elizabeth went to see the attorney, listening intently to the details of the Will and who was entitled to what. She made it clear to the attorney she wanted Susan and the children to be taken care of, making sure Susan would get the house because of the children. Then she told the attorney about Toby Blake, Richard's son. The attorney remembered the lawsuit and was no longer surprised at anything Richard had done. She told the attorney to send Sarah and her son a specified amount of money immediately for past support she should have received from Richard a long time ago and to send a monthly payment after that. She also had another separate amount put into a trust fund in Toby's name. The attorney advised her to have another DNA test done but Elizabeth said she didn't feel it was necessary.

She thanked him and said she would call and follow-up with him in a week. She drove back to the house, feeling good about what she had done. Her brother may have denied Toby a father, but he wouldn't be denied anything any longer. She went back to the house and checked on her sister-in-law. She told her briefly about what the lawyer said and told her the house would be hers to do with what she wanted. She also assured her she would have enough money to take care of the house and children without worry and that each of the children will have a trust fund set up with money for college. She told Susan they would discuss things in more detail when she was feeling up to it.

Susan seemed to feel a little better after they talked. Elizabeth hoped she had relieved some of her worry. She returned to her room and sat to write a letter to Kelly and Angie to thank them for everything they had done for her. She missed them already, wished them well and told them should they ever need anything to give her a call.

After she wrote the letter and left it on the foyer table to be mailed she decided to go for a walk on her beloved beach before dinner. She needed some time to think about William and decide what she wanted to do. She walked along allowing herself to remember the weeks she had spent with William and how she had felt when they were together. She wondered if she could forgive him and try to love him again. He had told her he loved her and he truly wanted to marry her. He had known that she was pregnant without being told which had caught her off guard but he had lied to her which directly resulted in her pregnancy and a lot of the complicated issues she had to deal with afterwards. He had risked himself and almost died trying to warn her about her brother. "Shouldn't that mean something?" she asked herself out loud.

After going round and round in her mind without resolution, she returned to the house for dinner. She sat with Susan and the children, trying to make jokes to lift their spirits. Elizabeth knew they would just need time and hoped the children wouldn't be subjected to harassment from the other kids when they went back to school. She went to bed that night, thinking about the children, hoping they would be okay. She remembered how angry she had been when her parents had died, although they still had their mother.

Elizabeth woke feeling more relaxed, having made her decision. She would never be right if she didn't confront her feelings for William. She had decided to go see him and see how things went. She showered and dressed, taking extra time grooming, needing all the confidence she could gather. She pulled out her secret box and put the bracelet on that William had given her.

She found a long gold necklace in her jewelry box and put the engagement ring on the chain like a pendant, tucking the ring under her blouse.

She went downstairs and had some grapefruit and toast with coffee before summoning the driver. She gave him the address Sarah had given her and sat in the limousine, nervous at the thought of seeing William again. She spotted William immediately as they pulled up in front of his house. She smiled as she watched him tossing a baseball in the front yard with a small boy she assumed was Toby Blake, her nephew. The boy stopped when he saw the large car pull up in front of the house and pointed at it in awe.

William turned and saw the limousine his nephew was pointing at, suspecting who was inside. "Toby, go help your mother with lunch," he ordered.

"Okay," the boy said, disappointed he couldn't stay to explore the large car and ran inside to help his mother. William stood nervously as he watched Elizabeth emerge from the vehicle, thinking how beautiful she was. He walked towards her, meeting her half way. He swallowed hard as his mouth grew dry, wanting to pull her into his arms.

"Elizabeth," he said nervously looking down at her. He was stunned when she slapped him hard across the cheek without a word. He knew he deserved it so did nothing but stand and take her wrath as she slapped him a second time across the other.

"Feel better?" he asked smiling down at her as his face stung from the blow.

"Not yet," she said and raised her hand to slap him again which he caught in mid air, pulling her close to him.

"Enough, woman! I know I deserve it but my face is stinging pretty good already," he said smiling as he bent to kiss her. She tried to pull away but he wouldn't allow it. He trapped her gently in his arms, kissing her softly, waiting patiently for her anger to melt away. After a few moments he could feel her body start to relax and he kissed her more deeply. Finally she was returning his kiss with passion and he pulled her even closer to him. When he forced himself to release her she had tears running down her face. "Oh, Elizabeth. I'm so sorry for everything. I love you and have missed you so much. I thought you were dead! I only knew you were okay when I saw you on TV," he said softly as he hugged her. "Please forgive me."

Elizabeth pulled away from him still angry for all he had done. "I'm not sure I can forgive you William. I'm trying but it's hard. I'm pregnant because of your lies!" she said angrily.

"You're pregnant? I knew it!" he exclaimed happily and twirled her around in his arms. She couldn't help but laugh at his enthusiasm but was quick to scold him once he placed her back down on the ground.

"You're proud that you got me pregnant by lying to me?" she asked angry again.

William hung his head with a serious shameful look on his face. "I'm truly sorry for lying to you and putting you in that position. I love you, Elizabeth and I am happy that you're having my child. I'll take care of you both and spend the rest of my life making up for what I did, if you only give me the chance!"

She wasn't sure what to say, still unwilling to forgive him so easily. "I would like to meet my nephew," she said firmly dodging his plea for forgiveness.

He smiled and escorted her into the house to meet Toby. She was greeted warmly by Sarah which took her by surprise. Elizabeth had felt so bad about what her brother had done to her she half expected her to tell her to leave. "Will you join us for lunch, Elizabeth? There is plenty," Sarah asked warmly.

"Thank you," she smiled awkwardly as she took a seat at the table. Elizabeth watched Toby carefully carry the plates and set them on the table in each place.

"Toby, this is a friend of mine, Elizabeth," William introduced them. Toby looked her over and smiled.

"You have pretty hair," he told her nonchalantly which brought tears to Elizabeth's eyes.

"Thank you Toby. I saw you outside throwing the baseball around. You're pretty good," she told him trying to return the compliment. Toby beamed with pride at her comment.

"Do you play baseball?" Toby asked curiously.

"No but maybe you can teach me," she answered liking the boy immediately.

"Sure! Uncle Willy taught me. That's why I'm so good!" he said looking proudly at his uncle. Elizabeth laughed when she heard him call William 'Uncle Willy' and couldn't help teasing him about it.

"Oh, Yeah? Well maybe Uncle Willy could help me out too," she said laughing at William as he groaned at the obvious dig about his nick name. "Maybe we should start calling you Aunt Willy instead." This last comment caused all of them to burst out laughing while William turned bright red in the face.

"I knew I would never live that down!" he said, laughing himself, remembering how silly he felt dressed as an old lady. They sat and chatted while they enjoyed the lunch Sarah had made then went out on the back porch to talk while Toby played outside.

While Toby was safely out of ear shot, Elizabeth apologized to Sarah for what her brother had done to her and Toby. "I want you to know how sorry I am for what my brother did to you and Toby. I'm ashamed to know he was my blood. Hell, I might have to change my name just to get away from the scandal he created."

"You're not responsible for your brother's actions, Elizabeth. You don't have to apologize. However I understand where you're coming from since my own brother has recently made his own mistakes I feel obligated to apologize for," she replied smacking her brother hard on the leg.

"Ow! Jesus! Between the two of you I'm going to end up black and blue again," he said, exaggerating his pain, trying not to laugh. Sarah and Elizabeth laughed at him for a moment.

"I'm sorry William that my brother tried to hurt you. I'm glad you're alright," she said as tears welled in her eyes again. William put an arm around her protectively.

"I would go through it twenty times over for you, sweetheart," he said seriously, bringing another swell of tears to her eyes.

She controlled her emotions and looked at Sarah. "One of the reasons I came here today is because I wanted you to know that I have made arrangements for you and Toby to receive some money from the inheritance. I have also arranged for a trust fund so Toby can go to college if that's his choice."

Sarah looked at her with surprise while William immediately got angry. "No. Sarah doesn't need Richard's money! I have enough to take care of my family!"

Elizabeth was a little shocked at his angry objection. "I'm sure you could provide for them just fine but the fact is that he is Richard's son and is entitled to that money so he can have security of his own," she explained, hoping that would calm him.

William calmed a little knowing Elizabeth was right but his pride and hate for Richard refused to let him give in so easily. "No. I will not stand for it!"

Elizabeth annoyed and angry lashed out at him. "You will not stand for it?! You listen to me you bull headed mule! You don't have any say in the matter! It's up to Sarah to decide what to do with the money!"

William glared at her realizing she was right and he was out of line. He walked away grumbling unwilling to admit he was wrong. Sarah sat quietly during the explosive argument and was amused at how fast Elizabeth had deflated her brother's pride driven protest. Sarah liked that Elizabeth didn't hesitate to stand up to William, knowing herself how stubborn he could be.

Once her brother was out of ear shot, she laughed. "If you don't know this yet, that grumbling means he knows you're right and he is wrong but his pride won't let him admit it to you just yet. I have had many arguments with him over the years that sent him away grumbling."

Elizabeth laughed at Sarah's explanation which allowed her own frustration to subside. Sarah took Elizabeth's hand gently, "Thank you, Elizabeth."

"You should have had help from Richard years ago. I feel like I'm just giving you what was already yours...and Toby's," she said kindly. The two women sat together as Sarah told Elizabeth stories about Toby growing up. Elizabeth was growing fond of Sarah Blake and her adorable son. It surprised her how comfortable she was with them. It reminded her of Kelly and Angie and how comfortable she had been in their company.

Eventually William returned to the porch and flopped down in his seat, pouting like a child. Sarah and Elizabeth looked at each other and laughed. "What's so funny?" he grumbled which made them laugh harder.

"Nothing, Aunt Willy," Sarah teased, giggling as William groaned then laughed, letting go of his stubborn pride.

They avoided the subject of money the rest of the day, concentrating their attention on Toby. Elizabeth allowed him to show her how to throw and catch the baseball, laughing at how funny she looked trying to use William's rather large baseball glove on her tiny hands. She enjoyed spending the day with her nephew and told Sarah she was doing a wonderful job. She had a moment of panic hit her as she wondered if she would be able to do the same with her own child. After seeing William with his nephew, she thought he would make a good father. He was so patient and loving towards Toby. She could almost forget what he had done to her. She felt her guard lower and her reservations begin to melt away.

Thomas showed up around dinner time with some excuse he no longer needed. Sarah's face glowed when she greeted him at the door. Elizabeth immediately noticed the mutual attraction between them. William and

Sarah had told her about Thomas and how he had saved William's life. William introduced them and Elizabeth greeted him warmly. "It's nice to meet you. I've heard a lot about you today. William is lucky to have such a good friend."

"It's nice to meet you too, Elizabeth. I feel as if I know you already," he said smiling at her.

"Thomas, would you like to join us for dinner? Elizabeth, I would love it if you would join us as well?" Sarah extended invitations to them both, happy when they both accepted.

"I'll only stay if you allow me to help with dinner," Elizabeth told her without hesitation.

"You have a deal!" she replied then Elizabeth followed Sarah into the kitchen as the men went outside to talk and watch after Toby. She chatted happily with Sarah as they prepared the meal and again found herself surprised by how comfortable she felt. They served the meal outside on the back porch, chatting happily. William was attentive but reserved, afraid to push Elizabeth too hard and scare her away. After the meal she helped Sarah clean up the dishes and serve ice cream to everyone for desert. They all laughed at Toby when he smiled from ear to ear as he gobbled the ice cream and smeared it all over his face.

"Well, I guess it's time I get home. I should call my driver to come and get me. May I use the phone?" she asked politely. She noticed William's look of disappointment as did Sarah who immediately intervened.

"Must you go? You're welcome to stay the night in the guest room. We would love to have you," Sarah invited hoping she would choose to stay. Thankfully Toby also wanted Elizabeth to stay.

"Lizbeth, please stay. I haven't even showed you my room yet and you need more practice with the baseball!" he begged innocently which made everyone laugh. Elizabeth found it difficult to say no to the child but hesitated, looking at William. He gave her a hopeful nod, silently begging her to accept their invitation.

"Are you sure it wouldn't be an imposition?" she asked, not wanting to intrude.

"Absolutely not! You're welcome anytime for as long as you like!" Sarah said firmly before anyone else had a chance to respond.

"Oh, well, I don't have any clothes with me," her last excuse to escape was quickly dismissed as Sarah told her she would be happy to lend her something to wear. "Okay then. I guess I'll stay." Toby immediately jumped up and down beaming that she had agreed to stay.

"Yeah! Lizbeth, come see my room?" he asked taking her hand. She smiled at him fondly and allowed him to drag her to his room where he proudly showed her all of his toys and books. Sarah came in shortly after he finished showing her all his favorite things and ordered him to go take his bath. Elizabeth promised to play baseball with him again before she left the following day.

"Sarah, may I use your phone? I just want to check on my sister-in-law and the kids. Make sure they're okay and let them know I won't be home this evening."

"Sure," she replied without hesitation. Elizabeth went downstairs to call Susan from the phone in the kitchen. She felt better after speaking to Susan who seemed to be in better spirits today. After her call she joined everyone on the porch where she relaxed in a lounge chair feeling quite tired after the long day of playing with Toby and the emotional turmoil caused by seeing William again. William noticed she was looking tired and instantly became concerned.

"Are you alright? Tired? Cold? Can I get you a blanket?" he asked, fussing over her which made her laugh.

"I'm fine. Just a little tired. I find I get tired earlier than I used to since…." her voice trailed off afraid to say the words out loud. She had to keep it to herself for so long she wasn't comfortable with speaking of the situation freely.

"Since you got pregnant?" he asked finishing her sentence. She nodded and smiled shyly which made his heart skip a beat. Her shy smile reminded him of the first night they had spent together. He had to force the thought from his head as desire began to stir within him. "Should I rub your feet? They say pregnant woman like that."

Elizabeth laughed at the suggestion. "Thank you but I think my feet are fine but I may take you up on that in a couple more months!"

He gave her a brilliant smile, making her melt. She was glad she was not standing because her legs suddenly felt shaky and weak. She found herself drawn to William just as she had been before, wanting to hold him, kiss him and..... Elizabeth forced herself to think of something else since they weren't alone. Thomas interrupted just then having to leave himself.

"It was nice meeting you, Elizabeth. I hope to see you again soon," he said and gave his friend a quick handshake. Sarah walked him to the door where they shared a quiet moment together. "I'll see you Saturday." he said then kissed her softly. She smiled and said goodnight. Sarah was happier than she has been in a very long time. She was happy for her brother that things may work out with Elizabeth after all. She had watched through the window like a little old lady hiding behind the curtain as Elizabeth smacked her brother twice when she first arrived. Sarah had chuckled at his nerve when he pulled her too him and kissed her until her anger had subsided. They were a perfect match she decided after spending the day with them both. Sarah could tell Elizabeth still had feelings for William but her pride was not allowing her to completely forgive him. She hoped she would be able to work it out. She was sure they would be very happy together.

Sarah decided to go to bed and give them time by themselves so she said goodnight, making sure to layout some night clothes for Elizabeth on the guest bed before retiring to her room. She went to bed, smiling and looking forward to seeing Thomas again on Saturday.

Elizabeth felt shy once she was alone with William on the porch. It seemed darker now with only the soft glow of one light near the door, making the porch feel very intimate. William sensed her discomfort and asked her to join him on the swing. "Come sit with me?" he asked softly patting the seat beside him. "I promise I won't bite."

She smiled shyly but joined him on the swing unable to resist the opportunity to be closer to him. Once she was comfortable, he gently took her hand and ran his finger across the bracelet she wore, the one he had given her. He looked into her eyes tenderly, knowing it had meant something that she had worn the bracelet today. He grew very serious, holding her hand tightly afraid she may pull away. "Do you think you'll ever be able to forgive me?" he asked hanging his head low. "I know I don't deserve it but I need you so much and I've never needed anyone."

Elizabeth's heart betrayed her when she saw the pain on his face. Her heart wouldn't allow her to stay angry with him no matter what her head told her to do. She squeezed his hand and he raised his head to look at her. What he saw in her eyes made his heart sore and he felt dizzy when she gently took her hand and caressed his cheek. She gently pulled his head down towards her kissing him softly on the lips as she teased him with her tongue. He moaned, pulling her closer to his body. Their desire grew quickly, intensified by their time apart. He looked at her questioningly, making sure she was ready to give herself to him again. She simply nodded and smiled as he lifted her right off the swing and carried her up to his bedroom locking the door behind them.

He put her gently on his bed, kissing her all the way. He sat next to her, enjoying the sight of her in his bed. They took their time, caressing and getting to know each other all over again. He began to unbutton her blouse as he kissed her neck. He trailed kisses down her neck towards her breasts, teasing her as he slowly undid each button. He froze when he saw the ring hanging from the necklace that had been hiding under her blouse. He took the ring in his hand staring at it for a moment. He looked at Elizabeth lying next to him. She had tears running down her face. She had forgotten that she had the ring on the chain. William gently loosened the necklace from around her neck and removed the ring. He looked in her eyes as he took her hand and without saying a word he slid the ring back onto her finger. He kissed each finger then her wrist sending a shiver up her spine.

Elizabeth was melting in a sea of emotions and sensations. Only William could make her feel this way. She kissed him passionately, not able to deny her need any longer. She needed to feel the weight of his body on top of her. She began stripping off his clothes which ignited William's passion even further. He kissed every part of her, teasing her with his tongue until she moaned with delight. He caressed her everywhere teasing her nipples with his thumb of one hand while caressing her inner thighs with the other slowly moving upward until he reached the moist, sensitive area between her legs. Elizabeth moaned with pleasure as he expertly teased her with his fingers.

William couldn't deny his own passion and need a moment longer. He rolled on top of Elizabeth, gently making love to her. They fell asleep in each others arms, both feeling satisfied and happy. In the morning, Sarah smiled widely when she walked by the open guest bedroom door and noticed that the bed hadn't been slept in and the nightgown she had left had never been used.

"Breathe, baby breathe," William said as he drove his wife to the hospital. The pains were already so strong and coming so fast that William was concerned. She seemed to be so uncomfortable and he could do nothing to ease her pain. Even the classes they had taken together on natural child birth hadn't prepared him for the panic he felt. "We're almost there," he told her as another pain took her breath away.

He pulled into the emergency room parking lot, jumping out of the car to assist her. He helped her out of the car slowly, yelling for help once they were through the doors. A nurse brought a wheel chair and began to ask them both questions. She rolled Elizabeth into the maternity ward and helped her into the bed. She ordered William to go scrub up and gave him the required sterilized cover ups. The nurse assisted Elizabeth into her own hospital gown while they waited for the doctor.

Elizabeth was finding it hard to breathe and couldn't help groaning in agony as the contractions got stronger and closer together. The doctor came quickly after the nurse put her on the priority list because her contractions were so close. Elizabeth put her feet in the stirrups as instructed and William did his best to comfort her.

"Wow! This one is in quite a rush! I can already see the baby's head. Elizabeth you're going to have to push now."

"Already?" she said through gritted teeth as the next pain took her breath away.

"Take a deep breath and push," ordered the doctor, "Good, again...., one more time. That's it! Push!" The doctor smiled as the newborn let out a nice healthy cry. "It's a boy!" he yelled placing the baby in his mother's lap and congratulating them both. William and Elizabeth smiled at each other as they looked upon their newborn son.

Sarah, Thomas, and Toby came into visit once mother and son were settled into their hospital room. They congratulated William and Elizabeth hugging them both laughing at Toby's excitement at having a cousin. "A boy? Yeah! I can teach him baseball too!"

Sarah held her nephew tenderly, "Well what's his name?" she asked her brother.

William and Elizabeth shared a tender glance before answering. "William Thomas," he said simply.

Thomas was surprised and honored that they had used his name, smiling at them fondly. "Good strong name," he said, patting William on the back.

"Sarah? What's that on your finger?" Elizabeth asked, noticing the beautiful ring on her left hand as she returned the baby to Elizabeth.

Sarah smiled and looked at Thomas. "Thomas asked me to marry him and I accepted!" she told them proudly. There were cheers from Elizabeth and William as they congratulated them both. The commotion brought a nurse running into the room in a panic, "Is everything alright in here?" the nurse asked Elizabeth.

Elizabeth smiled, looking at her family proudly, "Everything is perfect!"